I0717092

Sorry I Kissed You

a romance

Natalie Keller Reinert

Sorry I Kissed You
Copyright © 2023 Natalie Keller Reinert
All rights reserved.
ISBN: 978-1-956575-33-0

Cover Art: James, GoOnWrite.com

Also by Natalie Keller Reinert

The Settle Down Society
The Weekend We Met
The Settle Down Summer
The Business of Fairy Tales (2024)
The Tropical Update (2024)

Catoctin Creek
Sunset at Catoctin Creek
Snowfall at Catoctin Creek
Springtime at Catoctin Creek
Christmas at Catoctin Creek

Ocala Horse Girls
The Project Horse
The Sweetheart Horse
The Regift Horse
The Hollywood Horse

The Florida Equestrian Collection
The Eventing Series
Briar Hill Farm
Grabbing Mane: A Duet
Show Barn Blues: A Duet
Alex & Alexander: A Horse Racing Saga
Sea Horse Ranch: A Beach Read Series
The Hidden Horses of New York: A Novel

Theme Park Adventures
You Must Be This Tall
Confessions of a Theme Park Princess

Don't miss the tunes!

Listen to the playlist on Spotify for music that inspired *Sorry I Kissed You*'s characters!

Visit bit.ly/sorryplaylist

Or, search "Sorry I Kissed You Playlist" on Spotify.

You'll find an ongoing playlist from indie artists of the 2000s through today!

Chapter One

THIS VIP EXPERIENCE ticket has a lot to be desired, I think, as my cheeks go pink and my heart lodges itself firmly in my throat, right on top of my vocal chords. Thereby preventing me from saying anything while Everett Torby is in the room, shaking hands and signing autographs and, let's be very honest, melting a few panties.

He's six feet away, as close as I've ever been to him, and now I can see the blue chasing the gray in his eyes, the lines criss-crossing his tan skin from years of squinting into the sunlight at music festivals and outdoor stages of all kinds; the grooves etched into his forehead from a lifetime of writing songs about lonely nights, lost loves, and broken dreams.

I'd like to stay focused on those artistic details, to remind myself that this is the musician and not the man, because that's why I'm here—to get over this dream guy I've been chasing since I was twenty-two years old—but then he looks up, two fans away, and our eyes meet.

Panty-melting doesn't even begin to describe this moment.

Those stormy eyes are suddenly fastened on mine, and as eyebrows just on the shaggy side lift up, a pair of perfect lips, not too thin and not too full, fall open to complete a look of perfect surprise.

I'm not breathing.

Something in my brain starts screaming, *He knows me!*

My brain is insane. Please forgive my brain.

But—why does he look like he recognizes me? Like he can't believe I'm here? Like—

He shakes his head, a gesture so slight I might have imagined it, and turns to the next fan with his poster held in shaking hands, his praise and thanks gushing forth in stutters and rushes while Everett smiles and listens with the cool demeanor of a bored messiah.

I should get out of here.

The less optimistic side of my brain has entered the chat.

This isn't what I expected.

I take a quick look around, taking note of the open door behind me. We've been lined up like hopeful extras before an open casting call for the past half an hour. Standing out there in the semi-industrial hallway of a municipal arena, where the sweat of athletes and rock stars alike has permeated the cement walls. Or maybe they just need to take the trash out. *Something* smells sour out there, and it isn't me, because I have checked. Often.

No way I was going to be anything less than fresh for my moment with Everett Torby.

We stood in that line for thirty minutes that felt like forever; it became our home. When the security guard finally opened the green room door, we filed inside with tiny, scuffing, frightened steps. I think we were all grateful for the line, for the order that kept us from acting on our own. What would we do if we were allowed to be feral and free and simply confronted with the singer of The Emergency in the flesh, no rules, no instructions?

I press my fingernails into my palm and make myself turn around. He's so close now that I could reach out and touch him, but luckily, I know it's not my turn.

The girl next to me bursts into tears as Everett says hello to her.

I'm jealous of her. Tears for Everett, that's *my* love language. Now she's gone and taken the only thing I know for sure I can say to him.

Blubbing; shameless overwrought sobbing.

What else is there?

He hugs her and the photographer snaps a picture of the two of them, his eyes cool and kind, hers red and filled with tears. Then he runs a hand down the front of his brown gingham shirt, as if checking the buttons are all intact, and takes another step.

To me.

I take a breath and look into the promised land of Everett Torby's unforgettable blue-gray eyes.

My whole body freezes up—well, almost my whole body. One part of me unfurls, stretches, and looks around with a leisurely, *Oh, are we doing this, then?*

Everett's lips open, saying those damning words: "Thanks so much for coming tonight. It means a lot to me."

He says that to *everyone*. I'm *no one*.

But he knew you, the rah-rah side of my brain insists.

You shouldn't have come, the other side snaps. *This will only make things worse.*

So, maybe I shouldn't have come. It's possible this was a mistake. But those eyes...these aren't the eyes I've admired in photos over the years. This is a person I know. Intimately. Forever. I'm not crazy. I just have a deep, cosmic connection to Everett Torby, indie rock star.

Lucky me!

The only part of me left alive and moving is warming up now, simmering with a   liquid heat that's spilling into my frozen limbs.

Our gazes lock, and his pupils seem to dilate, the blue rims of his irises growing brighter as the gray is forced to retreat into darkness, and for a foolish, hopeful moment I think, *You, too?*

Then his eyes flick downward, like my gaze was too hard to hold.

I'm left blinking in disappointment.

"You didn't bring anything," he says.

"What?" I gasp, sucking in air as if I've been underwater.

"To sign," he says, gesturing at my empty hands. "That's okay. Hang on; let me see if I have anything."

To sign. This is an autograph and photo session. A meet and greet. Not a gaze and dream.

And he turns away, bending to dig through a laptop bag on the dingy green room sofa. Everyone left in the queue is treated to a view of his butt in skin-tight jeans. I don't think anyone in the room is mad at me for this. There's a sense of held breath as everyone waits for him to find some scrap of promo to sign for the weird girl near the end of the line.

I *did* have something for him to sign, earlier tonight, but that was before the evening went colossally wrong. I lost the vintage handbill for one of Everett's early shows as a frontman for The Emergency, watched it go sailing down the street in front of the arena's main entrance, as I stood on the top steps and argued with Barry one last time.

What's one more argument between a terribly matched couple?

He was mad at me because of this: that I was more excited about meeting Everett, without him, than I was of seeing the show with him. "The Emergency were my favorite band, too," he sniped, as I turned in my ticket at the box office, holding the plastic VIP lanyard card they handed me with something like reverence for a holy relic. "So you can quit acting like you own them or something."

"Barry, I'm not going to fight with you over this," I'd lied, pressing my thumb into the word *Everett*. It said *Meet and Greet*

With Everett Torby. Me. Meeting and greeting. Soon. "And I'll only be gone for like half an hour after the show. You can wait —"

"You want me to stand out here on the street while you go in there and fondle Everett Torby?" Barry sneered. He always has such a practiced sneer; he makes the same face whether he's talking about the L.A. traffic or the New York Rangers or coleslaw—he hates them all, equally—but tonight, when he turned that undiscriminating lip-curl on me and my love for Everett, I felt something snap.

The last frayed rubber band holding our on-again, off-again, I'm-lonely-tonight relationship together, I suppose.

"Yes, that's exactly what I want," I snarled, and he dove at my envelope, the one holding my handbill, the one I wanted Everett to sign so I could frame it and look at it every day (*his fingers touched that,* I'd think), and his fingers plucked the envelope open and the handbill slipped out and then the wind came and that was the end of it.

I hoped some other fan picked it up; I hoped it wasn't destroyed.

Anyway, that was the first time I cried tonight.

I cried more during the show, because of, oh, catharsis and camaraderie and the dreamy cult-like sense of belonging that I always got at an Emergency show. Even though this is Everett's first solo tour without the rest of the band, we are all united as Emergency fans first and foremost. Everett is simply the secret sauce that makes The Emergency our passion and our poison.

And crying at The Emergency shows is a rite of passage. If you don't cry, you're not a fan.

Barry has never cried at an Emergency show, and I doubt he cried tonight, and I seriously doubt he'll cry over me. He'll probably call tomorrow like nothing happened. But I'm not going to pick up.

(I've told myself that before.)

Anyway, I'm not crying now, because Everett is turning around, a promo card in his hands, a smile on those luscious lips, and as our eyes meet again, that shudder runs through my melting-hot core and my panties melt *again* and I think, *I'm just going to straight-up tell him I love him,* and I open my mouth and a huge, shrill scream comes out—

No, thank god, that's not me!

Flashing white lights, and the scrambling of shoes on scuffed tiles, clues me in.

That unending scream is the fire alarm, and we're being hustled out of this room like puppies getting shushed out of a kitchen. I see a security guard collar Everett as if he's just robbed a bank and push him through our unruly line, making sure rock stars are out of harm's way first. Then it's time for us to file out, as the warren of rooms opening onto the hallway spills their maintenance workers and custodians and assorted staff into the evacuation route.

It's over. This is the VIP Experience: a handshake and a meaningful look that can't be explained and a totally unsatisfying climax.

Okay, *now?* Yeah, now I'm crying.

Chapter Two

"WOULD YOU REALLY have felt better if you'd gotten a hug from him?"

My sister's face is skeptical, as if even from a thousand miles away (or however far away the Columbus suburbs are from Orange County) she can read my thoughts and knows I'm obsessing over something I can't help.

Again.

"I would feel so much better, Angie. I promise you. I just need to touch him. Not in a weird way! Just to know...he's real, and we've hugged."

"I have to say, I think it would have made things worse. I think you dodged a bullet with that fire alarm."

I study Angie's face for a moment. At age thirty-eight, she's ten years older and a million years wiser than me—and since we look so alike, she's a weird magic-mirror to what I'll look like in a decade. Reddish-brown hair that's prone to curl in humidity lies in a soft bob around her chin, while mine is still halfway down my back; a pointed chin and round cheeks remind me that I'll never have cheekbones, no matter how hard I Keto; serious hazel eyes beset with long lashes assure me that they'll be my best feature well into my mature era.

But we're alike in looks only. Angie is a mom of three with a good job as a lawyer in Columbus, Ohio, while I'm a mom of none with a bad job running the events calendar for a community theater in a canyon town outside of Los Angeles.

I mean, it's a bad job on paper. It's an interesting, if frustrating and low-paying job, in real life.

And it suits my personality, which is, well, *dramatic.* I moved to L.A. in college for two reasons. One, to be immersed in the world that created my favorite things: music, movies, media of all kinds. And two, to get away from Ohio's dreary gray skies.

I became who I am in Los Angeles (or her low-slung suburbs). I am stereotypes: tanned despite the warnings, a squeezer of avocados, vicious when provoked in an overcrowded parking lot.

But I'm also intensely myself, or so I hope: my skinny jeans have real holes in the knees, that I put there myself kneeling down to help lizards cross the road or watch bees bumbling through flowerbeds. My music selections in my car might be the electronic mania of a 1970s-era Disneyland parade score or the doom-washed post-punk of The Emergency. And I refuse to identify as either a cat or a dog person...I love them both, equally.

I love Tilda, my cat, the most, of course.

My sister knows all my sides, and they worry her. "I think you should come home for a visit," she says now, cocking her head to look beyond the phone camera. She's probably watching one of her girl-children run amok in the living room.

"I can't come home," I say contentedly, because Ohio in autumn does not sound appealing, and if I have nothing else, at least I have Southern California. "We're gearing up for our holiday season. I have a lot to do at work."

"You shouldn't be alone right now."

I tsk. "I'm not having a nervous breakdown," I inform her.

"That's what you think, but this whole thing with this singer...I just think you're too invested."

"I'm a fan," I say. "You've been a fan of things! It gets personal."

"You broke up with your boyfriend so you could meet him," Angie says. "If that is personal, I think it's a little too far."

"We were breaking up, *anyway*." This is almost certainly true. Barry and I were constantly breaking up. This one just feels real. I won't even notice he's not in my life anymore until around seven o'clock, when I have to pay for my own dinner. "Everett was just an excuse," I say. "A convenient reason to fight. We were both looking for it."

Angie's attention is lost by now; her eyes are following the exploits of some rugrat on a mission. I sense the end of the call coming on. She says, "Come back anytime, okay? I have to go. Rosie is—I don't know where Rosie is, actually. Love-ya-bye," and the screen goes blank.

"Love ya, bye," I murmur, starting to pocket my phone—then pausing. Real quick, I'll check my email. And my socials. And the weather...

Half an hour later, I blink at the sun's angle and realize my lunch hour is up. I head back to my desk, which sits alongside a big picture window overlooking the bougainvillea-clad front wall of my apartment complex, and click the mouse to wake up my iMac.

Photoshop is still open on my screen, waiting for me to get back to designing the fall and winter lineup posters. The theater is doing a production of *Pinocchio* first, then *White Christmas* for the holiday season, with a smattering of local choruses and orchestras to fill in the open weekends. It should be good, even well-attended...if I can get people to come.

I genuinely love my little theater, which sits in the same historic building where it began operating as the opera house back in the 1890s. And I love the people who work inside the brick building, all of them working in theater because it's their passion, not for the money.

Hah, the very idea of working at this job for the money is laughable.

I poke at the leaves of my spider plant, Charlotte, which is slowly creeping around the windowsill and reaching for my iMac's glossy screen, and then get back to work.

Or, I try to.

But my interest just isn't in the design this afternoon.

It wasn't this morning, either. I move text boxes around and adjust some vectors, but nothing seems to stick.

Nothing will convince the good people of Phoenix Canyon to leave their living room sofas and sit in the tiny, hard seats of our historic theater to watch *Pinocchio.* It's hard enough getting them out when I'm inspired; if the work won't come, crowds certainly won't either.

The fact is, I called Angie on my lunch hour because I was feeling so stuck, and things aren't any better now.

I haven't been functioning properly since Saturday night, and that's the hard, sad truth. Now it's Monday afternoon, and I'm still caught up in the moment that Everett started to hand me a promo card, his lips parted to say something to me that *wasn't* part of the stock spiel—hey, a girl can dream—and the fire alarm went off, ending our one and only interaction in this human life.

It shouldn't have ended that way.

Unlike my relationship with Barry, which was stunted and mean and lasted way too long, I felt like in the minute or so I was breathing the same air as Everett, we had something real. When we looked into each other's eyes, we knew each other. I didn't make that up.

Or maybe this is a nervous breakdown, like Angie thinks.

Or *maybe* I really felt a connection, and he did too.

That's what *I* think.

I recognize that my belief in this does not make it more likely or even sane.

"Charlotte," I say to my spider plant, "*you* believe me, don't you?"

Charlotte quivers gently. It could be an affirmation, or it could be that the A/C just switched on and she's right in the breeze from the duct.

Come on, would an insane person allow for the interference of air conditioning?

It's clear I'm not going to get any work done from my desk this afternoon, so I throw my computer bag over my shoulder, call goodbye to my cat Tilda, who is sleeping in a ball of gray-and-white fluff on my bed, and head out to the parking area behind the apartment building. My Prius is green, dusty, and boasts several stickers letting every driver on the road know that I'm a huge fan of The Emergency. And even then, they don't know the extent of the fandom.

I'm not sure where the dust comes from. The wind, maybe.

It's a half-hour drive to the theater, which is nestled in a block of brick buildings making up Phoenix Canyon's historic downtown district, so I have thirty minutes to rock out to Everett's new solo album. It's ten songs that are essentially about being depressed and stumbling through life and love, plus one song that is weirdly upbeat. I wish I could have asked him about this upbeat track, titled *"Dream or No Dream"*. It's not like his usual stuff at all. It's almost...silly.

But of course I didn't think of that when he was standing in front of me.

Stupid of me, to waste that time daydreaming that we were having some sort of soulmate connection, when I was just another woman in line with a VIP ticket I'd paid for solely so I could shake his hand and get a selfie.

Out here on the freeway, in the unforgiving light of a SoCal late-summer afternoon, I can see how silly I've been.

It's a relief to get out of the car, shake off my Everett obsession, and stride through the theater's side-door. The warm air inside settles on my skin; we've had to turn up the thermostat this year to keep energy costs down. Ticket sales haven't been robust since the pandemic, while the cost of running the theater has skyrocketed. So we pay to keep our theater going with some very real sweat equity.

I slip off the cotton shirt I was wearing over my camisole and fling it over my arm, then head into the little maze of offices on the second floor, above the lobby. It's even warmer up here, and I'm just starting to regret my decision to work in the office when I realize there's a weird silence to the building.

Usually at least six or seven people are working here—they either can't work from home, have meetings to attend, or just prefer to get out of the house. But other than the sound of a box fan whirring in our shared office space, there's no activity at all in here. I look at the messy desks, the posters from old engagements tacked to the walls, the light spilling through a set of broken blinds, and wonder where everyone's gone.

For a moment, the loneliness courses through me like a physical thing, like the way I felt when I was standing on the pavement on Saturday night realizing I'd lost sight of Everett and I'd never see him that close again.

And then the conference room door opens and five people walk out. Four are coworkers—they shoot me worried glances. The fifth is a bald man I know to look at, if not in person. The chairman of the theater's board of directors, Alan Holmes.

He gives me a brisk little nod as he walks by, but doesn't say anything. I hear the door to the stairs whine open, click closed.

I look at my colleagues: Heidi, our accountant; Milton, our business manager; Sam and Lee, who work in client relations. They look like they've just walked out of a funeral.

Or a hospital room, one where the news isn't good.

Milton is the first to sigh and toss his notebook on a nearby desk. "Don't make this tougher than it has to be," he says to the room at large. "Just tell her."

"Tell me what?" The cold, lost feeling is back, filling my stomach with dread.

"The theater's closing," Sam says, looking at the floor, at the walls, anything but me. "We didn't bring in enough to fund the fall and winter season."

"But the winter season will *save* us," I remind them. "That's why I came in, to finish the posters—"

"We can't get there," Milton says. "It's not happening."

I don't have to ask what that means for my job.

It's over.

Chapter Three

EVERETT'S LYRICS ARE often described as the soundtrack to a nervous breakdown, and it's exactly what I need right now. The tears that I held back as I ran down the theater steps finally trickle down my cheeks when I slam my car door. But when I let Everett's rich baritone roll out of the speakers, he does all the hurting for me until I get home. That's good, because it's not safe driving on the freeway with blurred vision.

Back in my apartment, with the air conditioning set to an uncivilized sixty-five degrees—I only truly feel alive when I believe the PG&E police might come banging on my door—I put on the first Emergency album and let their raw chords and college-age anger spill through the studio apartment. At least, the first few songs. Then my natural, courteous nature takes over, that Ohio inherent niceness that makes me afraid I'm disturbing any neighbors who are home right now. I turn things down.

It's fine. I can still feel sorrow and anger emanate from the speakers without the whole building shaking.

Tilda sits in the front window, watching the neighborhood's outdoor cats stalking lizards, while I make myself a fresh pot of coffee and dump milk, vanilla syrup, and ice into it with the abandon of a woman who will only ever wear stretchy pants from here on out. Why go out of this apartment ever again? I have no job, I have no boyfriend, I have no true calling to work in TV or film or music, or I would be gainfully employed in some shiny building with an address in Burbank or Glendale, not out in the wilds of the canyons.

I'll stay in here with Tilda and Charlotte, I think, and listen to Everett and The Emergency, and that will be enough.

For how long?

Long enough.

I sip iced coffee, sickly sweet, and sing until my voice is hoarse, and then I flick open my phone and thumb through my socials, looking for something to take my mind off the dead weight of my life.

And then I see it.

An email from Everett.

Okay, not *from* from Everett, it's not like he is sending me personal emails—if he was, would I be in this state of mental debauchery? But it's from his fan club, a very small group compared to The Emergency's fan club, and the subject line is SECRET SHOW TONIGHT.

I exhale and I swear my heart goes fluttering out of my throat and into the ice-cold air of my apartment. Even Charlotte's leaves shiver a little, confronted with all that raw emotion and bone chilling A/C.

It'll be in New York, I think, jamming my thumb down on that email, willing it to open faster, stop spinning, wheel! *It'll be in Portland, it'll be in San Francisco.* How long would it take me to get to any of these places? I glance at the time. It's just past five. I might as well be in lockdown for the next three hours.

The email opens.

Everett Torby welcomes fans to a secret show tonight at the Desert Palm Motel in Palm Springs. Doors at nine p.m., hope to see you there!

My jaw drops.

Palm Springs—how far is that? I try to remember the last time I drove out there; it was a solid six or seven ago, when I was still new to California. I'd loved the retro town with its palm trees towering against a dramatic backdrop of mountains and the empty desert all around...but life was busy, and I'd never made time to go back.

Two hours, I think. With traffic? Even if it's double the usual mass of cars, if I leave right now, I can get there.

I don't even have to consider any potential downsides. It's *Everett.* And truly, besides Tilda, what else do I have now but Everett?

I grab my purse and run for the door. The only thing between me and my car is a stop at my neighbor Ronnie's door, asking her to feed Tilda tonight. She's delighted.

So, everyone wins!

This is traffic.

This is beyond traffic.

There should be a new word for this level of traffic.

Or maybe just "Hell" will suffice.

I resist the urge to beat my forehead against the steering wheel, but only barely. I know, I know: L.A. traffic is bad, blah-blah-blah, but seriously, doesn't the universe know I've been given one more chance to be near Everett? And once it's over, it's over. There won't be more secret shows in SoCal. I have no illusions about that point. This is just some fluke, some one-off.

At twenty past eight, when I'm starting to give up all hope, my line of traffic passes a police cruiser with its lights flashing and then, impossibly, daylight opens between the car ahead of me and mine. I watch the growing line of pavement between its bumper and my car's hood and then I realize *we're moving*.

Not at a crawl, not at the speed limit, but at something close enough to a decent pace that if I can find a parking spot near the hotel, I'll actually get to the show before the doors open.

With a laugh, feeling unusually light-hearted for a woman who just lost her job, broke up with her boyfriend, and is harboring a dangerous delusion that her soulmate is the lead singer of a rock n' roll band, I flick the album track ahead to that goofy, soppy, improbable song *Dream or No Dream* and belt along with Everett.

I just need one thing to go right

To catch this dream I have every night

Dream or no dream, I know you're the one

Dream or no dream, under stars, under sun

It's not a great song, is it?

But it's perfect for what I've got going right now.

Air conditioning spills from the doors of the Palm Desert Hotel's glass-fronted lobby. This retro-styled motel looks like an expensive idea of what a dive should be: chrome and neon and funny angles abound.

A desk clerk glances at me, immediately takes in that I'm not dressed expensively enough to be a guest, and says, "The Everett Torby show is in the lounge, through those doors and to your left."

"Thank you," I gasp. It's just past nine o'clock, and the lobby is deserted; if a crowd has shown up, I've missed my chance to be front of the line and muscle my way to the front near the stage. But I'm here. And that has to be enough. I give the clerk a nod and speed-walk through the tiled lobby, brushing against the potted palms at either side of the doorway off one side. The hall is wide, dimly lit, and empty; I'm immediately reminded of a movie theater late at night, after everyone's gone home. But there's conversation and music spilling from the open doorway ahead, so I make a beeline for it.

My people are in there.

I round the corner with a sigh of relief: here are the fans, men and woman of all ages, plenty of them wearing Emergency shirts, most of them making wide-eyed and animated conversation with the people around them. There are no strangers at Emergency shows, and at an Everett solo appearance, that rule goes double. But before I can get sucked into a chat with someone who loves the band like I do, I scope out the space, looking for the best spot to enjoy the show.

Under cool blue lamps that give the lounge a noir-mystery glow, the tables and chairs have been set back against the walls to free a square dance floor. The stage behind it is no more than a foot off the ground, and the stool where Everett will sit for his slower songs is so close to the edge, if I can elbow my way to the front I'll be able to gaze into his eyes as he sings.

But of course, there is already a thicket of girls there, and *their* elbows are out at their sides like sharp thorns, ready to defend their territory.

I sigh and turn to the bar against the wall to my left. If I can't be front and center, I'll take a vodka and tonic to settle my nerves.

With a glass and a spot just a few rows back, I'm feeling prepared as I can be for Everett's impending appearance. I sip my vodka and sigh to myself. *Soon.* That's all I've got right now.

Soon I'll see him again. Soon we'll make eye contact again. Soon I'll know, once and for all, if I was just out of my mind on adrenaline on Saturday night, or if there's really some strange flash of recognition between us, like he knows me and I know him.

The thought makes me tremble ever so slightly. And because I know I must look like a deranged fan-girl, I stare into the fizzing bubbles of my drink and try to stop my thoughts from buzzing around inside my brain. Some conversation from the front-and-center girls filters through the haze and I try to focus on that.

"I love him so much," a girl gushes. "Like, I don't think there's a hotter guy on the scene. He's so underground and sophisticated, you know?"

I realize, with a start of horror, that these are actual girls. Like, *maybe* eighteen years old? They are teenagers in belly shirts and stacked-sole sandals. They are here to ogle the forty-one-year-old man who sings about holding it together through another quarter-life crisis *"until you can't see where the midlife crisis took over"* and I am deeply, deeply confused and concerned that I'm somehow of their ilk. If I opened my mouth, would I sound like a teenager?

The vodka turns hot in my stomach and I swallow reflexively.

And then the lights go down and I don't have any more time to reflect on my shortcomings as a human, because here he is.

"Oh, Daddy," one of the teens moans, just before the clapping and cheers drown their chatter out completely.

Ick, I think, my toes curling in my Cons, but at the same time I'm instinctively moving forward, taking that crowding step that every GA audience makes the moment the band comes onstage. My chin is practically in the girl's pigtails before she gives in and steps forward, crowding her friends, who in turn shove against the stage. Everett sits on the stool, props his Doc Martens on the bottom rung, and looks out over us with a casual smile. It's magazine-ready, practiced, the perfect shot for any media who made it out here tonight, and as he scoops up the nearest guitar waiting on a stand near his stool, his gray suit jacket stretches over his shoulders in a way that makes my breath seize in my lungs.

I'm gross, I think.

But I can't help it.

With the crowd's help, I'm now within ten feet of him, just the sharp shoulders of two scrawny teenagers blocking me from the stage. Still, it's close enough to get what I need.

I hope.

He strums his guitar, looks out over the crowd, over my head.

Look at me, I think, along with two hundred other people.

His gaze drops, and our eyes meet.

A prickle of sensation ripples across my skin, as if he's stroked my cheek with the back of his knuckles, ever so softly.

He blinks, and his smile stiffens for a moment. And I know he feels it, too.

Doesn't he?

Everett Torby opens his mouth to sing, and for the next hour, he manages to avoid looking me in the eye for even a millisecond.

Chapter Four

BY THE LAST song, I know it's time to give it up. Possibly all of it —fandom, The Emergency, music in general. A small price to regain sanity, I figure. I came here tonight like a madwoman, convinced the singer of a moderately famous indie rock act was my soulmate and just in need of a little eye contact to help him figure it out. Not a healthy position. My sister has been telling me this for years, and if I would only listen, probably my coworkers have been, too.

Why did I think spending *more* time in his presence would fix me? I have been going about this all wrong.

The only real answer is to turn to audiobooks and podcasts, as dry and scientific as possible, and maybe adopt some more cats, maybe some dogs. Three each should keep me busy, for starters.

Yeah, this is the right move. I can invest in myself as a crazy animal lady, instead of a fan-girl, before I *really* take things too far. Today I drove to Palm Springs at the drop of a hat. Who knows what I might do tomorrow?

Freshly buoyed by this self-knowledge, I watch Everett walk offstage without looking over his shoulder. He's tired, he's spent, he's done with us. I tamp down the normal feeling of sympathy that always overwhelms me at this moment, when he is so clearly done with being a rock singer. It's not my place to feel sympathetic for him. I'm supposed to buy the records, scream at the end of songs, and leave.

Fans who have not reached my enviable level of self-awareness are clustered at the bar, unwilling to leave the venue until they know that he's left the building. The bartender opens the kitchen door and shouts for help. For a moment I waver, my desire to be part of them warring with a need to be better than them, a chosen one, and this new resolution I'm playing with, this life in which I'm not obsessed with Everett Torby.

None of them are good choices, I think, but they're all I've got.

Reluctantly, I toss my cup into the trash and head out the door.

I used to love being one of them, a willing member part of the cult, but clearly I can't be chill enough for this scene anymore.

The palm trees surrounding the parking lot and planted against the low-rise motel are rustling in a soft desert breeze as I trudge out to my car. Palm Springs at night is cool, dry, scented faintly with some exotic bloom I can't place. It's not so different from my own neighborhood, but there's an exotic feel to this town that has been cultured by nearly a century of Hollywood excess. It feels like a place where crazy things can happen, probably because so many stars have come here to blow off steam. There is an aura of potential sin, like Las Vegas without the crowds and jingle-jangle of casino games.

Earlier tonight I'd parked on a side-street a short walk away from the motel, not willing to give up a single minute of Everett's show by searching for a closer spot or finding room in the municipal parking garage. The stroll back to my Prius takes me past mid-century houses squatting behind stone-patterned front yards, blue lights of TVs and monitors shining through their plate-glass front windows with the same glow as the lounge I just left. Every house has a camera by the front door, a luminescent electric doorbell that gazes onto the stoop and the street beyond.

I wave at them, one by one. *Hello, computer, hello, hello.*

I stop where my car should be and look at the empty spot.

I realize there are no other cars parked on the street, either.

I look up the block and see the *No Parking 9 PM - 9 AM* sign crouching near the stop sign at the corner.

I turn a slow, sorrowful circle and wonder if today is just the start of a spectacular run of bad luck.

"Saturday, too," I reflect, looking up and down the empty street, watched by the luminous blue cameras. "It all started going wrong on Saturday. When my handbill blew away."

Like a lucky talisman I didn't know I held. I should have chased it down.

Well, there's only one hotel I know of within walking distance. "Credit card," I say to my pocket, where my slim wallet is stowed, "this is gonna hurt."

"No rooms," the clerk behind the front desk of the Desert Palm Motel says diffidently, looking anywhere but the computer. "We're completely sold out tonight."

"Did everyone check in?" I ask, feeling a level of desperation that is only slightly enhanced by the sound of fun coming from the lounge. *Is he in there?* I don't dare go find out.

"Everyone has checked in," the clerk replies, sighing at me for even trying to find a loophole.

"Can you recommend anything for me?" I could get an Uber back home, I suppose, but suddenly I'm so exhausted, the idea sounds impossible. I just want a place to lay my head. And coming back tomorrow to pick up my car makes the thought of paying to get all the way back to my apartment even less palatable. I'd be saving money by staying at this overpriced hotel. "My car was towed and I just have to stick around until nine a.m. so I can find where they took it and bail her out."

"Her?" The clerk eyes me for a moment.

Yes, I think, *I am the kind of person who names her car, and Lime Lucinda is probably alone and scared in an impound lot right now, and I'm incredibly guilty over that fact.*

"Please," I say. "I recognize that I screwed up, but I am asking for a little help here."

The clerk lowers his gaze and his tone, as if he's trying not to get caught by unseen spies, and says, "The pool deck is through those double doors just down the hall. Towels in an unlocked cabinet right outside. You fell asleep on a lounge chair after a fun night; it happens all the time."

I scramble for words to tell him how grateful I am, but he won't meet my eyes and that makes effusive thanks difficult to verbalize. "Okay," I say at last, "thank you so much."

"Goodnight, madam," he replies, eyes on his computer.

It occurs to me that if he doesn't know what I look like, it'll be easier for him to deny he ever allowed me to trespass and sleep on the hotel grounds overnight. That's fine. He can take our little secret to the grave as long as I can just get off my feet for a few hours.

The pool deck is easy to find; the towels, thick and luxurious, are right where he said they'd be. I find a chair half-hidden by palms and spread one towel out, and roll up another one for my head.

This is okay, I think, feeling cozy in the wraparound grasp of the hotel courtyard. It's only three stories tall, the balconies winding around the pool deck's tall palms and casting a dim light down on the blue water, so there is plenty of sky overhead. Even with the lights of the hotel and the surrounding town, the big desert sky presses downward, stars pulsing to their own beats.

I have to make some changes to my life, and this is probably the best place to lay quietly and ponder what they'll be—where I'll go, how I'll start over, what I'll replace Everett with—

because this can't go on. I'm stranded in his hotel on the other side of the mountains, no car and no room, because I chased him here. And for what? The way his presence gnaws at me, drawing me towards him, isn't just fandom. It's something else. Something darker?

If I'm obsessed with Everett, and I think most people assessing the situation would agree that I am, that sounds bad. But it's hard for me to really see my feelings as trouble in the making. For me, maybe. But for Everett? He's going to continue floating through life, making music and melting panties. And I'll be the girl on the pool chair, my life paused indefinitely while I try to figure out how to live without him.

The only one who gets hurt in this is me.

And I'm content with that.

Chapter Five

THE CHAIR NEXT to me creaks, cutting through a weird dream, and I flicker my eyes open. The shape beside me is long and bulky in the dark; my heart starts hammering and I draw back in panic.

Then the figure shifts and the soft light from a room above brushes his features with a golden glow, and the panic turns to... well, to more panic.

It's Everett.

It's *Everett Torby*.

My brain is screaming frantically, making a lot of incoherent noise. This would be a great time for those rah-rah brain cells of mine, the ones who have been telling me all along that Everett and I have a chance, to make some suggestions. But of course, now that I need them, there's no advice, good or bad, cutting through the clutter.

So I just stare at him, my eyes so wide I can feel them straining at the corners. I probably look like a lemur. I blink a few times, trying to get my expression back under control.

Everett sighs and turns on his side, as if settling in for the night in some comfy bed. I'm staring right at his face, just inches from mine.

Be asleep, I think. *Do not wake up and see me staring at you.*

As if he hears me, Everett's eyelids flutter open.

He looks at me.

Right at me, cool and calm.

If he realizes I'm the girl who has been stalking him for the past two shows, he doesn't give anything away.

"Sorry I woke you," he murmurs, his voice husky with singing and whiskey.

"No, it's fine," I whisper, hardly believing I'm actually awake.

"I know what you're thinking," he says. "There are a lot of pool chairs. But these are the best hidden, which is probably why you're here, too."

"Yeah," I say. "I mean…just from hotel management. Not like, the law or anything."

His cheek dimples. "Let's just remember that you're the one who brought up running from the law, alright?"

"Sure," I agree, trying desperately not to read some kind of future into the words *let's just remember.*

Everett shifts on the pool chair, wincing a little. "Maybe I'm too old to sleep on the pool chairs," he says regretfully, voice still low. Just for me. "This thing is reminding me of a time I fell off my bike in sixth grade and bruised my hip all to hell."

"Ow. But...don't you have a room?"

"I have a room," he says, "but I'm not welcome up there right now."

I blink at him. He shifts again, his face slipping out of the light. The darkness gives me courage. "What do you mean?" I ask.

"I had some messy ex stuff to deal with here...that's why I'm in Palm Springs, really. We had some papers to sign, some stuff we owned together getting sold off. She didn't want to come to L.A., though. Insisted I meet her here." Silence for a moment. I wonder if he's said all he's willing to share. Then he continues, his voice slightly strained: "She wants to get back together. I didn't expect that."

I take a breath to hide my very unreasonable disappointment. I know Everett and his girlfriend broke up six months ago; that's not stalker-knowledge, it was just available information. He has mentioned it at shows; it's been in music blogs and magazines. He has added lyrical footnotes to some of his songs on his solo record, sharing how they've helped him get through his breakup. I *swear* it's general knowledge.

Now, should I have harbored a deep, secret, embarrassing hope that since Everett and indie singer Liz Astra broke up, I might have a chance with him?

Of course not, but that's why it's a *secret embarrassing* hope and not one I share with friends or coworkers or the fellow fans on our judgmental subreddit.

They're getting back together, though?

For a moment, I let myself flounder around in a sea of despair. Then, I remember that Everett *isn't* upstairs having a passionate resumption of affairs with his ex-girlfriend. Instead, he's on the pool deck, talking to me.

Well, this can't be real, my last rational brain cell remarks, just before it's pummeled into dust by all my spiraling, love-struck, out of control rah-rah brain cells. They're back and better than ever.

I hesitate; then, as my triumphant gray matter shrieks, *Nothing ventured, nothing gained!,* say, "It's really uncool of her to put you on the spot like that."

"Thank you!" Everett exclaims, lifting his head from his chair again. The light from above caresses his sharp cheekbones. "That's what I think, too. I told her as much."

"You have to be honest," I contribute.

"Yes, you have to be honest." He sighs. "And she was probably being honest when she told me she never wants to see me again, then kicked me out of my room."

"And the hotel's full."

Everett chuckles dryly. "So I've been told. And it's my fault, apparently. So I have no one to blame for any of this but myself. If I hadn't craved approval so badly, I wouldn't have set up this secret show tonight, and there'd be a room for me to barricade myself inside after Liz played her usual head games."

"It was a good show," I say, feeling more at ease with him now. Everett's just a person, after all. A person who gets blindsided by his ex, a person who has been denied a new room by the stiff clerk in the lobby. We have one thing in common, anyway. "I'm glad you put it on, anyway."

"Well, thank you. I always appreciate hearing that." He shifts again. "Damn, this chair is really uncomfortable."

"You should try doubling up a towel under your hip," I suggest, lifting my head from my towel-pillow to point out the offending spot.

"I think you're right," he says, and he swings his feet to the ground to adjust the towel. He's leaning forward, his upper body dangerously close to me, when his gaze suddenly rakes across my face and his eyes widen with surprise. "Wait a minute. It's *you*."

Yes, in a few of my wildest dreams, I've imagined Everett saying those very words to me, but possibly in a more romantic, relieved, let's-go-home-and-make-babies tone. He doesn't sound horrified, thank goodness, but he doesn't sound thrilled, either.

"It's me," I confirm, smiling as lightly as I can. "This is awkward."

"No, I'm making it that way and I'm sorry," Everett says. "I thought your voice was familiar. I should have recognized you before. It's just so dark over here."

"It's fine, really—"

"Let's start again." That dimple pops out again, filling my insides with heat. "I'm Everett, and you are...?"

"Cassie," I whisper, hardly believing we're doing this. Real introductions. Real names. "I'm Cassie."

"Cassie," he repeats, and my name in his husky voice is enough to send shivers up my spine. Shivers and heat, I'm doing great here. He says, "It's good to properly meet you, Cassie. You know, at that meet-and-greet thing on Saturday, I had the funniest—"

He stops.

"The funniest?" I prompt, desperate for him to say it. Say *feeling*. Say *feeling that you and I have met before*. Say *feeling that you're my soul-mate*.

Okay, he's not going to say that, but, I mean…

"Nothing," Everett says, shaking his head. "Never mind. I'm just happy to have you as a pool deck-mate tonight, Cassie. Seems only fair, after the whole fire alarm thing at the coliseum."

"That was pretty traumatic," I say, sighing. Oh, the things he might have said. Lost forever. Was he going to say he had the funniest feeling we'd met before? Already knew each other? I could understand why he wouldn't admit that—I wasn't exactly bursting to admit that same feeling to him, after all.

But now I was going to wonder about us, more than ever, when just a little while ago I'd been planning the big, full life I'd have for myself once I forgot him.

Fat chance of that happening now.

Everett's still leaning towards me, his elbows against his knees and his hands loose in front of him. They're almost touching me, and as I slowly straighten up to sit and face him, I feel his closeness like our bodies are pressing together. I let my knuckle brush his, just to experiment, and the full-body buzz whips across my skin like an electric shock.

His lips fall open, and all at once I can't stop myself, don't have any reason why I should stop myself. There are no more dissenting voices left in my brain. He's here, I'm here, and there's clearly something between us. I press my hand onto his right knee for balance, lean forward, and kiss Everett right on those luscious, spare lips of his.

Chapter Six

I'M KISSING HIM. I'm kissing Everett Torby.

And for the moment, anyway, he's into it!

At first it's just lips on lips, a middle-school kiss, but when he doesn't shove me off him, that's all the encouragement I need to lean in, pressing my spare hand against his left knee so now I'm practically in his lap, my lips cajoling his to split open ever so slightly and give me something to work with. His mouth is soft and hot and silky-smooth and all I want is to know what's beneath the surface, to press my tongue against his shiny rock-star teeth and then slide beyond, to taste him after a night of singing and god-knows-how-many whiskies.

His lower lip buckles and mine scoops him up, our mouths meshing in a way that feels as perfect as two puzzle pieces clicking together. I feel his breath come hard through his nose, and I know in my bones he's just a second from opening his mouth and letting me in—

And then his hands are on my upper arms—*yes,* I think excitedly—but instead of squeezing and pulling me against him, he's pushing me back. Gently, and, maybe worse than that, kindly.

I don't want kindness right now. I want passion. Wherever that might lead.

"Cassie," he says, slowly freeing his mouth from mine. I feel my name against my lips. "Cassie, we can't."

And suddenly I'm myself again, the horror of what I've just done raising goosebumps on my arms. I fling myself back into my pool chair with so much violence that it rocks under my weight and then, with a silent acquiescence to the cruelty of the universe, it flips over, taking me with it.

I'll just stay down here until he's gone, I think from beneath my cover of towels and pool chair.

But no, the chivalrous Everett refuses to allow me to die with dignity. He's over me in an instant, hands extended, and I can't help but grasp his fingers and let him help me up.

I dance back from him the moment I'm on my feet. Wouldn't want him to think I'm coming back for another kiss.

"Sorry," I mumble, scooping up the towels I've spilled across the pool deck. "Look, I'll go find somewhere else to sleep."

"No, no," he says, sounding unhappy. "I'll go back upstairs. I think I need to put my foot down with Liz, anyway. She's just trying to provoke me into getting mad at her, because when we're mad, we—" He stops abruptly, but it's enough for me to know where he's going.

Great, they're one of those angry-sex couples. Talk about knowledge I never needed.

Please, just leave me to die inside in peace.

But even as he turns away, giving me what I thought I wanted, I feel a surge of terror at the idea of losing him again. For good, this time.

"Everett," I say, "please, wait."

He lifts an eyebrow at my request, but holds in place. Waiting.

There are a thousand things I want to say to him, but only one will make any sense. It's the weakest line of all, and still my voice cracks a little when I say, "I'm sorry I kissed you."

Everett shakes his head. "It's fine."

"But—"

But what?

He seems to know why I'm stalling. "It was a good kiss," he admits after a moment. "You're a good kisser. And...you're a beautiful girl, Cassie. A good kisser, a good listener, a beautiful girl." He grins. "You're the whole package."

A rah-rah brain cells sticks up its hand. *Call on me, please.*

No, I tell it. *He's still leaving.*

And sure enough, Everett turns to leave. But not before he says, "Thanks for talking to me tonight. I mean that."

While I'm still standing there silently, flustered by his compliments, Everett heads inside the hotel and disappears from me.

Forever, this time.

That's a promise I am making to myself.

I wake up with a backache to the sound of hip hop, playing at a whisper-level from a boombox sitting at the feet of the pool boy. He's humming along to his music as he sweeps the pool with slow, practiced motions, enjoying the predawn silence. A streak of pink in an otherwise deep blue sky is the only giveaway that day is on the way; this isn't a hotel of early-risers. I wonder if the pool boy even saw me. After Everett went back inside, I tugged the deck chair deep into the landscaping against the hotel wall, hoping that if he came back, he'd think I was gone.

Of course, he didn't come back, and I am surprised I got any kind of sleep with the way I was beating myself up over that kiss. I guess I just exhausted myself.

Well, it's a new day, time to start the self-chastisement fresh. *Cassie, what in God's name were you thinking?*

"Oh why," I murmur to myself, because this kind of embarrassment has to go fully verbal. "Why did I kiss him? We were having a nice chat. I ruined things."

On the other hand, my brain says thoughtfully, *you got to kiss him. That chance wasn't coming again.*

"That's probably true." I roll up my towels, planning to drop them into the hamper as I make my quiet escape from the hotel. The towels, and my kiss, will be the only lingering signs I was here—if he even remembers it—and that's for the best.

But when the doors slide open, a cloud of air conditioning scented with sausage and eggs wafts out. And I remember seeing a sign for a breakfast buffet at what I'd consider a very reasonable price.

It's too early to go search for my car, anyway. Breakfast it is.

I follow my nose to the buffet, which is being set up in a room beyond the lounge. I don't even look at the closed doors to the lounge; there's something sad about a venue after the concert is gone, like a haunted space that will never be the same, and I know I'll never see it again. Nothing will ever induce me to come back to the hotel where I kissed Everett Torby. Probably even Palm Springs will have to be dead to me now; the whole damn municipality must disappear from my mental map if I'm ever to move on from this.

The buffet room is comfortingly empty and devoid of emotional connections, just some black-and-white prints on the walls depicting the hotel in her early days and a window, tinted dark to keep out the desert sun, that overlooks the landscaping around the parking lot rather than the pool. I can choke down a nice breakfast if I'm not staring at the scene of what might have been.

A white-shirted server glances curiously at me as he sets out napkins on the tables, and I give him a little shrug to say *yes, I know it's hellaciously early, but what can I do?*

No one is asking for room keys or proof of residence, so I just pick up a plate and start moving my way down the buffet line. Eggs, sausage, watermelon, blueberries, a tiny bottle of hot sauce, and I'm on my way. To a table in the corner, where I can sit facing the blue-tinted palm trees outside, and hopefully not be spotted as an imposter posing as a hotel guest.

I'm watching a lizard scurry through the palm fronds outside, hotel-buffet eggs gluey in my mouth, when I hear him say good morning to the staff.

It's an effort not to drop my fork, since all the nerves in my body simply stop their usual work and instead put all their energy into flooding my brain with flight messages. *Get out, get out, get out!*

But where would I go? He'll see me if I pass through the room on the way to the door. Well, what about the emergency exit next to the window? I look thoughtfully at the sign that reads ALARM WILL SOUND and consider which is more embarrassing: seeing him again, or turning the entire hotel upside-down with a false fire evacuation at six o'clock in the morning.

I can't do it; there have already been too many fire alarms between us. The lizard vanishes up the tree, a waiter sets a cup of coffee on the table next to mine, and Everett says, "Thank you," in his charred-honey voice.

Why is he sitting next to me?

Does he want my attention? Maybe he feels just as bad about how last night went as I do. Maybe he wants to kiss me again?

No, that's not it. I've just taken the most secluded spot in the room, and he's going for the second-best place to avoid being spotted by fans the moment they enter the breakfast room.

I suppose I'm a known threat that has already been neutralized, what with the embarrassment of a lifetime just a few hours ago.

But of course I can't help but slide my gaze towards him. I mean, he sat next to me. That's on him. I make myself look at his food first, as if I'm just curious about what the other early-riser in Palm Springs eats for breakfast.

He has a plate of eggs and a little waffle; between them rises a tiny pyramid of blueberries. It's a light meal, and I feel a little self-conscious about the sausage links on my plate; there's just about enough here to build a little log cabin. If I played with my food. Which I most certainly never do—ahem.

My eyes stray from the plate to the man. Everett has changed his shirt since he left me last night; in fact, he looks freshly showered, with damp curls right behind his ear and along his shirt collar. I try not to think about who he might have showered with, focusing on his shirt instead. It's perfect for Palm Springs: white cotton with a subtle print of pale green cactus dotted over it, short sleeves, buttons, a loose collar.

In fact, I think I've seen him in this shirt before. On Instagram. I can't decide if that fact is icky or intimate.

Maybe both.

He glances at me and gives me a small, knowing smile. "Good morning."

Okay, he's acknowledging me. It's time to panic, people!

I open my mouth to reply, but find my tongue is tied in knots. "Good—hey—I—"

He chuckles and shakes his head, like it's no more than he'd expect of me. And that gives me a new rush of adrenaline that spikes from my toes to my fingertips. *He has an opinion of me.*

I've made a fool of myself, sure, but I've also gone from anonymous fan to someone he's got a baseline for.

Even if that baseline is unasked-for kisses and awkward apologies.

Suddenly, I wonder where his girlfriend is. Of course, I know who she is. It's public knowledge that Everett Torby previously lived with Liz Astra, an indie singer-songwriter, for two years. She was the reason he moved to L.A.—I can remember when his photos changed from Brooklyn to the beach. Probably every fan of The Emergency thought the band was going to break up and everything was changing, but as it turned out, the move didn't wreck anything and the next album sounded fantastic with that fresh dose of Vitamin D in Everett's lyrics.

When Liz and Everett split—again, public knowledge, check his Instagram—he stayed in his Venice Beach bungalow, saying that California was in his blood now.

And now?

Is California in his blood and Liz Astra in his bed? Did they get back together last night? Is she asleep in his bed, nestled up into his pillows, deliciously happy that they've kissed and made up? I torture myself with a carefully constructed imagining of the scene. She's kicked off the covers, and she sighs as she rolls over. The door clicks open and Everett comes in, sunshine at his back, bringing her a cup of coffee and a dish of fresh strawberries...

"She left," Everett says.

I gape at him. "What?"

"Liz," he says, lifting his coffee cup. "My ex. I went upstairs, and she was already gone. I was relieved, because I wasn't sure I could take another fight." He gives me a sardonic look with those gray-blue eyes, takes a thoughtful sip of coffee. Winces at the taste. "You know, if you hadn't talked to me out there, I might have gone up before she decided I wasn't worth the trouble and took off. I think you might have saved me, Cassie."

"Oh, well, I, uh—" I *saved* him? I saved him! I'm the hero now. Things are looking up. I take a breath and try to speak like a human instead of a glitching robot. "Happy to be of service," I assure him.

I pick up my coffee to take a calm, casual sip and instead my lips encounter a small bug and I spit it out. "Ugh, what was *that?*"

Everett's laughing now. He leans over, inspecting the small wet creature that tried to steal my caffeine. "I have to tell ya," he says, "this hotel is not the cleanest place in the world."

"Well, now I need more coffee." I look around for a server and notice one hovering near the buffet. I wave my coffee cup in the air, hoping he won't make me get up and refill it myself. I can't just walk away from this conversation.

"That's your reaction? More of their coffee?" Everett shakes his head, still amused. "It's got me thinking maybe I should head up the road in search of a more sanitary place to get a latte. Also? I really want a latte." And then he pushes back from the table, tossing his napkin down. "You ready?"

I stare at him. "For what?"

"There's got to be a cafe on the main road. Come on. It's still cool enough to take a walk. Won't be this nice again until the sun goes down. Want to join me or what?"

He's inviting me to take a walk with him?

Every brain cell I possess stands for an ovation.

"Yes," I say, possibly with more force than necessary. "Yes, I'm coming."

A second chance? With Everett Torby?

My life just turned around.

Chapter Seven

I KNOW WE must make an odd pair—I'm wearing a crumpled sleeveless blouse with denim capris that are loosening with every passing second, and he's wearing a perfectly crisp cotton shirt and a pair of blue linen shorts that probably cost more than the ransom on my poor impounded Prius will be. But as we saunter along the sidewalk, savoring the final moments of a cool desert sunrise, I know it doesn't matter that we're dressed differently or that we live in different spheres. He asked me to come with him. I'm not a stalker, and I'm not a fan. I'm a girl out for a walk with a guy.

That fact, as unlikely as it seems to the more rational side of my brain (which frankly is really struggling right now), soaks through my body like a cool bath on a hot day. I give myself over to the fantasy. Everett and me. It could happen?

It could happen.

Palm Springs is sleepy this early in the morning, but after a couple of blocks we find where everyone awake is hanging out: a funky-looking cafe called Smiling Lizard Coffee. The building is squat and brown; the front door is marked by a four-foot-long green lizard carving. He's got a mug of coffee and a blissed-out expression.

"This has to be the place," Everett says, pausing at the steps. "You feeling it?"

"As a lizard appreciator, I don't see how I could miss this place."

"You appreciate lizards?" Everett grins and opens the door, letting a cool rush of air blow over us. "*I* appreciate lizards!"

"No way! Are you also a member of the Los Angeles Lizard Appreciation Society?" I slip past him, up the stairs and into the cafe. The scent of coffee, rich and warm, is like a soothing burst of incense.

"Are you kidding? I started the Venice Beach chapter. And I bring all the snacks to our meetings."

"Your meetings have snacks? No way! I'm moving to your group." I tear my gaze from the lizard-heavy decor in the cafe and laugh up at Everett. "It's just not as much fun without cookies."

"You make me wish it was real," he says, smiling down at me.

"I wish a lot of fake things were real," I admit, and then the truth of that statement hits me a little too hard and I have to look at the chalk-written menu before I say something stupid.

"Like unicorns," Everett suggests, perusing the board from my side.

My fingers could brush against his if I just—I ball them up and put my fists behind my back. *No touching.* Don't do anything stupid. "Like birds."

"Oh, I totally wish birds were real."

The barista looks over her espresso machine at us. One eyebrow pops up as she takes in Everett. I bite back a little smile. Everett's not exactly a household name; indie singers are famous to a fairly select audience. But this girl knows exactly who is standing in front of her, taking on the entire birds-are-real establishment before seven o'clock in the morning. "So," she says with a conspiratorial twist to her lips, "I hear you know birds aren't real."

"Oh good, honey, she's one of us!" Everett announces, and even though I know it's part of the game, the *honey* throws me off balance for a moment.

The barista nods smartly, enjoying her moment in Everett's sun. "I have to tell ya, I saw a bird outside yesterday, and if I were you, I'd avoid."

"Ten-four, comrade," Everett agrees.

Okay, maybe it's getting a little out of hand. "Could I get a smoked honey latte?" I ask. "That sounds amazing."

"For sure," the barista says. "And for you, Ev—sir?"

He grins. "Hey, my grandmother calls me Ev."

The barista is lit up from within. "Oh, now that's cute!"

"I think you just wanted a latte, right?" I interrupt, unwilling to share a second of this little dream world I'm currently inhabiting. *Get your own Everett, Barista,* I think. *I worked my ass off to get this one.*

And I don't know how long I can keep him.

"Yeah," Everett agrees. "A large latte with four shots and maybe, like, a quarter-foam? So not a cappuccino, but, you know..."

"A wet cappuccino," the barista says, pulling out a few paper cups.

"I actually hate that term," Everett says apologetically. "Don't you think it's kind of gross?"

"Hey, I don't name 'em, I just make 'em. But yeah, it's pretty gross."

"What if it was a 'moist' cappuccino?" I ask. "Would you order it that way?"

"I would absolutely," Everett says gravely. "I love the word 'moist'—I wish I had more opportunities to use it."

The barista glances up and says, "What if you wrote a song called '*Moist is My Favorite*'? That would be cool."

There's a moment of silence while we all reflect that the barista made it weird. She knows it, too. There's some extra emphasis to her banging as she empties the espresso wand and prepares new shots. It's an old-fashioned machine from the days before even espresso had to be computerized, and I hope it can stand up to her embarrassment, which clearly has a physical side.

A few more customers enter and stand behind us, which helps her hurry things along, and a few minutes later Everett has pulled out a chair for me in the back corner of the cafe. A clay lizard spills out of a pot of geraniums and smiles up at me. "I thought this one had the cutest lizard," he explains, booping its nose.

"I like the stripes." I run a finger along its back, fingering the rough paint strokes in purple and blue. "How's the moist cappuccino?"

He takes an experimental sip. "Surprisingly moist! How about that smoked honey?"

"It has to sit for a few minutes. I'm afraid of burning my tongue."

Everett lowers his eyelashes, smiling to himself.

"What?"

"Oh...I was just thinking...forget it. Silly."

I've never wanted to know what another person was thinking more in my life, but I don't have the courage to pry. I'm afraid to make a single wrong move that might send Everett Torby walking out of my life again. "Okay," I say. "So, about this lizard cookie situation—"

"I want to take a year off."

"What?" I blink at him.

Everett rubs a hand over his face. "Sorry. I just—this will sound crazy, but I have no one to talk to. Not about this. Can I trust you? I feel like I can trust you." He laughs. "I think I just made it really clear I trust you, so maybe I should have asked first."

"Of course you can trust me." My heart is thudding. Am I Everett's confidante now? Is that a good thing? What if I give him the wrong advice? "A year off, from what?" I ask, hoping he doesn't mean The Emergency.

"From music, from public life, from everything," he says, sighing. "And I know that sounds privileged as hell, maybe even a little over-the-top, because it's not like I'm, oh I don't know, Bruce Springsteen or something. I don't exactly have the press driving around after me when I go to Ralph's to pick up a loaf of bread. But I still feel…I feel like I need permission."

"From the band," I suggest.

"From the fans," he says. "From people like you."

I drop my gaze, looking down at my coffee cup instead of his earnest eyes. I'm a test subject. He wants to know what his small but mighty army of mega-fans will do if he deletes his social media and goes off to live in Tibet for a year.

"Everett," I say, savoring his name because I know I won't get to say it to him many more times, "if you need a break, you have to take a break. And you don't have to justify that to anyone."

"I feel like I do, though. Is that…I don't know, is that arrogance on my part? To feel like I'm that important in other people's lives?"

I sigh and sip my latte. It's good. It's good, but it doesn't drown out the screaming in my head. Everett brought me out this morning to ask me if he can disappear without hurting people like me. And the truth is, no, he can't. But at the same time, I know I can't tell him the truth. Because it's not fair to him, nor is it his fault. The crazy is *our* problem.

I take a breath before saying, "It's going to be hard for some people to deal with, but if you're not able to refresh yourself, it's going to be a lot harder on everyone in the long run when you retire because you're exhausted, and leave us all in the lurch. So, yes, if you need the break, you have to take the break."

He nods. "Thank you. That's really helpful. It's *my* rationale, obviously, but I didn't know if...fans...would see it that way."

"I think in the end, everyone will understand."

"You'd understand?"

"I promise I would. I already do." I sip the latte again. "Yo, this is *really* good. You should try it."

I mean he should order one for himself, but Everett simply reaches across the little table, picks up my cup, and takes a sip.

"Mmm," he says, while my mind reels that he just put his lips on the same lid where mine have been. "Damn. That's *really* good, you're right."

He pushes the cup back to me, unconcerned. Maybe the kiss canceled out any thoughts of germs? Or maybe he's just the kind of person who always accepts a drink from someone else's bottle or glass?

"Well, I'll think about the break, then," he says, drumming his fingers lightly on the table. "I just think it would be healthy, after all the touring we've done over the past year. Everyone else in the band is ready to play with their own side projects. Zander has a baby on the way. If I was going to do it, this would be the time."

I try not to react, but I have to ask, gently, "Zander has a baby on the way?"

Everett gives me an apologetic grin. "Yeah, whoops. That's not public yet. Our secret, okay?"

"Okay," I agree. "Our secret."

We have a secret.

"Listen," he says, and I lean forward, full of anticipation.

"Yes?"

"I'm going to get one of those avocado toasts. Do you want one?" And Everett points at a person sitting a few tables away, looking blissfully happy with their avocado toast.

It's time I just accept that this is breakfast with a guy I'll probably never talk to one-on-one again, and enjoy it for what it is. "If you're buying," I agree, giving him a genuine, not-freaked-out, smile. "I'm going to have to save my money for my car's ransom."

"Oh my god, I forgot about your poor car!" Everett stands. "Let's have breakfast and then I'll help you find it, okay?"

"That's really kind of you, thanks. Hey, Everett?"

He looks back at me. "Yeah?"

"Sorry I kissed you." I feel like it had to be said one more time. Just to clear the air between us.

He smiles. "It's no problem, Cassie."

Which makes me wonder if maybe, just maybe, he liked it.

Dammit, Cassie!

Chapter Eight

THE AVOCADO TOAST *is* wonderful, served on slabs of fresh sourdough bread and drizzled with olive oil and more of that smoked honey. I'm feeling very full and happy when Everett glances at his phone and suggests we walk back to the hotel.

"It's nearly eight," he says. "I'm sure the car lot opens at nine. So you can freshen up in my room, then we'll go find your car. I drove myself here, so we have wheels."

The idea of going up to Everett's room gives me a full-body electric shock, but I just nod and say, "Honestly, that would be awesome of you, thanks."

"More coffee to go?" He picks up my empty cup and heads for the register without asking. I have to jog after him to make sure he gets me a cold brew for the road. One milky, sweet latte is enough in a day.

Turns out he had the same idea, so we emerge onto the street and leave the lizards behind with cold cups in our hands, condensation already sweating from their sides as the desert heat rolls over us like a smothering blanket. "Phew," I gasp. "How do people live out here?"

"Where do you live?" Everett asks casually. He looks at me as he takes a sip of coffee, his mouth pursed into an *o* on his pink straw.

I resist the urge to laugh at his face. "I live in Orange County, far enough west to get a decent sea-breeze most of the time. You know where Phoenix Canyon is?"

"Yeah, I've been to the theater there," Everett says. "It's pretty cool, actually."

My footsteps stutter for a moment. "No way, Everett, I *work* at that theater!"

"You do? That's so awesome! I love how historic that place is...and you get great players. What's next, anyway?"

I stare at him, stricken. Because for a moment, I'd forgotten. But now it all rushes back—the theater is closing, I'm about to be out of work, I have no idea what I'm going to do next. The things I was supposed to leave behind when I came to Palm Springs for one night of rebellion at Everett's solo show.

"There's nothing next," I say. "It's closing."

"*What?* That's insane! How is the community allowing that?"

I shake my head. "It's a cute little town, but it's still the O.C. —not exactly known for its high-minded theater-goers. I don't know if anyone who lives in the town actually comes to shows."

"God." Everett looks genuinely upset. "That's really depressing."

"Community theater is a tough gig," I say pragmatically, as if my heart isn't broken over it, too. "And also I guess I have to find a new job, but I haven't given that much thought yet. I only just found out yesterday."

"Yesterday, huh?" He looks at me thoughtfully. "You were really dealing with some stuff when you decided to come over here, weren't you?"

I have to laugh at that. "Honestly, it's more like I *wasn't* dealing with my stuff. I just decided to come here instead."

"If I can be someone's break from reality, I've done my job."

"That's really nice," I tell him, and I mean it. "More breaks from reality, please."

"Okay," Everett laughs. "As soon as I take a year off. That's *my* break from reality."

"What do you think you'll do?"

"Maybe travel? I don't know, that's kind of what I do for work, isn't it? Maybe I should stay home instead. That would be a novelty."

"Get to know *you*," I suggest.

"Oof, or not."

"Have you not met my friend Everett? He's lovely."

Everett gives me an appreciative smile. "That's really nice, thank you. But you've only just met me. I'm sure the real me is just waiting to jump out and surprise you."

"I didn't realize you were a goblin in a human body. That's cool."

"Yeah." Everett takes a long, noisy slurp from his coffee. "They say I'm cool, you know."

I laugh and smack his arm, hardly realizing what I'm doing, and Everett cuffs back at me, and for a moment we're mock-sparring in the street like a pair of kids, trying to keep our cold brews safe from each other's swinging paws, and I'm so happy I can feel it bursting through my skin like I'm filled with an incandescent lightbulb.

And then someone shouts, "Everett Torby!" and we both stop and look up.

It's not, as I first feared, a mob of fans from the hotel. Probably still too early for them. Instead, there's a couple of guys leaning against cars in the hotel parking lot. One of them holds a camera with a long lens. As we stare at them, the guy with the camera lifts it and aims it in our direction.

No, not ours. Everett's.

We just stare for a moment, deer in the headlights. And then Everett has the presence of mind to shout, "Can I help you?"

"Yeah," the guy with the camera calls back. "Looking for Liz. You seen her?"

Liz *Astra*?

Something isn't right here. Neither Liz nor Everett are famous enough for paparazzi. They're indie performers, not mainstream acts. And in California, there's no time for photographers to chase anyone but the A-listers, anyway. He'd have to attain Mick Jagger-status to warrant getting followed to a hotel in Palm Springs. Liz would have to be, I don't know, Madonna?

Everett shifts beside me, swapping his coffee between hands like he doesn't know what to say. Finally, he answers, "Not today."

The guys look at each other, then back at Everett. "You sure about that, bro?" one of them asks. "Because her car's in the lot."

His brow furrows. I struggle to keep a straight face. He told me she left, but we aren't going to get into that now. Possibly ever; it's not like I'm going to pick a fight with him on this one and only morning we're spending together.

But I feel a little bit like I'm gagging on my own heart here. Yeah, gross metaphor for a gross feeling. Why did he lie to me? And where is she staying?

Everett holds up his hands. "Listen, boys, I don't know what to tell you. Liz left last night. We aren't together, haven't been in almost a year. And why do you want to know where she is, anyway?"

The camera guy laughs. "Do you really not know? She didn't cough up any details when she was snuggling up to you last night?"

I'm close enough to Everett to feel his whole body stiffen. "What are you talking about?"

The camera guy shrugs and looks at his buddies. "He really doesn't know. Let's get out of here, grab some breakfast." To Everett, he says, "Google it, buddy. See what your old girl's up to now."

They climbed into a pair of beat-up cars and backed out of the lot, heading into town. Everett and I look at each other. I can see the confusion in his expression. He's pleading for answers, and despite my reluctance to even mention his ex, as if I might conjure her up somehow to ruin my day, I know I have to give him some reassurance.

Or at least confirm he's right to ask questions.

"I really don't know what they're talking about," I say. "She didn't have any news for you?"

"She didn't say much, just that we should be together." Everett rubs his mouth. "Damn. I wish I knew what brought that on. I wonder if she's in trouble, somehow."

"She's a grown woman," I say, hoping he's not going to get an attack of the chivalries. "I don't think there's some kind of trouble she could get into that would be fixed by you two dating again."

"Yeah, you're probably right. Come on," he says, starting across the parking lot. "It's roasting out here."

We skip the lobby and, I assume, the potential for a bunch of fans to jump on Everett the moment we step through the doors. Everett leads me around the side of the hotel and up an outdoor flight of stairs. On the third floor, he walks briskly to an end unit overlooking the pool and pops open the door.

Cool air blows out, followed by a stench of alcohol that makes me look at Everett in alarm. Is this guy an alcoholic? I never knew—

He goes to shove the door closed again, but something catches it. No, *someone*, with long red nails and thin white fingers. A ring dangles loosely on a middle finger, its chunk of ruby giving her away before I even see her hollow-cheeked face. Looking as thin as a Hollywood actress and as hungry as a wolf, Liz Astra is gripping the turquoise hotel room door, her huge hazel eyes boring into Everett's.

"I knew you'd be back," she laughs. "Well, come on in. Leave the groupie, though." Her gaze flashes to my startled expression, a look acidic enough to eat through metal. "Hope you had a good time, honey, but it's time to go back to the real world."

Everett makes a strangled sound, as if something is caught in his throat. And then, before I can move or say anything, he turns to me, sweeps me up in his arms, and kisses me.

Chapter Nine

Everett's kiss makes my faux pas of six hours ago seem like a joke kiss between two friends. By the pool, I had to press my lips encouragingly against his, asking him to open up and let me in. Here on the balcony overlooking the scene of last night's shenanigans, Everett's lips demand rather than ask, and I give into him without a single qualm, my mouth opening beneath his, inviting him to devour me whole.

The heat between us sings like a blade slicing the air, buzzes like a live wire cut loose from the safety of its tall pole, melts in my center like a rock turning molten in the onslaught of a lava slide. Without even stopping to ask my brain for permission, my body presses close to his, molding us tightly together. My fingers are in his hair, digging into his shoulders, wrapping around his back, everywhere all at once as I desperately try to take him in, fold him into myself, wear him like a coat and drink him like a cool bottle of water. I can feel his hands gripping my hair just behind my ears, palms cupping the base of my skull, his pinky fingers pressing against my neck and pulling me into him.

Our tongues meet, clash, and tussle. A moan escapes my throat, something animal and wild and indescribably full of need. His answering groan is all I need to know. He wants more of me, too.

This isn't a game.

"Disgusting *whore!*"

I'm snatched back to reality by her furious tone. It's like a bucket of cold water has been thrown over our heads as we stumble backwards, our confused bodies protesting the sudden daylight between us.

Suddenly there are three of us where a second ago there were only two, and she's looming larger than life over us, eyes narrowed at me with unmitigated hate.

Everett is the first to find his voice. "She's not a whore, you nasty bitch," he bites out. "And you said you were leaving. What else do I have to do to get you out of my hotel room?"

"This is plenty," Liz retorts, her voice shaking—with shock? With horror? With rage?

I don't know, maybe it's all three, but either way, she's backing away from the door, picking up a handbag, kicking on sandals. "You've made your point, bastard. I'm gone. Just forget I was ever here." This time I hear a real wobble in her voice as she pushes past us, stalking towards the stairwell.

Everett sighs and rubs his head like a migraine is coming on. "I'm so sorry that happened to you," he tells me. "The thing is, she told me she's done with me twice in the past few hours. It doesn't seem to stick. Maybe this time?"

"It's fine," I say.

"It's not fine," Everett says, "but thank you for saying so. Please come inside."

I can't help but feel sorry for Liz, whose hunched shoulders are the last thing I see of her before Everett gently guides me into the hotel room. Breakups are no one's favorite, and she seems to be taking this one particularly hard.

Who wouldn't? It's *Everett.*

I hung up my first poster with Everett on it when I was twenty-two and a year out of college, freshly disillusioned with life and newly obsessed with music that reflected my personal misery. Okay, maybe that's more serious than it really was, but suffice to say, the real world was not as exciting as everyone said it would be.

The third Emergency album had just come out, and I was in the right place to receive its moody lyrics and brooding beats and that husky, whiskey-on-coals voice of the lead singer. *Everyone's A Liar* featured their breakthrough college radio single "Something Suburban" and as I faced the horror of moving back to my parents' house if my job-hunt in L.A.

continued to fail, it seemed like Everett Torby and his band were the only ones who understood me.

When I was turned away from my sixth studio interview empty-handed, I went to Amoeba Records in Hollywood and bought everything they had by The Emergency, the first two albums, a couple of CD singles, and the poster of them standing, in glorious gray-scale, against a battered brownstone somewhere in their adopted hometown of Brooklyn.

They were part of the New York indie scene but on the literary fringes, attracting a certain kind of wistful college grad with a lot of used Penguin Classics on the shelves and Criterion Collection DVDs stacked next to the TV. In other words, perfect for me.

I couldn't afford the things I bought at Amoeba, but when I had that poster on the wall of my rented room in an apartment inhabited entirely by screenwriters, some failed and some prospective but none actually in production, I knew I had a lodestone. Whatever else went wrong—and it was all bound to go wrong—I had them.

I had Everett, guiding my disappointment.

Times changed. I got the job in Phoenix Canyon. I eventually upgraded my car and moved out to be closer to work. Everett and the band put out more records, experimented a little with sound and tone, stayed true to their bummed-out roots, but got a little more grown-up, too. We were growing up together, I thought. I kept that poster up in my new apartment, even when it began to look like something out of date with my maturing tastes, my potted plants and my vintage store furniture mixed with carefully chosen IKEA pieces. The Emergency, and Everett, were still my constant.

I met guys. I dated them. We broke up.

Everett still scowled from my bedroom wall.

I couldn't imagine ever taking him down.

Until today.

"Well," Everett says, surveying the damage to his room, "I don't think she *drank* any of it."

The overwhelming smell of liquor in the hotel suite isn't from a wild party or some over-imbibing on Everett's part, much to my relief. It's just that Liz broke everything on the kitchen counter that runs along the back wall, including the two-tier bar stocked with full-size bottles of whiskey, rum, vodka, and assorted other booze.

Everett picks up the top half of a smashed tequila bottle and shakes his head. "This is always her go-to when she's mad."

"Tequila?"

"No, breaking things."

"Still destructive, just in a different way."

"Exactly." He sighs. "I'm going to really have to tip the staff, huh."

"I saw an ATM in the lobby," I joke lamely.

Everett chuckles at that. "Well, let's see what the bedroom looks like—" He swings open the door that would have made any other hotel room into a set of adjoining rooms, and walks into a bedroom suite with a king-sized bed, a sofa, and a few nice pieces of mid-century furniture. "She didn't trash the bedroom," he says. "I guess she wanted to keep that intact for later. Liz isn't known for being subtle."

Please stop making jokes about having sex with your ex. "Well, that's something," I say with a little shrug.

"No, it's good. You can take a shower in there while I get housekeeping up here to help with this mess."

I glance at him uncertainly. "Shower in here?"

There's something almost *too* intimate about the idea.

"I'll be in the other room," Everett assures me. "Take your time. And then we'll go and get your car."

And with that, he shuts the door gently behind me, leaving me alone in the bedroom suite.

Alone in Everett Torby's bedroom suite.

After the most earth-shattering kiss I've ever experienced in my life.

Initiated by *him.*

"Okay," I say aloud. "Right."

The furniture stares back at me. No answer.

Well, brain? Any suggestions on what the hell is going on with my life?

This time, my misfiring neurons have absolutely no answer.

The only downside to my shower is putting on the same set of clothes I had on yesterday, and slept in outdoors, and have wandered the streets of Palm Springs in during (hot) daylight hours.

Oh, that and there's nothing of Everett's in the shower stall. I would have loved to pick up a bottle of shampoo and thought,

Okay, now I know Everett uses lime-cucumber Dove, but no such luck. Looks like he uses the little complimentary bottles just like the rest of us.

On the other hand, I do have the pleasure of knowing I smell just like him as I step onto the bathmat and tug a towel around my chest. For today, at least, we are hotel soap buddies.

My hair is dripping onto my shoulders; I pause and look for a hairbrush on the bathroom counter. Everett's hair is longish, and it doesn't get finger-combed into those smooth waves in back or above his ears. I spot a brush and pull it through my hair, feeling as dangerously deviant as I have all morning. The towel slips through my fingers and falls to the floor.

I'm in Everett's suite, using Everett's brush, looking at myself naked in Everett's mirror.

It means nothing, and it means everything.

I can hear him directing hotel cleaning staff on the other side of the wall: "Be careful," and, "There's more over here," and, "I'm sorry, but we're still missing half a Jack Daniels bottle." I decide to stay hidden in the bathroom until everyone's gone; it probably wouldn't be great to be seen by the hotel staff with wet hair coming out of his suite. Maybe it wouldn't make *Variety,* but I'm pretty sure a few music blogs would love to spread the word. And with the craziness that came out of his ex-girlfriend a few minutes ago, I figure poor Everett needs a break from female controversy.

I find some lemon-scented lotion in a drawer and start working that into my elbows and neck, thinking about how many weird things have happened this morning. What was with the paparazzi looking for Liz this morning, anyway? Is it possible she's gotten a movie deal? Or been spotted with some A-lister? If so, that might explain the camera around that one guy's neck. Liz Astra on her own might not be much news for the general public, but a lot of people might be really invested in Liz Astra dating their favorite leading man or lady, then ditching them for her ex in Palm Springs.

Well, that's not how it's ending, I think smugly. *Because her ex was with me.*

I still can't believe this is happening. Not that I'm sure what's happening…and I'm not going to allow myself, for a second, to relive that kiss. Or believe that kiss was real. Even though it felt real. Even though it felt like my body was melting into his and we were the only two people left on earth…it's still possible it meant nothing to him. A kiss to piss off his ex.

Well, if it was fake, the man should be in pictures. That's all I can really say about that.

As the sound next door fades and I hear the front door close, I slowly hang up the towel on its peg and think about getting dressed. My capris are really so loose from being worn for almost two days that they're going to hang off my hipbones, but there's nothing for it. I sigh and pick up my shirt, which has also lost all shape.

The bathroom door trembles slightly as the door into the suite opens and closes, and I hesitate. "Hello?" I call. "Everett?"

"Housekeeping," a woman replies. "You okay in there?"

I feel my brows coming together in confusion. "I'm fine. Where's Everett? The man staying in this room," I add, in case she doesn't know who he is. Most people don't. It's better that way; I'd never have met him otherwise.

"No Everett," she says. "You better come out."

The door handle rattles, and before I can grab hold of it, the door opens, a camera *click-click-clicks,* and a red-haired woman smirks, says, "Bye, sweetheart!" and gallops out of the suite, leaving the door between the bedroom and living room wide open.

I stand like a statue, the cold air of the suite licking my naked body, utterly confused at what just happened. It's not until I hear the front door of the suite open and close again that I think to jump for the dividing door, my right hand reaching for my towel as I swing for the handle with my left.

I miss and hit the door square in the middle, shoving it all the way open. *Going down!* my brain screams helpfully. I'm toppling over, pulling the towel down with me. It catches on the hook and the fabric makes a tearing sound. On my way to the ground, I have just enough air-time between me and the floor to hear Everett grunt as the door slams into him.

There's an ice cube by my nose. I blink at it, then push myself into a kneeling position, taking stock of the situation. I'm naked, and the floor is cold, but actual ice seems like a step too far. Then I realize there are ice cubes scattered everywhere, and a bucket a few feet away. The bathroom door is open next to me. "Everett?" I ask cautiously, picking up my torn towel and pressing it to my chest. "Are you okay?"

He groans in reply.

I crawl around the door and find the carnage: poor Everett took that living room door to the face. He's sitting back on his haunches with one hand pressed to his eye. "I was coming to see why the door was hanging open," he mutters. "I promise I wasn't sneaking in while you showered."

"Let me see your face," I whisper, one hand pressing the towel close to my chest. The girls are in check; I'm just going to have to hope the rest of me is covered. I'm not hurt, but if he is, that takes precedence way above any chance of Everett seeing my naked butt.

Everett doesn't take his hand from his eye, so I gently pull at his fingers, ignoring the excited buzz this sets off in my skin just as best I can. He resists me, but finally gives in with a sigh. His eyes flutter open. I take a close look at the skin around his eye and breathe a sigh of relief.

"Aside from a little redness, there's nothing here—"

His gaze flicks down and I clutch at my towel, realizing I'm completely naked as I'm bent over his lap. The towel is probably only *just* covering my breasts, and not much else, as it's falling forward from my chest.

"Sorry," I murmur, slipping backwards so my weight is on my heels. The towel flattens against my front section.

Covered, but now I'm stuck here, with nothing covering my back half.

Everett rubs his face. "This is a very strange morning," he says.

"You're telling me," I mutter, plucking at the towel so it drapes over my knees. Who knows what else I'm going to show him by accident? "Someone takes my picture in your bathroom, and then I hit you in the face when I fall on the door—"

"Wait," he cuts in. "Your picture? What?"

"Oh." I realize that something really bad has happened. "Everett, do you ever look at social media?"

"Not a ton," he admits. "Instagram, mostly."

"That's wise," I say, "but I think we need to know what's going on with your ex. Because there is a lot of photography going on around here, and I think my chest is involved."

He gives me an appraising look. My body warms.

"Tell you what," he says at last. "I'll go in the other room and take a look at my phone while you get dressed. It shouldn't take too long to get some answers."

"Perfect," I agree, but I stay on the floor, in my kneeling position, while he rises, scattering a few more cubes of ice across the floor, and heads into the living room.

When the door closes behind him, I count to three, then race to the bathroom.

Chapter Ten

FINALLY DRESSED, I take a steadying breath before heading back into the living room. I'm getting used to being in Everett's presence, but the in-between periods, when he's in another room, are still weird. That's when I remember that I'm about to go talk to the man I've idolized and dreamed about for years, and it's impossible not to get a little shaky and worked up about it.

But when I open the door, he just glances up at me with a welcoming smile. Nothing crazy happens. Nothing weird going down.

He's just Everett, a regular human man.

I smile back and join him at the round dining table. "Find anything on Liz?" I ask.

"You're not going to believe this," he says, pushing his phone to me.

I pick up Everett's phone with the same sense of disbelief I felt knowing he was on the other side of the door. *Is this all really happening?* I have to keep asking myself that, even though the answer, incredibly, is always yes.

But the news on the phone quickly outruns my sense of unreality. This is really happening, and now I'm absolutely in the thick of it.

Indie Songstress Skips Line With Surprise Casting.

I look at the URL. It's *Variety*. The real official newspaper of Los Angeles.

Sorry, L.A. Times.

"She has the lead in a Brad Baylor film," Everett says, his voice heavy with disbelief. "How does Liz get the *lead* in a movie like that?"

I skim the rest of the article. Brad Baylor's known for popular movies that have an art-house feel; basically, he makes non-movie people feel like they're movie people for about ninety minutes. He has a quirky way with story and cinematography that shouldn't work, but somehow always does. He's also one of the nerdiest hipsters in Hollywood. No one has chunkier glasses, scruffier ankle boots, or tighter jeans than Brad. It would stand to reason that he knows indie music, if only to maintain his image.

But Brad usually commands superstar casts. All-star ensemble films that place comedians in straight-man roles and

Shakespearean-trained actors in comedic roles. He plays with the status quo.

The one thing he's not known for? Launching new ingenues in his films.

"The movie's about a singer," I say finally, reaching the end of the story. "So, he must have listened to her already and decided she'd be right for the role. I mean, there's no chance Brad is listening to Top 40. It makes sense that he'd know about Liz."

And you, I think, but I'm really trying to concentrate on Everett as himself, not as the singer of The Emergency. It's not easy, but I think with some effort I can get there.

"Yeah, you're right," Everett says, taking his phone back. He shakes his head at it. "I just...this is not what I expected. She was always interested in getting into acting, but...this is jumping all the way up the ladder. I hope she knows what she's doing."

I press down against the coil of jealousy in my stomach. "She'll be fine. She knows how to perform for an audience."

"The fame, though. I mean, what little bit we've got is hard enough sometimes."

We. Jeez, man. Way to kill the vibe by showing solidarity with your ex-girlfriend, who called me a whore about an hour ago. I shrug, saying, "I don't know. Kind of outside my realm of expertise."

Everett nods absently, scrolling through social media with an idle roll of his thumb. I glance around the suite, wondering if there's coffee in the pot, and what he wanted all that ice for. It's melting into the carpet behind us, forgotten in the confusion of slamming doors and naked encounters. What a morning, I think, and then snicker to myself at the inadequacy of that phrase.

Today is shaping up to be *insane.*

And we haven't even talked about finding my car yet.

"Whoa." Everett's thumb stops scrolling. "Uh. Hmm. Humph."

That's a series of concerned sounds that I never expected to hear come out of Everett Torby's mouth. I crane my neck to see his phone screen. "What's up?"

He's looking at a picture. A woman, a color scheme alarmingly familiar, a shocked expression, *bare boobs—*

"Oh, my god," I gasp, snatching the phone from him. "Don't look at me!"

Everett looks at me with a shellshocked expression. "How the hell did this happen?"

"It was while you were getting ice! This woman said she was with housekeeping and opened the bathroom door—" I stare at the picture until my shaking hands make it impossible to focus any more.

Me. Naked. On the Internet.

This just became the worst day of my life.

"I *said* there was a photographer," I remind him, "and my chest was involved. I just—"

"Didn't think it would come to this?" Everett is looking at my chest. The real one, not the photo. "Where did you *think* a naked pic of you would go?"

"I really didn't know what to think," I say. "This is all new to me."

I look back at the photo. At least the girls look good.

Small blessings. Small, perky blessings.

"Well, at least we know why we've got paparazzi around all of a sudden," Everett sighs, taking back the phone. He minimizes my photo, but his eyes linger on the screen for a moment. At first I think he's admiring my nude, but then he reads the caption aloud. "Yeah. It says, 'Lonely at the top for newly crowned queen of hipster Hollywood as Liz Astra is dumped by long-time boyfriend Everett Torby and replaced in their Palm Springs hotel room.'" He looks at me, perplexed. "Why do they think we were still dating?"

The *we* doesn't bother me as much now. "Maybe they just got their facts wrong," I say. "It's not like they've had time to read every post from Pitchfork to find out all about you guys."

"Maybe," he says, but he sounds uncertain. "Or maybe she told them we were."

"Why would she do that?"

"Liz isn't always truthful," Everett says, with the air of a person who is trying to be delicate about dirty laundry.

"If you're talking about the time she fabricated a story about saving a girl's life in Greece..." It wasn't weird that I knew about that. All the indie rags picked it up. Liz was on tour in Europe, spent a few days at a Greek island, and shared a photograph of herself hugging a little girl she'd claimed to have rescued from drowning. Later, it came out that she'd made the whole thing up. For attention, most people agreed. Liz claimed exhaustion and canceled a few shows to prove she was taking care of her mental health.

But all that was years ago, before she and Everett even got together. Surely she'd grown up since then?

"Let me tell you," Everett says with a sigh, "that is the tip of the iceberg. I used to call it Liz's Overactive Imagination. But honestly, I was just putting a happy spin on a serious problem."

"You think it's a disorder or something?"

"I'm no doctor, but it certainly seems like something she can't always help." He shrugs. "Or she doesn't want to help herself."

I add *Liz Astra is a pathological liar* to the list of things I didn't expect to have intimate knowledge of today, along with what it feels like to have a paparazzi post my photo on Twitter and the intensity of Everett Torby's kiss.

Everett looks past me, towards the bedroom suite. "I forgot about that ice."

"Too late for it now."

"Too bad," he says. "Because I could really use a drink."

Leaving out the fact that it's barely nine a.m., I could, too. "We could see if the bar's open," I suggest.

"Better," Everett says. "Let's get a bungalow."

Chapter Eleven

THERE ARE THINGS I should be doing besides letting Everett lead me around Palm Springs. Things like getting back my car, and driving home to deal with my closing job, and putting on clean clothes that aren't practically falling off my body with the exhaustion of cheap fabrics that have been on the go for over twenty-four hours.

But when he calls a hotel across town and asks if he can reserve a poolside bungalow for the day—"Just this once," he wheedles, when told they're only for hotel guests, "and I'm having a bit of a day so I won't forget this next time I'm booking a show in Palm Springs," —I go with it. I walk downstairs with him and get into his car. I watch him drive us through the sunbaked streets to the hotel. Smile at the valet. Walk through the sliding glass doors and make a quick detour at the lobby's expensive boutique, where I buy the least expensive scrap of Lycra I can find.

I don't even wince at the price, all three numbers in it higher than they should be. I just take it into the changing room and slide it on.

Because this is my one and only day with Everett Torby, and I'm not going to waste it on the real world, or worrying about buying a black bikini I cannot afford, or thinking about getting a new job while I close up shop on the one I am losing, or even about where poor Lime Lucinda is being held for ransom by a cruel tow-truck driver. I'm definitely not going to think about my naked body and shocked face being spread around the world via digital signal, or the potential for trouble raised by an indignant ex-girlfriend who is also a pathological liar *and* Hollywood's newest star.

It's actually really easy to forget this stuff exists: I just look at Everett and the familiarity of his face, transferred from photographic to real in the past few hours of closeness, takes over every other thought in my brain.

I'd do it all again for this day, I think, as I walk out to our bungalow in my new bikini, and this day is only a few hours old.

So, that's saying something.

The bungalow is modeled after an architect's idea of an old California beach shack, with one small studio room hung with oceanic art and a wooden porch across the front where we can sit in plush chairs and admire the pool. It's not exactly hidden; there are other bungalows here, and plenty of beautiful people in the blue water, splashing or swimming or just staring, glassy-eyed, up at the sky from the center of a doughnut-shaped float.

There is already a tall daiquiri glass on the table, and another one in Everett's hands. He has his legs crossed and is leaning back in his chair, eyes closed.

"Hey," I say, coming up the steps. "Thanks for the drink."

His eyes flutter open. They fasten on me. For a moment, we are both still. I'm arrested by his gaze, and he seems fixated on me.

"Cassie," he says huskily. "You look gorgeous."

"Thank you," I murmur, blushing a little. But it's the sweet heat in my middle that has me pressing close to the porch railing as I walk past him. Somehow, I'm afraid he will see how taut with longing he leaves me after the slightest compliment, as if all he has to do in order to drop my panties is to whisper my name in exactly the right tone.

I mean, that's the truth. I don't know why I bother phrasing it as a hypothetical.

I settle into the second deck chair and brush my hands over its soft fabric, admiring the floral pattern as if it's the most consuming subject in the world to me. The fact is, I'm just waiting for my skin to stop tingling and my limbs to stop trembling so that I can pick up my daiquiri without showing him I'm in desperate need for his touch.

Although maybe he wouldn't find my shaking fingers that surprising.

I mean, we've already kissed.

Twice.

And I apologized for the first one...but he hasn't said a damn word about the second one.

The one that was all *him*.

"The drinks are good here," Everett says. "A little heavy on the rum, but I don't think anyone complains about that."

"I certainly won't," I agree, as if drinking by pools before ten a.m. is my standard Tuesday morning. I go for the frosty glass and take a healthy slurp on the straw. "Mmm, coconut goodness."

"I love coconut everything," Everett remarks. "Coconut ice cream, coconut water, coconut milk in espresso..."

"I do too! Coconut is the world's most perfect fruit. I would put it in everything if I could."

He reaches into a drawer in the table and pulls out a tube of very expensive-looking sunscreen. "You can even smell like it and everyone just smiles and says you make them think of being on vacation."

"Exactly!" I uncap the sunscreen and give it a sniff. "God, it's like perfume. You smell," I say, handing it back.

Everett gives the sunscreen bottle a discerning waft and nods his approval. "Use it up. You don't want to get a burn from the water's reflection."

"You say that with an air of experience," I chuckle, leaning forward to rub the sunscreen on my bare legs.

"Painful experience. I didn't know that was how pools worked at the time. I thought if you sat in the shade, you were good."

"I actually have had the same thing happen. You know, in Ohio we didn't spend a lot of time by the pool, so it's a hazard of moving to L.A."

He looks across the table at me, interested. "You're from Ohio?"

"Unfortunately. You know Columbus?"

"I've played some gigs there."

"Well, imagine growing up an hour from Columbus, and that's as interesting as your world gets."

Everett gives me a sympathetic wince. "As a child of Kansas City, I salute and respect your childhood plight."

"Thank you. It was rough. We had a fenced backyard, and we were allowed to ride our bikes until the street lights came on. Those were the highlights until I turned eighteen."

"And then?"

"College, escape, the west coast, a lot of disappointment, my own apartment and a cat, a job I liked, but it's over now." I tick off my adult life on my fingers; it's pretty short and boring. "Not exactly the stuff songs are written about."

But even as I say it, I know Everett will sit up straighter, and I can almost mouth along with him when he says, "That's exactly what all my songs are about."

"I know," I laugh. "That's why I like them, I guess. You get me."

"Hey, those songs are about *my* disappointment, not yours," he informs me with a grin.

"Well, I claim them. They're mine now. Write some new ones for yourself."

"Maybe I'll have to," he says. "Something completely different."

"*Un*-disappointed, this time?"

"Sounds crazy, but it just might work."

The sunscreen smells like my drink; I dive in for a much longer second slurp on the pink straw. The rum goes straight to my head, giving me a pleasant tingle in my fingers and toes. Like being turned on, but not.

I say, "What would you write about it, if you weren't always thinking about how life didn't go the way you wanted?"

His eyes are more blue than gray right now, and they're boring into mine, making me want to push aside the table between us, drinks and all, and grab him by the collar. Why's he still wearing that cute cactus shirt, anyway? It's time to strip off, put on some sunscreen, and show me what he's got.

"I'd write about getting exactly what I wanted for once," he says, that warm honey simmer in his throat coating his words in just the right way to send my nerves singing. "Or better yet, seeing what I want and taking it, no consequences, no questions, no answers."

It feels like the song is already starting.

A moment turns into a minute, and we're watching each other like two cats circling, tails twitching, wondering who will make the first move.

And then a phone on the table between us starts to buzz.

I look at it like an alien just dropped into our midst, but Everett sighs and picks it up. "The hotel concierge," he explains, hitting the speaker button. "This is Everett," he says, all business.

"Mr. Torby," a silken voice purrs. "We hope everything in the bungalow is to your liking?"

"It's just fine, thank you." He makes a wearied face at me, like he can't wait to get this nice person off the phone. And do what? Drag me inside and make love to me?

Yes, my tipsy brain cells shriek. *To the bed, to the bed!*

"And would you like another round of drinks? Perhaps a fruit tray? Or a selection of biscuits?"

He raises his eyebrows at me, asking if I want any of those things. I shake my head. I only want one thing.

Him.

In that bed.

Is that so wrong?

I mean, he's already seen me naked. It's only fair I get to see him unclothed, right?

Unclothed, and above me, his eyes dark with passion—

"We're good, thank you," Everett tells the concierge in a polite voice utterly devoid of any passion. "Bye now."

He glances at me. I shrink back a little, afraid he'll see the heat coming off me in sizzling waves. My imagination got busy *fast.* I manage a weak smile. "Seems nice," I say.

"Oh, very. They always think I'm going to be more demanding than I am. And I think it bothers them a little that I'm *not* a diva, because that's their clientele."

I suppress a sigh and take another sip of my drink. He's still making small talk, so bed isn't on the agenda.

Yet.

"Do you stay here a lot?" I ask after a moment's contemplation of the pool. "I mean, it does seem to be a pretty high-end clientele, not that I'm saying you're not high-end…"

He laughs. "Not high-end like Jasper Pikeman over there, right?" He points out the mustachioed movie star who has just splashed into the shallow end of the pool. "No, I don't stay here a lot. But every now and then. I was gifted a room here once years ago, on our fourth tour, when things were kind of crazy —"

I nod, remembering that The Emergency's fourth album, *Mood Killer,* was a breakthrough release that netted them a Grammy nomination and an arena tour. As a fan from the third album, I was self-righteous enough to be irritated with the wave of new fans and the graduation from clubs to arenas, but I should probably keep that to myself.

Everett says, "Now I kind of keep this place in my back pocket for when things just seem too crazy to deal with in a rational fashion. I just put it on my best credit card and try to expense some of it to the record label, although I don't think being on my solo tour is going to be much help this time." He grins. "Small artist woes. My solo label doesn't have the deepest of pockets."

"I'd say I'd help with the bill," I say, "but you might have heard I'm about to be unemployed."

"Well, that's lucky for me," Everett says. "Because otherwise I'm pretty sure you'd have ditched me and headed to the office by now, and I kind of gambled on you sticking around for the rest of the day when I booked this place."

Silver linings are crazy things, I think. Never what you'd expect.

"Don't worry," I say, rum making my tongue lazy and prone to slipping out the truth. "If I hadn't been pink-slipped yesterday, I'd have quit this morning before I let you soak up all this luxury by yourself."

He laughs again, his gaze lingering on my face—then dropping ever so slightly to my chest before he gets control of himself again. I can't help but smile at the way his eyes rise and fall, and I'm happy about the bikini, even if it cost roughly six times what it should have in that hotel boutique.

I can take it all—the credit card bill, the impounded car, even my bare breasts on the Internet—if it gives me a shot at something more than fandom with Everett Torby.

And I might have said that, or something equally embarrassing to admit out loud, if his phone—his actual phone, not the hotel phone—didn't start buzzing with an overabundance of purpose. He catches it before it can buzz itself right off the table and grimaces. "This is my manager," he stage-whispers. "I'm about to get in a lot of trouble."

"Why, does he see the credit card charges?" I reply, but he's already answering the call.

"Sheila? Yes. No. I mean—yeah. But—wait. *What?*"

Everett sits bolt upright in his chair, the color draining from his face.

The bed inside seems farther away than ever. Flirtation hour just got canceled.

Chapter Twelve

Everett gets up in one fluid movement and heads into the bungalow, the phone pressed close to his face. Even with the window closed, I can hear him saying, "Uh-huh, okay, uh-huh," over and over, as if he's receiving a precise set of instructions. It makes me nervous. Could something new be going on with this Liz situation?

It seems almost certain that he's going to be involved in some kind of celebrity gossip explosion after all the events of the past twelve hours, but at the same time, how is any of this Everett's fault? Liz showed up, shouted at him, left, came *back* and yelled at him some more, and then left again.

And somehow, I was the one who had my boobs plastered on the Internet.

If this is fame, it's confusing.

I imagine poor Everett feels the same way. After all, he has spent the past ten years as an almost-famous singer. Not a household name, but pretty damn popular amongst a subset of indie music fans. He *can* get recognized on the street, but he probably won't be. This feels like a fairly comfortable version of fame. Just enough to know you're doing something right.

Illicit photographers and shouting paparazzi on the street would not be a step in the right direction, especially when it's not even about his career or success…it's about *her*.

A woman he isn't even in love with, isn't even dating.

I finish my daiquiri and poke at the whipped cream left in the glass, trying not to look over my shoulder at what's going on inside the bungalow. I can hear his footsteps on the tile floor, pacing back and forth.

I want to get up and offer him my support, even wrap my arms around him and tell him everything will be fine. But, of course, that's not my place.

I'm just the girl he found himself next to last night on a pool chair, who has somehow been insinuated into his life for twelve hours or so, and who he'll never see again once he heads back to his life in L.A. and I head back to my life in Phoenix Canyon, a world apart even if on a map we look pretty close.

It sucks. Even though I've been trying really hard to live in the moment, to tell myself that it's only for today, I'm sad to think it's going to end now, before we even make it to lunch.

I'm lost in my thoughts, watching movie stars splash each other in the pool, when Everett finally comes back onto the porch. His phone is in his hand; his face is set in grave lines. "Some things have come up in L.A.," he begins, then pauses.

"I guess you have to go back," I say, trying to make this easy on him, since it sure won't be on me.

"Not quite," he says. And to my surprise, Everett sits down again. He picks up his glass and drains it, then puts the glass down, seemingly lost in thought. After a few moments, he turns to me. "What do you think about staying here with me for a week?"

I blink at him. "What?"

I'm so shocked it's a wonder I even thought of *that* word.

His smile is self-deprecating, as if he understands I couldn't possibly want to be his roommate for a week—boy, does this guy misread the situation—and he continues, "Sheila—that's my manager—has brought up a few things that would make it smart to stick around Palm Springs instead of going home right away. And if I'm staying with you, so much the better."

Well, I couldn't agree more with that statement, although I suspect our reasons are different. "Why am I important?" I ask.

His cheek creases like he's biting back a grin. "Not that I don't want to get into the existential, but right now, can we focus on my problems?"

I have to laugh. "Okay, bad wording, smart guy. Why does Sheila think I should be here, too?"

"Because I need a girlfriend to stave off whatever craziness Liz is up to right now," Everett says. "And right now, the world is very open to the belief that *you're* her already."

* * *

I'm quiet long enough that Everett clearly thinks there's a problem, because his face gets very apologetic all at once. "Look, I'm sorry, I didn't mean—clearly I misread the situation, and I feel awful. Do you want to go? I mean, do you want me to take you to your car? I totally get it if you're done with me now."

I wish I can hide the hurt on my face, because it's embarrassing. To want to spend time with him as much as I do, and to know that he's asking me to stay with him as a *fake girlfriend,* to keep Liz from dragging him in the tabloids or whatever it is she's planning...it's just brutal. Like a hammer on my heart, which has already been feeling pretty bruised by the events of the past twenty-four hours or so.

The VIP debacle, the theater closing, and hell, I even feel a little bad about losing Barry's occasional dinner time conversation.

I know my face will give me away, though, so I look down at my feet instead, bare toes which could really have used a pedicure before they were exposed at a swanky Palm Springs resort, and say, "No, I don't want to go."

"Okay." He exhales. "Okay, well, forget I said anything. Please. It was Sheila's idea, and she doesn't know you as a person."

I glance up at him through my eyelashes. "And you do?"

"I mean—" Everett rakes his hands through his hair, ruffling those gentle waves. I remember the feel of his hair in my fingers, as I grasped at him with everything I had, like he was the only buoy in a typhoon intent on taking me under.

Of course, he's the typhoon, not the buoy.

Whether I stay or go, I'm going to get hurt.

It's something I realize and accept in the same instant. But it's all fate. Not a thing I can do about it.

Because nothing in the world can stop me from opening my mouth and saying the dumbest thing I could possibly say: "Everett, stop. I'll do it."

He's shaking his head. "No, you don't even know what she wants you to do. It's crazy. I shouldn't have asked—"

"Tell me, then," I say, way more calmly than I should be able to speak right now. What's wrong with me? Clearly I'm in shock. I should be wrapped in a blanket and fed cookies and orange juice. "What does Sheila want me to do? I'm listening."

Everett considers me for a moment, like he's weighing the badness of his request against the vulnerability in my face. I try to toughen up, to look like a badass girl who can deal with the subterfuge of *pretending* to be into him. Sure. It's all a big game to me. I'm not playing Russian roulette with my heart or anything.

Finally, he sighs and nods. "Here's the deal," he says, leaning forward, elbows on his knees. The position of a man with a plan, even if he doesn't like it very much. "Sheila says that Liz was all over L.A. last night before she came down here, and her sources say she was looking for me. If I hadn't decided to play that show and sent out an email, she wouldn't have found me last night. Well, that's on me."

Neither would I, I think. *That's on you.*

Nice to blame him for something, really.

"And last night was key to her, apparently, because—and this is just Sheila speculating but she's been in this town a long time—there's going to be a big rumor that she's sleeping with Brad Baylor and that's where the surprise casting in his movie came from."

"Oh, okay." The caption from the photo with my hotel-room ambush comes back to me: Liz Astra *dumped* by long-time boyfriend. "Liz was going to get back together with you and tell everyone you guys have been exclusive all along, so how could the casting couch rumor be true, is that it?"

"Exactly." Everett shakes his head. "You know, my mom was right. I should have stayed in New York. None of this Hollywood bullshit there."

"I hear New York is one hundred percent bullshit-free."

He grins at that. "Yeah. That's the way I remember it, too."

"So, Liz wants the world to think you guys have been quietly dating for the past year," I prompt. "Instead of broken up."

"Right."

"And you don't want anyone to think that."

"Well, we haven't been." Everett lifts his eyebrows at me. "Don't you think it would raise some questions with, like, everyone I know? The entire band, for starters."

I get it. It's easier to lie about me from here on out than to create a backstory for an entire year's worth of lies. We are working with fresh, new lies.

I say, "That makes sense. So what does Sheila want me to do?"

"Stay here with me for a week," Everett says promptly. "In Palm Springs, not necessarily at this bungalow, which I can't afford for more than today. But she can hook us up with a house rental. I doubt it will be super-swanky, but I can probably guarantee a pool. And we'd have to be seen in public a few times together, so dinners out would be a good plan."

"We get photographed together, make it look serious, like we're on a lovely getaway in Palm Springs after your solo tour. Is that it?"

"Pretty much. Oh, and..." Everett looks so embarrassed I want to hug him. "Sheila said to tell you...we'll pay you five thousand dollars. For the week."

"Five *thousand*—no way, Everett," I say. "I am not taking your money for this. Bad enough you're going to have to pay for the house." I know he's not rich. Everett is the singer of an indie band with one solo record on an art-house label. Every music teacher I've ever had would be crying laughing if someone suggested he's making bonkers cash.

"Well, it's not my money," he admits. "It's my labels coughing it up for the house and for your payment, apparently. My solo house and The Emergency's are both in on it. Sheila says they don't want this kind of notoriety on me. Kills my indie cred, she says, if I'm dealing with movie stars."

"Liz isn't worried about losing hers," I point out.

"It's not what Liz ever wanted. She always hoped she'd make it big." Everett shrugs, like he doesn't get it. That's not his journey, that shrug says.

I don't think there's anything wrong with wanting to make it big. I kind of hoped I would, once, too. Just on the production side, not as an actress. But my big studio dreams got knocked down to local theater after just a couple years of banging my head against locked doors. Part of me still wishes I could break into the Hollywood scene. I guess part of me always will.

Everett's content out of the mainstream. That must be nice. But of course, it's a different story when you're already behind the mic. Even without the power of a big music label behind him, Everett has the positive reinforcement of tens of thousands of fans who love him.

And me, for whatever that's worth.

But as much as I love him, I don't want money to be his fake girlfriend. In the back of my silly brain, there are still a few drunken cells carousing and hugging and crying, *But what if he falls in love with us for real?* and I'm not going to ruin their party by turning this unexpected friendship into a business transaction.

"No pay," I tell him. "That's final."

Everett grins. "Okay, okay. I won't insist. But if you change your mind at any point, the check is written, so to speak."

If I had a check with Everett's signature on it, I'd never cash it and keep it forever, but I know that isn't how money works anymore, so I just nod. "And of course, I have to get back to my place for my things—"

"Sheila says she's going to courier a company card so you can buy some things—"

"—and to feed my cat," I finish, raising my brows at him. "And make sure my neighbor can feed her the rest of the week."

"Oh, I didn't know there was a cat," Everett says apologetically.

"But you should've guessed, right?" I say. "I've got cat spinster written all over me, don't I?"

"You really don't," Everett says softly. "But even if you did, I'd say you wear it pretty well."

We look at each other for a moment. I watch the blue in his eyes outshine the gray, and my pulse quickens.

He's the first to look away, blinking at the bungalow around us for a moment. "It's a shame to give this place up," he says, "but I guess we better get your car and feed your cat."

"We can come back, unless checkout is early," I suggest, feeling regretful as I eye the unused bed.

He brightens. "Checkout's at eleven p.m. on a day rental," he says. "So, should we get going so we can come back and enjoy it later? This place has super fish tacos. We could order in dinner and get to know each other a little better, so, you know...so we look convincing when we're out in public this week."

"Sure," I agree. "I'd love to look convincing with you."

I'm heading into the unknown on this, but there's one thing I know for certain.

This will either be the best week of my life or the worst. I highly doubt there is any in-between.

Chapter Thirteen

TURNS OUT, IT'S pretty helpful having a pair of panicking record labels at your back—especially when they're small labels who probably wouldn't survive without the guy at your side. Everett fields several texts and calls from Sheila as we change back into our day clothes (separately, in the bungalow bathroom) and by the time we're heading to his car, we know exactly where my car is. We're assured the impound fee has been handled and it will be waiting out front.

"I expect a wash and wax," I joke as Everett buckles his seatbelt.

He looks at me and grins. "Right now, it feels like I could make that happen. Want my phone? You can send the text."

"No, no. I was only kidding. That's too much power."

"I feel drunk with it. Let's make Sheila drive to Venice Beach and get us cookies from this one place I like, then have her bring them here."

"Absolutely not!" I laugh. "Poor Sheila is already chasing her tail to make this week work out. Does she even have a house for us yet?"

"She hasn't sent me anything yet."

"Then leave her alone, or we won't have a place to stay. I'll have to stow you away at my apartment and stage photos to make it look like a forbidden love nest."

Everett glances at me with interest. "How much work would it take? Are you already living amongst silks and velvets?"

I feel my cheeks redden and try to laugh it off. "Please, I'm as practical as they come. Cotton as far as the eye can see."

"Shame," Everett says, turning down an industrial-looking road. "But the budget probably extends to fur-lined handcuffs and silken panties if you want to go that route."

I *absolutely* want to go that route.

"Let's settle for the house Sheila finds for us, first," I say.

Oh, bland, vanilla Cassie! If only you were as bold as your imagination! This could be the adventure of a lifetime, but if I'm not careful, it's just going to be the letdown of a lifetime, instead.

Or rather, if I'm *too* careful...

"That's her!" I spot my Prius in front of a chain-link fence, parked right next to a little guard shack. "Lime Lucinda."

"Your car's name is Lime Lucinda?"

"Yes. What's your car's name?"

"Patrick Purple-pants."

"Wait, really?"

"No," Everett says, putting the car in park. "It's not even purple. Lucinda like in 'Light Up Lucinda'?"

I bite my lip. Ugh, why did I have to say her name out loud? "Light Up Lucinda" is a track off The Emergency's first album, the one only really hard-core fans even have a copy of, let alone listen to. And name inanimate objects after. "Well, and because Lucinda goes well with lime, and she's green," I mutter. "By the way, your car isn't even purple. It's gray. Which is disappointingly boring."

"I know," Everett agrees. "I have to admit something to you. I *like* the color gray."

"Because it's the color of storm clouds and foggy days on the ocean?" I ask hopefully.

"Because it's standard and doesn't cost extra from the dealer," he dead-pans. "Did you think *everything* in my life was lyrics and poetry?"

"I guess I just assumed." Out of the car, the desert morning is ferociously hot. I hope Sheila's search for a house with a pool doesn't come up short. Staying in Palm Springs without a cool-down option could mean a *lot* of Netflix.

A guy with a clipboard and a set of keys meets us by my car and I sign a couple of things, take possession of my car again, and unlock the doors. Everett hovers near me, and I realize we've left out something really important: what comes next.

"Should I just find you back at the bungalow?" I ask. "I should only be a couple of hours."

He looks around, as if there's something fascinating in the gleaming sun glinting off the hundreds of impounded cars. Why are there so many locked-up cars in Palm Springs? Finally, he says, "I guess I'll be there, yeah."

"You guess? I thought that was your favorite spot to chill out. Where else would you be?"

Everett glances at me briefly, then flicks his gaze back to the ground. "It will just feel a little boring without you there, that's all."

I feel my mouth fall open. "But I—"

I was about to say *But I'm nobody to you,* and I'm so glad I stopped myself, because not only does it sound ridiculously melodramatic, but it's clearly not true.

In the past twelve hours, we've already shared so much: two kisses—one he hasn't apologized for, by the way, even though I apologized for mine—and a threatening ex-girlfriend and a walk through quiet streets to a cafe where we had an excellent breakfast together. We've never had a moment where there wasn't something to talk about; we've never (at least I've never) had a moment when we wished we were alone instead of together. I feel like I've known Everett for years, and I kind of think, based on the easy way he talks with me, he feels the same way about me.

For a moment, I consider asking him to drive back to Phoenix Canyon with me. He can meet Tilda, give her some attention while I pack my things and arrange for Ronnie to take care of her during the week. He can see my apartment, which is small but cute, and—

No, that won't work. I think of my stack of Emergency record albums—I've been working on my collection and there is an embarrassing number of rare color vinyl piled on the sideboard where I display my records. I think of the three framed Emergency posters hanging in the living room, along with the framed, signed solo album that I ordered from the fan club the moment it was available. Everett's signature is inked across the front in gold. Every so often, I'll walk over to it, look at the album he touched, and smile at it. I think of the old poster still hanging in my bedroom—my bedroom!—like I'm sixteen years old.

He's standing right next to me, a real person, and he can't know how much value I place on those reminders of his rock-star self, scattered through my living space like trophies.

"You know what," I say, "you go back to the hotel and have a nap and a nice lunch, and I'll text you when I'm on my way inside so you know to order me a drink. How does that sound?"

Everett smiles. "That sounds pretty good. But you better give me your number, or I won't have that daiquiri waiting for you."

I smile and reach for his phone. He gives it up without a protest, and I tap my information into Everett Torby's contact list, making myself part of his life in the most official way I know.

I call Angie as soon as I'm on the freeway.

"Things have happened," I say when she picks up.

"Things? That sounds worrisome."

"I went to a secret Everett Torby show last night." Last night. Incredible. That show feels like a hundred years ago.

"Oh lord! Did you get your hug? Get some closure on this thing?" My sister sounds absent; she's probably typing up some legal brief while her kids destroy the house behind her.

"I wouldn't call it closure, no," I say, thinking of Everett's lips on mine. I have to shift in my seat to relieve some pressure.

"I'm driving the terrible twos to their sitter so I can finish a case. Get to the point, okay?"

A child wails in the background.

"Okay, from start to finish?" I take a breath. "My car got towed, I slept on the hotel pool deck, Everett came down too, I kissed him, he—"

"You *what?*"

I keep going, ignoring her crazed outburst. "We had breakfast together, his ex-girlfriend trashed his room and called me a whore, he kissed me, I showered in his room, his manager and record label want us to spend the week together posing as a couple, and I'm on my way back to my apartment to pack a suitcase. Oh! And he helped me get my car out of the impound lot. Since it got towed. Remember that part?"

There's silence for a moment. Even my crying niece has put a sock in it. Doubtlessly awed with my perfect, perfect story of a night and a morning that can never be equalled.

Then Angie says, "I think you should get out of California."

This isn't what I expected. "How is *that* your takeaway?"

"The sun is clearly getting to you. You need some midwestern gray skies to bring you back to reality."

"I didn't make *any* of that up. In fact, I left stuff out. For brevity and because you told me I had to."

"So you expect me to just believe that you met Everett Torby, he kissed you, and now you're on vacation with him in Palm Springs?"

"You don't have to just believe me," I retort. "Look his name up and you'll see a naked picture of me in his shower."

"WHAT?"

It's the perfect moment to hang up, so I do it.

Angie calls back a second later.

"There's a naked picture of you on the Internet, Cass!"

"Proof," I say. Folds of brown mountain slide past on either side of me, fawn-colored slopes crumpled like an old napkin. The sky above them is so blue the word isn't sufficient. *Southern California, I love you,* I think with supreme satisfaction.

Go back to Ohio, indeed. Angie's out of her mind.

My life out here is just getting started.

"Cassie, this is proof that things are spiraling out of control," Angie says, each word bitten out with perfect enunciation. "I really think you're making unwise decisions right now. Do you need me to come and get you?"

That's an idle threat if I ever heard one. "Absolutely not, sis. I'm fine. Everything is under control. You concentrate on Space Station Angie and all your little cadets, okay?"

She sighs. "I'm really worried about you, Cass."

"Please don't be," I say. "I wanted you to know it's all working out, not get you upset."

"How can you say it's all working out? You were supposed to get *over* him!"

And now, I think smugly, I'm going to get under him.

"He likes me, Angie. This has potential."

"No, Cass. No, no, no—"

"Just because you can't imagine it doesn't mean it isn't happening," I tell her. "This is my freshman formal all over again."

"This is nothing like that. You had a date to freshman formal. I didn't mess anything up for you."

"Revisionist history," I tell her. "You convinced me he only wanted one thing, and I was scared of him the entire night."

"He only wanted one thing, and you were wearing that backless dress that was so racy you had to sneak out with a blouse over it so Mom wouldn't find out—"

"He only wanted one thing, and it was Garrett Kingsley," I say. "How is Garrett, by the way?"

Angie sighs, because Garrett Kingsley works in her pediatrician's office and his husband, my freshman formal date Ian Hoffenbacher, coaches her older kid's soccer team.

"He's doing great," she says at last. "And that doesn't prove anything but that you have terrible judgment, or you never would have tried to seduce Ian with that sexy dress."

"He picked out the dress, Angie!"

"Well, I did not know that part."

"You have to leave," I remind her. "You have to take your offspring somewhere important."

"Camp," she says wearily. "Cassie, please just—"

"I will," I promise.

"But I didn't finish—"

"Love you, Angie!" I end the call.

California rises and falls alongside the freeway, the traffic thickening. I feel terrifically alive.

I crank up Everett's album and sing all the way back to Phoenix Canyon. I love my sister, but she's not bringing me down off this cloud with her lawyerly logic. Not this time.

This time, I'm going all in on crazy, bad ideas and the possibility of the impossible. No one can stop me from making this amazing, remarkable, once-in-a-lifetime mistake.

Chapter Fourteen

"I'M NOT LETTING you go."

My next-door neighbor, Ronnie Louise, ladies and gentleman.

She shakes back her head of graying curls and steadies her stance, both arms across the doorway like she's ready for me to put my head down and ram her like a billy-goat.

"Ronnie, do not be so dramatic," I sigh, putting down my handful of panties. I was sorting through my dresser for my cutest pairs (mainly my least tattered pairs) when she knocked on the door. Assuming she wanted a cup of sugar or to tell me the latest gossip she'd seen on her favorite show, I am now regretting ever giving my sister Ronnie's phone number as an emergency contact. Earthquake threat, blah-blah-blah.

"I'm *serious*," Ronnie warns. "Angie said you're making a huge mistake! I can't have that. If you disappear into the desert, I'll end up with a new neighbor and it might be some noisy guy who fixes his motorcycle on the weekends. You *know* I sleep in on Sundays."

"You can keep Tilda forever, though. Think about that."

Ronnie glances at my cat, who is watching us from the center of the kitchen table with something like disgust in her pale green eyes. "Tilda, would you like to come and live with me?"

Tilda wraps the tip of her tail around her front paws and does not blink.

"I think that's a yes," I say. "So we're agreed? You let me go to Palm Springs, and if I don't return, Tilda's all yours. We good now?"

"Hmm...no! You tried to lull me into your trap. Nice try, girlfriend."

I sigh and go back to my bedroom. Ronnie will follow me and I can explain the whole situation. She likes gossip too much to forego the chance to lap up some honey *this* local.

I'm heaping clothes on my bed when she finally comes in, hands on hips, no trace of defeat on her stalwart face. "Tell me everything," she commands.

So I do, from the Saturday night breakup with Barry to the kiss last night—the one I apologized for—and the kiss this morning.

The one I haven't received an apology for.

I can't let that little fact go, can I?

"And so we're going to be fake-together all week," I finish. "You might even see us on TMZ if things get really crazy. We're going to be living like Palm Springs is our honeymoon."

Ronnie's enchanted now. *Take that, Angie.* "I can't believe all this happened! Angie was sort of thinking you'd just had a nervous breakdown and hallucinated it."

"She *always* thinks I'm having a nervous breakdown," I say, folding some light sundresses into the mix. "Should I bring a cocktail dress, do you think?"

"Oh, heavens yes. They're terrible fancy in Palm Springs." Ronnie springs into action, rummaging through my closet and finding all my oldest, most out-of-fashion clothes. "This one, this one, this one," she says. "Oh, ruffles!"

"That's my prom dress," I say, putting a hand out to stop her from adding the cough syrup-colored confection to the pile. "My mom mailed it to me when she was cleaning out my old room."

Ronnie thumbs the garish satin. It's really violently purple. I don't know what I was thinking when I was seventeen. She says, somewhat wistfully, "Do you think it will still fit? Because you'd look so classy—"

"No chance. I think I'll stick to the classics." I hold up a plain black dress that has been my fancy-date workhorse for the past three years. Not that it saw much work in the last few months with Barry as my escort. I say, "Old Bessie here will get me into the nicest clubs in Palm Springs."

"If you say so," Ronnie says doubtfully. "But at least dress it up with a scarf or something. Hang on, I have just the thing."

She hustles out and I hear the front door open and close. Perfect timing. I pull a truly scandalous scrap of silk and lace out of the bottom of my underwear drawer and slide it beneath the shirts in my suitcase. I don't need Ronnie to know *everything* going on under my clothes.

She's back a moment later, waving something peacock-blue.

"Oh, wow," I exclaim, impressed with the color. "Is that a scarf?"

"Vintage, you'd call it," Ronnie says proudly. "Look at that detail."

"It's Hermes!" I take the silk scarf as gently as I can. "My god, Ronnie, this is gorgeous!"

"You can tie it around your neck, or wrap it around your wrist, and it will give you such a pop of sophistication!" She shows me how to make a little knot in the delicate fabric. "This is a look that will never let you down. See—"

She maneuvers me in front of the mirror and I see what she means. From the shoulders up, I'm a suave and dangerous beauty. From the shoulders down, I'm just wearing yesterday's sleeveless blouse. "I'm obsessed," I tell her. "Truly. Thank you."

Ronnie waves her hand. "I mean, if my neighbor's gonna be on TMZ, I have to make sure she looks the part!"

I kind of think the TMZ look is more sweatpants and giant sunglasses, but I don't watch it with the same religiosity as Ronnie, so I take her at her word. "I think I'm packed now," I say. "Just need an outfit to wear back. You're good with Tilda?"

"As always," Ronnie says, glancing into the other room for a glimpse of the cat she adores. "Tilda and I always have such a nice time when you're away."

"I'll bet you do." Tilda really does love Ronnie. She'll curl up around my neighbor's arm and snooze with her for hours on end. It's perfect, because now I don't have to feel a bit bad about leaving my cat for a week while I'm pursuing love and bad ideas in Palm Springs.

I'm free to go crazy.

My phone rings as I hit the road, waving goodbye to Ronnie while she lifts Tilda's paw in a little wave back to me.

I look at the number on my dashboard screen. It's work. Oh, right, *work!* It's one p.m. and they must have just noticed I haven't responded to any emails yet today.

"Hey, Milton," I answer, the phone on speaker. "Before you say anything, I'm taking the rest of my vacation days. This week. Right now."

There's a sigh. Then he says, "Cassie, we kind of need you to help. There are a million things to do for closing. It's kind of ironic how much work it is to shut something down."

"I have six more days of vacation in my bank, and I'm using them." I figure I'll need next Monday to recover from this week. Or planning my wedding. I'm not picky. "I'll put in the hours later." I'm pretty sure I packed my laptop.

Did I pack my laptop?

Maybe?

"When I get to it," I amend, to cover my bases.

"You're supposed to get approval from the department heads for vacation time?" Milton says, in a tone which is meant to remind me he *is* a department head.

"So fire me, Milton," I tell him. "Seriously, fire me, so I don't have to go through the misery of closing up this theater."

There's a moment of silence, then Milton says, "So, I guess we'll see you next week."

"Next *Tuesday*," I correct him, and hang up.

I drive in silence for a few miles, the freeway hurling me through the canyons, and then I turn up The Emergency so loudly that I can't hear my own thoughts, all the better to drown out the sadness of losing the theater and the last excuse I had for living in Southern California.

This week, that doesn't matter.

This week, *nothing* matters but making the most of my time with Everett.

I pull into the parking lot of the resort and put Lime Lucinda in park, then look at my phone. I have his number and I'm ready to hit the button. Call him. For the first time. My pulse quickens, then races. It's too much. Nope, can't call. I opt for a text instead. Texts are normal. He's expecting a text. It won't change the world.

It only takes a second for him to text back. *At the bungalow. Drink is ordered.*

Smiling, I hop out of the car and run through the desert heat to find my man.

My key-card opens the side door and I'm through in an instant, staring down the security cameras trained on the passageway between the parking lot and the pool deck. This place has heavy-duty restrictions on it, as if the celebrity guests playing here are members of royal families or national governments—well, I suppose some of them probably are—and the behind-the-scenes vibe is definitely something out of a spy thriller. But as soon as I turn the corner onto the pool deck, the concrete walls are covered by trellises of billowing green leaves and the cameras, if there are any at all, retreat into the architecture. Blue water beckons, tiny bungalows gleam, and nodding palm trees oversee it all.

It's so easy to forget all of this is fake. The desert oasis, the smile on the face of the man waving a daiquiri at me from the nearest bungalow.

No.

That's not fake.

"Hey, you," I call as I tap my card and the gate unlocks. I'm up the three steps to the porch in a quick hop, and he's taking my bag with one hand, handing me a drink with the other hand, and leaning for a kiss on the cheek with his smooth, lovely lips. I almost turn my head to turn it into a lip-kiss, but lose my nerve at the last minute.

His mouth brushes my cheek with a sensation like passing my finger through a candle's flame.

I flick my gaze up to his, wondering if he feels that tingle too.

Judging by the way he widens his eyes, then lowers his lashes as if to cover the response, I'd say yes.

"You were quick," he observes, his tone light.

"Didn't want to miss any pool-time," I reply just as airily. "And my neighbor made it easy for me by coming over and helping me pack my things."

I'll leave out the part where she tried to stop me; it wasn't even sincere, anyway.

"And you're all set with work?"

"Yup, work is covered. I'm all yours this week."

I hazard another glance. He's looking down at me with an expression I can only interpret as satisfied.

Oh, I'll satisfy you, Everett Torby.

The thought comes out of nowhere; it's not like I haven't fantasized that this could be something real, but the sudden confidence that I can make him fall for me, really and truly, is new. I wonder where it's coming from and give my daiquiri a suspicious glance. But I've only had a sip and there's no way a taste of rum could suddenly give me this kind of courage.

Maybe this is just fate, the gods, the universe, or whatever, giving me the go-ahead to get what I want for once. Like, *Sorry we took your job and your ambition, Cassie, but we're ready to pay you back now. Here's one more chance to live a dream life.*

Thanks, guys. I won't let you down.

I wink at Everett and he laughs, startled.

"Ready for a day of sun and fun?" he asks good-naturedly.

"I'm going to wriggle back into that black bikini I paid way too much for this morning," I inform him, "and then, what do you say to a dip with me in that gorgeous pool? Splash around, get each other wet?"

Everett's eyes darken. I'm not imagining it; he has the kind of eyes that give away his mood changes, and I am pretty sure I just turned him on.

"A dip in the pool sounds perfect," he replies, with the husky gravel in his voice that drives me wild on a record and makes me burn in person.

I'm thankful now I didn't get in the pool earlier; it would have been awful to try and pull on a cold, wet bikini. In the bathroom, which is swagged with white muslin and faux tiki torches for lighting, I pull it back on, give my bikini line a critical glare, then decide it doesn't matter. If he's going to stick his face in my crotch out there, we'll be way past wondering if I trim the garden enough.

My mind is getting more and more heated, and I don't know if that change is going to excite him or turn him off. I can only assume that if we're spending a week together, and we've already kissed with the kind of sparks that can set off fire alarms, Everett has thought about me with, well, his dick, if we're going to be crude.

And frankly, that's exactly where I want his brain right now. I am not playing this game for some kind of wacky roommates sitcom pilot. I don't plan on sitting around a Palm Springs living room furnished with uncomfortable mid-century furniture playing Parcheesi with this guy.

I might have one chance at happiness with him, or I might have one chance at a week in bed with my rock'n roll idol— either one will do, I tell myself. But the one thing I am *not* doing is throwing away my shot with some maidenly ploy to intrigue him into wondering what's under the chaste hood.

I want him. I want all of him—I can admit that to myself now, with the prospect of a week with him actually in-hand, it's no longer embarrassing or teenage of me to say that I want every inch of Everett Torby, body and soul, for life and forever. I want all of him, but you'd better believe I'm going to take what I can get.

If it's only his body, so be it. Better than nothing.

One more steely look in the mirror. I flutter my eyelashes.

"Let's play this game," I whisper.

Chapter Fifteen

IT'S EASY TO talk a big game to my reflection in the mirror, especially one with such flattering lighting. As soon as I step back into the living area, though, I feel a nagging, annoying sense of reality take over. I might be ready to embark on the sexual Olympics trail with Everett, but first I have to make sure he's on my team, and not just a nice-looking bystander.

And how am I going to do that without flirting my way into oblivion? This guy is used to groupies. This is a man who has stood on thousands of stages for the past decade while women scream and sob and shriek out his name. I am one in a million, literally. Just one more woman in a sea of women, and men for that matter, plus a generous helping of non-binary people, who want Everett Torby's body in their bed, their backseat, or behind the bleachers—literally none of us would be picky.

He's looking at me from the doorway, his face silhouetted against the blinding desert light outside, and I wonder, with a touch of desperation, what he *really* thinks about me right now. Hot girl in bikini who he happens to really like? Or am I just another crazy, one he's shackled to for the week due to some weird events beyond his control?

I decide I have to believe it's the former. He kissed me and didn't apologize. Sheila told him to spend the week with me and he didn't tell her no.

It has to mean something.

"Well, I'm ready for that swim," I tell him, doing my best to sashay across the room.

He grins down at me. "You don't have to shake that ass of yours, you know," he says lightly.

Oh, god, I'm going to melt through the floor with embarrassment. My cheeks flaming, I look down.

"I already noticed it," Everett continues blithely, "and I'm already watching it."

What? My eyes fly back to his.

Two dark pools of black and blue, pupils dilated like a jungle-cat watching his prey.

Something deep within me catches fire at that moment.

He sees it; his eyes narrow and his smile catches with something like satisfaction.

Oh god, am I being played by *him?*

* * *

It's starting to feel like I walked out of that bathroom ready to be the aggressor, and instead have quickly found myself in the crosshairs of an accomplished hunter. Something about him has shifted since our casual, comfortable breakfast and chatter this morning. Maybe it's just the bikini—jeez, things that cost more really do make you look better, how unfair is that?—or maybe he has come to the same conclusion I have, that if we're going to spend a week together, we might as well make it count.

It could be my agreement, to him, was a sort of sexual carte blanch. Well, if that's the case, I am heartily ready to sign on the dotted line.

But with the true practice of an accomplished flirt, he doesn't just toss me straight onto the bed and ravish me from head to toe and everywhere in-between. Instead, he turns away, letting me take in the lines of his back and muscular shoulders—I must ask if he lifts, and hope he doesn't get too boring about it—as he heads down the steps and opens the gate to the pool deck.

I follow him, feeling like I'm in the thrall of a poetic devil. He's always been so sexy to me, being turned on by him isn't surprising, but right now I'm in such a cloud of excitement, pulsing right through the center of me like he's already pulled down my bikini and placed a feather-light finger against my skin, that even I am astonished by the intensity of my reaction to him.

"Coming?" he murmurs, in the huskiest honey-on-hot-coals voice I've ever heard, and with a blush I think that I could probably answer *yes* and it would be right on two counts.

The pool water is almost warm—not bathwater, but not cold, either—and there's no need to hover along the broad steps, waiting for our bodies to adjust. We both just plunge right in, until we're up to our chests—well, I am. He's more up to his rib-cage. We're facing each other. He is wet, glistening, gorgeous. I can only hope I am this beautiful when damp.

I swirl the water with my hands, suddenly nervous. What's the plan, now that we're in the water? I'm kind of a boring pool-person; my idea of a good time is leaning against the side just enjoying the contrast of sunny heat and wet coolness, possibly with a book in hand. But he's eyeing me like he's more of a chicken-fight kind of guy.

Barry's always like that, too. Why do men suddenly become teenagers again when you add water?

He grins at me and glances around the pool. "Want to see if Russell Brand over there wants to get up a game of Marco Polo?"

My gaze follows his and I freeze. "That's really Russell Brand," I say.

"Uh-huh."

"You're not serious about asking him to play with us, are you?"

Everett laughs. "Oh my god, no. I don't know him. Like I said before, this place is a splurge for me when things feel rough, not a regular hangout. Don't make the mistake of thinking I'm an A-lister, Cassie. I'm a solid F, at best."

I have to laugh at that, even though a little swirl of lust lights up my insides when he says my name. "Being indie isn't all bad,"

I suggest, sending a tiny wave of water against his chest. "For example, at least Russell Brand isn't over here *demanding* you play Marco Polo with him. I hear he's kind of a cheat at it, anyway."

"That bastard! Anyone who deliberately disrespects Marco Polo is no friend of mine."

"Thank god you feel that way. For a minute there, I was afraid this week was over before it started."

Everett gives me a grin. "So, what *is* your favorite pool game?"

I hesitate. Will he be annoyed if I reply that it's called Closing My Eyes and Relaxing and it's best played by one? That's probably not the answer he's looking for. I glance at his swimsuit and an idea pops into my head.

"I absolutely love playing Untie the Knot," I tell him.

"Untie the Knot?" He frowns. "What's that?"

"It's this," I say, and I take a breath, pop underwater, and tug loose the knot on his swim trunk laces.

"Yow!" he shrieks as I pop back up. "Untie the knot is very—uh—invasive!"

I laugh, even though I'm freaking out a little inside. "Oh, come on, it's fun! Good clean fun."

"I don't know about *clean*," Everett says, fumbling with his laces. "You almost showed this entire pool my *ahem*."

"That's what makes it fun?" I suggest.

He lunges at me. "Yes, that's what makes it *fun!*"

I shriek and dive underwater, pretty sure I can swim faster if I'm submerged. Everett grabs my ankle and I kick involuntarily, then picture myself bloodying his nose and stop as quick as I can. My head breaks the surface again, just as I feel the knot on the back of my skimpy bikini yank backwards.

He wouldn't!

My bikini top loosens as his fingers scrabble at my back, trying to gain purchase.

He would!

I leap forward again, water burning my nose as I try to swim away without kicking him. My bikini top is loosened but not off, and I have to stop abruptly with my hand pressed against the front to make sure the girls don't pop out for a little fun in the sun.

Everett's in front of me suddenly, water pouring down from his hair, his eyes and mouth fully laughing at me. "How about that? I decided to be a gentleman, but I think we're tied now."

"Actually, I think you win," I say ruefully, my arm straining a little as I try to get at the knot. Meanwhile, in front, things are getting dubious with one hand trying to keep everyone contained. "I'm officially disabled and can't play anymore. Will you fix the knot now, before we get kicked out of the pool?"

"Oh, it takes more than a little topless game to get kicked out of *this* pool," Everett says, but he gallantly moves behind me to fix the knot he has half-untied.

I stand still, feeling his fingers move across my skin as he fiddles with the straps, thankful for the cool water to keep the pink out of my cheeks.

His touch sets me on fire, and if we were just standing out in the desert sun, I'd surely burst into flame.

"Hey."

His whisper has my entire body at attention, from toes to nips. I stand rigidly still and concentrate on his mouth, which is just next to my right ear. So close it's nearly touching my neck. I'd die if it did—

"What?" I whisper back.

"Your game was a good idea. See if you can look past that far bungalow without turning your head...the one on the north side —"

"Which side is north, Lewis and Clark?" I demand, forgetting to whisper. Why do men always have to turn to cardinal directions? Is it just me or just the guys I am into or what?

"Oh, the left. That's a Telephoto lens over there, or else someone is trying to look at the planets at the wrong time of day."

I scan the bungalows lining the pool with only my eyes, careful not to move my head. His fingers have stilled, so I assume the knot is tied. When I finally see the long camera lens, which seems to be trained on us, I gasp and spin around.

"Everett!" I exclaim, but he isn't looking at me.

He's looking at my chest. And with good reason, because the girls have finally made a break for it and are floating merrily on the surface of the pool. I feel the straps of my bikini drifting apart.

He's not exactly a sailor when it comes to tying knots.

"Oh, god," I murmur, too embarrassed to react. And also just a bit pleased with how entranced he seems to be with my escapee boobs. I'm torn between asking if he likes what he sees or just pressing them against his bare chest. Luckily, I don't do either.

"Did you know boobs float?" Everett asks after a moment.

"Yes," I say. "That's how you know they're witches."

Everett bursts into surprised laughter, then moves his body close to me, protecting my renegade bust from view. He reaches around me and fiddles with the knot again, his chest close up against mine. I'm sizzling all over, my chin so close to his that I could turn my head and kiss him.

The idea makes my lips fall open.

Everett's too wrapped up in his work to notice my state.

"Sorry," he chuckles. "I really did think I had it…I guess I'm not great with knots. Maybe your next swimsuit should just have a clip, okay?"

And I don't know what has me more breathless, his arms and chest pressed against my half-naked body, or the idea he's just put out there, that we might be together longer than this week, longer than the longevity of this scrap of black nylon. How durable is a four-hundred dollar bikini, anyway?

"Nice tits!" someone calls, someone recognizably famous, and I feel myself blushing.

"I think it's time to get out," I say regretfully.

"What's the matter?" Everett asks. "You don't want your tits to outshine all the famous ones around you?"

"They're not used to being ignored," I say, "and it wouldn't be fair."

"Okay," Everett agrees, taking me by the hand. "For the other tits."

I look at my hand in his for a moment, then back at him. He smiles and shrugs.

"If I just showed your breasts to the entire pool, at least I can be a gentleman and escort you back to our bungalow," he says. "And anyway," he adds in a lower tone, "I am pretty sure we are about to make some waves with the pictures that photographer is getting. Your game was a good idea. Did you plan it that way?"

"Yes," I say, more caustically than I intended. "I wanted my tits on Twitter twice in one day. Thought it would be good for my job hunt."

"You never know," Everett says, leading me through the water. The pool steps seem to recede from us, as if we're traversing an ever-expanding infinity pool of gawkers, enduring laughter from a group of people who are used to being the focus of far too much attention. I feel myself shrinking back a little, but Everett ignores it. "Maybe your future employer is sitting out there, wondering where he can get a talented woman who both has a fantastic rack and a—what did you say you do, again?"

"What?" I'm distracted by his casual statement that I have a fantastic rack. I have a nice enough chest, but I wouldn't call my B-cup brigade a rack. "What do I do? I'm a small-town theater promoter, remember? I do marketing and graphic design and... well, everything, I guess."

"There you go. A small-town theater promoter with a fantastic rack. I'm sure the market is there."

We arrive at the steps and he leads me out. Dripping wet, with sagging shorts, he looks like a youngish dad who just took the kids into the pool on family vacation, and I love him even more for it.

Not lust this time, just the old, nagging love I've had for him for years, amped up to eleven by the reality of knowing him in person.

He's really everything I ever hoped and imagined, and then some.

I smile up at him, whisper, "Hope the camera's watching," and press my lips against his.

It's a tentative kiss, nothing like the mistake I planted on him last night or the whopper of a French he laid on me this morning. This one feels real in a way that I hope translates from my lips to his, a soft and seeking question—*do you want this?*—and a pause while I wait for his answer. A breathtaking second that lasts forever, while my heart thuds in my ears and the sounds of the rich and the languid recede into nothingness. A moment for the ages, a fearful and consequential wait that I'll never forget, for better or for worse.

And then he answers, a sigh that never leaves his mouth, a slight turn of his chin that deepens the kiss from soft pressure to questing push. He goes from the conquest to the conqueror, and I sigh in reply, my breath caught up in his mouth, in his heat, in the way he twists his lips and opens mine just so, as if he knows the secret that opens the genie's bottle. My fingers reach up and twine in his wet hair, cool and dripping, as his hands flatten on my cheeks, thumbs below my eyes, holding me still as if he's afraid I will run away.

But I'm a mermaid now, I have no legs and I'm just a weight in his arms, a sag against his frame, wet and hot and cold all at once, a moan escaping my throat and I think we might have kissed forever; I think we might have dropped to our knees and then onto our sides and then onto my back on the hot pavement, if it weren't for the hoots and howls of the Hollywood hundred, those voyeurs steeped in ennui, who tug us back to the present and leave us gasping, blushing, impossibly turned on and unforgettably public, on the pool deck of a Palm Springs resort where we have no business being in the first place.

Chapter Sixteen

BACK IN THE bungalow, there's a sense that we've come very close, and we'll get that close again. So I don't regret it when Everett takes a shower, then comes out again fully dressed. I'm going to do the same thing. Nothing is going to be forced in this week of fake-dating. I'm determined of that much. It's going to be natural.

"Want to go find the house?" he asks, opening a bottle of water.

"Oh, did Sheila get us one?"

"Yeah, I have a couple of texts from her." He glances at his phone. "About ten, actually."

"Oops."

"She'll survive." He grins at me. "The pool was calling louder."

How about our bodies? I think, but it's a silly thing to say out loud, so I keep it to myself. I am determined not to let things get weird. Not when they're going so well.

That kiss...that was something else. That was out-of-body. That was, well, in the words of one actress as we walked past, hand-in-hand, that was, "I thought they were going to fuck right in front of us, and frankly I was here for it."

I don't know that it gets more serious than that.

I do know that everyone who was on the pool deck during that kiss, and probably a few of their friends who hustled down when they heard what was happening with the indie singer and the nobody girl, is probably out there watching our bungalow like a whole flock of hawks, waiting to see if it starts rocking.

"It looks like a cute house," Everett says, holding out his phone.

I take it and admire the cream-colored rancher from Sheila's text. It has a low, flat roof, a red door, and a rock-garden for a front yard. There's a carport and, just visible through the gap, I can see the blue of a pool. "Another pool," I say, handing the phone back. "Maybe we can get in that game of Marco Polo."

Everett grins. "I bet you cheat."

"I do not!"

"You bring it up an awful lot for a person who isn't eight."

"You brought it up first!"

"Well, I have my eyes on you. That's all I'm saying."

"That's the *definition* of cheating in a game where your eyes are supposed to be closed."

He pockets his phone, that grin of his still gleaming. "You ready to get over there and get settled in, or what?"

We drive over in our separate cars; I keep Lime Lucinda pretty close to his gray sedan, because losing sight of him now would just be embarrassing...and take away from the little time we have together. In the course of one short drive, I manage to go from reveling in the week we have, to panic over only having one week with him. Seven days, and then I turn back into a pumpkin. It doesn't seem like enough time to convince this guy that I'm the one.

You shouldn't have to convince someone of that, not if they're really the one, an unhelpful contingent of my brain pipes up.

Why don't you shut the hell up? The more rah-rah side steps in. *We don't have time for your Debbie Downer shit! We have a man to win over!*

I am grateful for the rah-rahs right now.

Palm Springs isn't large and we're driving on residential streets, curving beneath towering palm trees, in no time at all. The craggy mountains are always just beyond, seeming to rise from the backyards of these low-slung, modest-looking houses with their million-dollar price tags displayed in the cars in the driveways, the expensive furniture seen through broad windows. The neighborhood Sheila has found for us has a weird vibe, like we've stumbled into a suburb for aliens—wealthy overlords who have come here for a little peace and quiet after running a galaxy for a few eons.

Of course, that's exactly what the movie stars and assorted celebrities who live here would like for me to think.

He finally pulls up to the house from the picture, and I nudge Lime Lucinda close to his car in the narrow driveway. It's all here: rock garden, red roof, pool glimpsed through the carport, and those sensational mountains rearing up as a backdrop.

"The sunsets are going to be amazing," I say as I get out of the car.

He turns his lazy smile on me. "I love a good sunset. We better enjoy it from the pool. What do you think?"

"Let's get a look at that thing," I suggest. "Since we're going to be spending so much time in it."

"Pool first, then unpack," he agrees, and we walk through the carport.

Behind a low fence, the blue pool sparkles like a magic carpet. Surrounded by the sandy, rocky native terrain, it seems unpredictable and strange—an oasis placed here by sorcery. Back at the bungalow resort, the pool area was made to look like a tropical island we'd stumbled upon, high walls closing out the surrounding desert. But here, the blue water is placed smack into the desert.

"I know this is an ecological disaster," I say, "but I really love it."

"Yeah, agreed," Everett mumbles, leaning against the fence dividing the carport from the pool deck. The slats wobble dangerously and he steps back. "Whoa. Just for show."

"I think it's to keep kids out, or dogs." I look back at the silent neighborhood baking in the sunlight, so many sleeping houses. "Although I'm not sure this place has much of either."

"Well, it's the middle of the afternoon in the desert," he says. "Give them time."

"What do people usually do in the middle of the afternoon in the desert?" I ask him.

Everett's smile quirks delightfully. "I think they make love," he says.

Well, *that* puts a spring in my step as I haul my bags out of the car. It's not too much stuff—an overnighter and a little rolling suitcase, but Everett still insists on taking them both from me and gravely carries them inside, as careful as a hotel porter.

"I work for tips," he says, placing the bags inside the front door. He holds out his hand.

"Oh, I don't believe in tipping, young man," I say. "Better luck next time."

"You Hollywood types are all the same." He flicks his gaze around the house. "Cute place."

Inside, a wide living room dominates the floor plan, looking towards floor-to-ceiling windows at the back of the house which show off the pool and the mountains beyond. I admire the long, low sectional sofa near the front, and a space-age looking table and chairs with fine, angled legs near the back windows. What a nice place that would be to eat dinner, I think, just before I follow Everett down a short hall. I wonder if we're allowed delivery, or if the fake-dating deal requires being spotted at trendy restaurants.

Bedrooms open on either side of the hallway. Everett hesitates at the doorways, then turns right. "This room faces west," he says. "So, you won't get the morning sunrise. You can sleep in. You're on vacation this week, so I figure you deserve that much."

Thoughtful, I think, but I'd rather share a room with him.

Everett sets my overnight bag on the bed, a king-size that takes up most of the bedroom's floor space. From the bed, I'll be able to look out the big window, which offers more views of the pool and mountains. The only other pieces of furniture are another space-age chair upholstered in a rich turquoise and a sparely built bureau with tiny silver drawer-pulls. The goal of this room, clearly, is to get in the bed and use it to its full potential, possibly while gazing out from time to time at the sunset.

Then to sleep long and late, while the sun rises on the other side of the house.

Everett looks around, then at me, waiting for my approval.

"I hate waking up early," I tell him. "And you must, too, since you're living that rock star life."

"I don't *hate* it," he says thoughtfully. "Sometimes I like to get up before sunrise, go for a bike ride before the streets are full of people, watch the fog rolling off the beach..."

"Oh, I see," I chuckle. "I forgot getting up early is optional and therefore doesn't suck when you're not working an eight to five. For me, it's just so I can get on some makeup before the Zoom calls start piling up."

"Not big on morning runs or coffee in the garden?"

"I mean, no, and I don't have one...I live in an apartment." *Let's focus, Ev.* "Okay, guess I should, uh, unpack? Then what?"

"Meet you in the pool," he says.

"Right." *Back into the bikini with me, then.* "I'll see you on the deck."

With the door closed and the curtains pulled shut, I busy myself hanging up the wrinkle-prone clothes and then wriggle into my damp bikini yet again. Miraculously, it hasn't started to lose its shape yet. Props to the A-lister nylon, I guess. I pluck at the fabric to get it sitting in the right places, taking in my reflection with a critical eye.

My mind is spinning through a million possible scenarios, most of which get me right back to this bed in the next half-hour or so. After the searing kisses we've shared today, surely a session between the sheets isn't too much to expect?

And yet—I smooth my hand over the thousand-thread-count sheets and nearly swoon over their softness—is instant sexual gratification really the right way to go? After all, this week is my chance to make Everett fall in *love* with me, not bed me and be done with me. Not that I believe Everett Torby is the belt-notching type of rock star, but I can still see that if we tumble straight into bed together, the entire focal point of our relationship changes.

Man, my mom was not kidding when she said undressing in front of a man takes away the mystery. Right now, I'm still all unknown potential to Everett—who could this girl be to him? But as soon as I strip out of this bikini for him, he'll have me defined, categorized, and put away in a drawer for the rest of my life.

Slowly, hating myself, I take off the bikini. I'll tell him it's still damp, and I hung it up to dry. From the bureau drawer where I already stashed my unmentionables, I take out the considerably more demure bathing suit I usually wear. The cheerful white polka dots on a navy blue bodysuit aren't exactly seductive, but hey, that's why boobs exist, right? And he already told me he likes mine.

Feeling like I am on the verge of starting something real, I grab a bottle of sunscreen and head for the deck.

Chapter Seventeen

"RIGHT," EVERETT IS saying, his phone pressed to his ear. "Right, right. No, I know. Right."

He looks at me from his perch on the kitchen counter and waves his fingers, a regretful smile on his face. I guess it's a call he couldn't skip, but I can't help feeling disappointed. I was ready to enlist his help to get my shoulders slathered in sunscreen. I waggle the bottle at him, just in case I can entice him to end his call.

He grins, then says, "Yes. I know. Right. Mm-hmm. Okay. Got it."

That must be the world's worst phone call. It sounds like he's receiving a dressing-down from his most judgmental aunt or something.

Finally, he hangs up and sighs, looking at me with a tired expression.

"Forget to turn in your homework?" I ask.

He cracks a smile. "Sheila was letting me know the parameters of the week."

"The...parameters?" The word adds a level of tension to our arrangement that I don't like. "I wasn't aware we were on a special ops mission," I say.

"Shoot to kill only," Everett says, rubbing his forehead, where a few lines have settled during his phone conversation. "No, it's fine. She just wants to make sure we're seen in the right places, we don't do anything stupid like get matching tattoos, we keep the partying to a low roar, that kind of thing."

"Well, damn. Now I want matching tattoos."

"I know, right?" He hops down from the kitchen counter. "It's like, I didn't know that was the thing I wanted until she said I couldn't have it."

"Do you *always* listen to Sheila?" I coo, wondering if I could really talk him into tattoos. It would be hilarious, and also— romantic? Adorable? A big regret if this week doesn't work the way I want it to? Hard to say. I'll keep the idea in my back pocket, and reanalyze later in the week.

"Always," Everett assures me. "She also said to be sure to wear a lot of sunscreen."

"Well, good news for you, Boy Scout." I wave my Ocean Potion at him.

He takes the bottle from me slowly, letting his fingers linger against mine, and a sizzle starts low and works its way through my limbs. By the time he has sunscreen in his palm and his fingers are on my back, I'm losing my mind to a hum of static that means all transmissions are being blocked by one loud, insistent beat.

"What's that sound?"

I blink my way out of my hypnotized state. "Huh?"

There's no way he hears my—

Oh, *that* beat.

"I think the neighbors are having a party," he says, walking over to the windows overlooking the pool.

In response, the beat grows deeper and the music overlaying it louder. "Is that...New Kids on the Block?" I ask, horror-struck.

"You're not a fan? I had the complete set of dolls when I was a kid."

"Really?" Time to rethink my life plans.

"No, not really. My sister did, though." Everett laughs, then sighs. I get it, I really do.

This is not the music I meant to romance him to, and I'm pretty sure if he has seduction on his mind, he was planning to use some indie crooning to get the job done. Believe me, I am ready for him to use that nuclear option on me, but New Kids? Hanging tough? I do not want to know how or what those plastic-haired boys are hanging, thanks very much.

"Maybe they're just going to play the one song," I suggest. "Let's wait it out."

Everett shrugs and comes back to finish the job. "You changed your bathing suit," he says.

I examine his expression for signs of dismay, but he's holding his cards close to his chest. "The bikini was damp."

"I liked it," he says. "I like this, too. Very pin-up model, like you're going to cheer on the troops."

"I'm hoping to get my portrait painted on the side of an airplane."

"Miss Cassie, the bomber from Phoenix Canyon." His fingers stroke my back and it's all I can do not to purr. "The boys all say she's worth fighting for."

I arch my back and lift my shoulders, leaning into his touch. The metaphor gets dropped fairly quickly, because I can't concentrate on World War 2-era witty banter when this man is massaging me with such dexterous fingers. I think about him strumming the guitar, then turning all those little moves on me, and let out a sigh that's a little more longing than I anticipated.

Everett's breath is warm on my neck. "Everything okay, Miss Cassie?"

"Just enjoying the massage," I admit. "You're very good with sunscreen."

"It's a gift," he says. "But I'm afraid you're all done now."

I knew I should have worn that bikini, anyway. All that exposed skin that would have needed a rubdown! What an opportunity lost! "I guess I better do your back, then," I say, turning around to face him.

I look up into his eyes and see a smolder that matches the fire in my skin. I feel my lips fall open; despite my decision to keep this session to light seduction, I can feel the potential for a tumble in those smooth, soft sheets rising with every beat of our hearts.

And I want it.

But my rah-rah section is oddly quiet, and I know they're right when those errant brain cells suggest, *Don't be another groupie, Cassie.*

I drop my gaze before I do something I might regret in seven days' time. The quick win or the long game? I have to stay the course. "Hand me the sunscreen," I murmur, and he puts the bottle in my hand.

Beneath his shirt, there's a muscular man who must blow off mental steam in the gym fairly often. I rub my fingers around the outlines of his shoulder blades, pressing lightly so that I can enjoy his shiver of sensation in reply. He seems to feel every touch keenly, and I suspect he would absolutely fall to pieces if I inflicted a little sensual massage on him. I make a mental note to read up on pressure points later tonight. It would be a real pleasure to touch him in just the right spot and watch his defenses crumble.

Not that he's putting up a lot of walls between us.

It's stunning to know that twenty-four hours ago I was depressed in Phoenix Canyon and now I'm a hair-breadth away from getting flipped on my back by Everett Torby. Life can really change in an instant. The hard part, the part I have to remember, is making the change *last.*

I can't go back to the way things were when this week is over.

If I thought I was getting him out of my system with one wild hurrah, I was sadly mistaken about how deep in my system Everett really is.

"Hey," he says suddenly.

"Hmm?" I dab sunscreen on the back of his neck, running my fingers beneath his wavy hair.

"The music stopped!"

"Oh, thank god." I hadn't noticed, too deep into my own musical thoughts.

"We should put on some of our own."

I imagine playing Marco Polo while the fourth Emergency record, the one with the wild drum machine beats that everyone called their dance phase, plays in the background. "I'm sure there's a stereo on the pool deck," I say, finishing up the sunscreen with a final swirl on his lower back. "You can probably Bluetooth it to your phone or something."

"Perfect," Everett proclaims, heading for the patio door. "Do you like Iron and Wine?"

Not exactly the music I had in mind, but of course I like Iron and Wine, and I'm not going to say no to some indie folk with an emotional edge that could sever an artery when Everett suggests it for pool time. When he opens the fridge and triumphantly removes a few cans of gin and tonic, I realize that we're going for a chill pool experience, not a splashy Marco Polo game. It's a good idea, actually, because the afternoon sunlight is starting to slant, taking on that golden quality of early evening, and I figure if we sit around having a few happy hour drinks now, we'll be soft around the edges and ready to enjoy a nice dinner out afterwards.

After all, we *have* to be seen in public. We can hardly order DoorDash and watch TV.

It would be nice, though.

The pool is warm, and the steps are wide and shallow, giving us plenty of room to stretch out and sit with our drinks. Sam Beam sings to us in his hushed and husky croon, "Naked as We Came", while Everett hums quietly along, as if he can't help being included. I want to ask about his relationship with the indie singer who goes by Iron and Wine on his records, but I also don't want to remind Everett of the stakes surrounding *our* relationship, that of star and fan, so I decide to keep things more general.

"If you could live anywhere on earth, where would you live?"

He glances at me and smiles. "Right now, I think I'd say here."

Just melt me already, sun. "Seriously, though. Like, I think I would live in the middle of Yellowstone National Park. In a cabin. But not where tourists could find me."

"Or bears?"

"Bears are a problem," I admit.

Everett peers at me. "I don't think you really want to live in the middle of the forest. You don't strike me as the hermit type."

"Maybe not forever, but it would be relaxing for a little while."

"Except for the bears."

"Except for them. Don't you ever want to just...disappear?" The words come out almost by accident. I glance at the can of G&T, assuming it's to blame. Did we have lunch? We didn't.

Oops.

"I do sometimes," Everett says, giving my question the gravity it commands. "But you know, I spend a lot of time all at once in front of people, and then I have to come home, close the blinds, decompress. It's hard. I think a cabin deep in the woods would be good for that. But also I'd need a personal chef or a delivery service or something, because part of my process is just ordering in a *lot* of food."

"Is that why you work out so much?"

He smirks. "Who says I work out a lot?"

"Your back muscles do," I say, with an unrepentant shrug.

"Okay, fine. I do. But it's part of the job. I'm up running around for a couple hours a night, singing, and it takes some strength and stamina. And also, I guess, all those hours on a bus going between towns. Tour food. Late night dinners. Drinking to come down off the performance high. It's hard on a metabolism."

I nod slowly, imagining joining that kind of circus. Could I be a tour wife? I do like staying up late. "I guess it would be," I say, "but better than an office job, right?"

"Definitely, but I'm no spring chicken," he teases, affecting a grandfatherly squeak in his voice. "I'm not twenty-two anymore! I can't just eat a whole pizza and call it a night like those whippersnappers in their rock and roll bands!"

"It's okay, grandpa, age makes a mockery of us all," I say with a smirk, and he snorts.

"So flattering. I guess I'll never have to worry about you inflating my ego, Cassie."

When he says my name, my body temperature rockets. Suddenly, the water is uncomfortably warm. I move up a step, so that I'm only just sitting in the water, and he glances up at me in surprise. "You okay?"

"Just warm," I admit. "I'm fine. I think I would actually just keep living in Los Angeles, if I could live anywhere. I like being warm, and it gets cold as hell in Yellowstone."

"Where are you from, again?"

I take a long swallow from my can. The G&T is sweet and goes down easy. It's a good thing it's not as alcoholic as one mixed by an actual bartender, or I'd be on my ass already. "Ohio," I say, giving the word all the misery it deserves.

"Ouch."

"Yeah. I told you already, but you forgot because it was so boring, the name simply left your brain."

"I'm sure it has its nice points."

"Occasionally. Fall leaves on sunny afternoons. Corn fields and little white farmhouses. A really good meal in Columbus. But then the sky turns gray, it goes all Ohio again, and you realize it was just fooling you."

"That could be a song."

"What's the opposite of a love song?"

Everett laughs appreciatively. "Do we all hate where we came from? Is that how we end up in L.A.?"

"I'm sure a few people are born there."

Everett looks skeptical. "Prove it."

"I can't. It's just math."

"Oh, I don't do math."

"Me neither. Might be why my theater is closing. I don't think any of us can math very well."

He sighs. "That's a real shame. I wonder if it can be saved."

I shrug. "I didn't get the details."

Didn't stick around long enough. There are probably Zoom meetings going on right now that I'm not part of, discussing the demise of my job. I should probably have a seat at that table, but it's not worth losing this.

Everett finishes his drink and looks at the can. "That was extremely sweet and now I'm hungry as hell."

My stomach rumbles in response.

"I guess that's an answer," he says.

"Did you skip lunch, too?"

"I sure did. Let's see what Sheila has planned for us, okay?" Everett hops out of the pool and walks over to the chair where he stashed his phone. I watch the water drip down his legs and think obscene thoughts. He nods to himself and laughs. "Looks like we have reservations at Melvyn's."

"What? *The* Melvyn's?"

Everett taps a few times. "The address matches up. Are you ready to eat where Frank Sinatra ate?"

"I don't have the clothes for this," I confess. Even my black number is too weak for such a date. "I'm pretty sure Melvyn's is still the kind of place where you dress up in your finest velour and polyester. The seventies glam that never goes out of style."

"Well, I think as long as you look like you tried, you'll be fine," Everett says, grinning at me. "Or you could always just pull a skirt over that cute little bathing suit and say you're going for a Fabulous Forties look…"

"No," I snort, getting out of the pool. "I'll find something. But I have to shower first, obviously, and dry my hair—"

"Hey," Everett says, grabbing my wrist as I start past him. My steps arrest and I look up at him. "You look great. Don't freak out, okay? I admit I get invited to places like this *very* infrequently, but when I do, they expect the rocker to be a little less than perfect. I'm not putting on a tie, and I don't think you should bother with a cocktail dress, either."

"What should I wear, then?" I can't keep the note of exasperation from my voice. But that's okay. He can know I'm human now and then.

"Put on a decent top and a pair of pants," he says, like he's talking to a third grader, "and leave your hair exactly like this." His gaze lingers on a spot just to the right of my cheek, and I put my hand up self-consciously, feeling where water and the desert breeze have tangled my locks into something slightly wilder than usual. "Yes," he murmurs, with that gravelly undercurrent to his voice that makes my insides clench together, "don't do a thing with your hair. Trust me."

Chapter Eighteen

I TUG AT my sky-blue blouse as the valet approaches Everett's side of the car. It's not velour, but we're definitely working with a man-made fabric here. And, since Everett saw me walk out of the bedroom wearing it and declared the top matched my eyes, I consider it a pretty nice choice for our night out at Palm Springs' most historic restaurant. The cut looks nice with jeans, but I'm pretty sure there's a dress code at Melvyn's, despite what Everett says about looking rock-star trashy, so I opt for a short black skirt instead. Now, I just have to avoid tugging at it all night; I've never been great with anything that stops above the knee, and this sucker only goes halfway down my thigh.

I've left my hair just as Everett asked; the tangle of waves concerns me a little, but he gave me such a lecherous look out on the pool deck that I have a sneaking suspicion I look like a mermaid goddess.

Beside me, Everett stretches his legs out of the car, and I can't help but watch his muscles flex beneath his neat, well-cut slacks. He wanted to wear jeans, but I convinced him that was a bad idea.

"Keys, sir?" The valet looks hopeful that Everett will like him. The staff will know the reservation list ahead of time at a place like this, and this kid recognizes Everett Torby. But he doesn't gush—I'm sure that's against the rules—and instead settles for a look of worship as Everett hands off the keys and opens the car door for me. The kid looks at me carefully, wondering if he should recognize me.

Nope, not yet, kiddo.

But soon.

We have time for a drink at the bar, so we let the hostess lead us into the lounge, which is dark and understated—from what I can see in the low light, which leaves me blinking after the blazing late evening sun outside.

Everett leans against the bar while I slip onto a stool. "There are people here wearing shorts," he informs me.

"Well, you look nice," I say, unrepentant. I pick up the cocktail menu and try not to pass out from the sticker shock. Twenty bucks for a martini! Thank god the record labels are covering this. I'm a little too unemployed to cope with the numbers, so I put it down again. Everett is still moping about his trousers. I shake my head at him. "How was I supposed to know that the dress code in Palm Springs allows shorts?"

"My poor legs are suffocating in a prison of khaki."

"Grow up," I laugh, smacking his arm lightly.

He gives me a hound-dog look. "Everyone here could be admiring my calves, you know."

"They can't see them," I say mercilessly. "It's too dark." *And anyway, they're just for me.*

Everett orders us a pair of the twenty-dollar martinis and two prawn cocktails to keep us from staggering to our dinner table later on. I'm starving and the starter sounds delicious, although a part of my brain has already moved into Dating Strategy 101 and the prospect of eating shrimp and horseradish, with its latent effects on one's breath, isn't ideal. But if he's eating them, I have to, too, right? Out of self-defense.

I just hope he isn't planning on making it a big escargot night. That much garlic is hard to overlook in the early stages of a relationship. Escargot is really more of a marriage appetizer, I think. Same goes for French onion soup and anything with anchovies.

"So, we talked about Ohio a little," I say as the bartender moves away to mix our drinks, "but we didn't get a chance to bash your home state of Missouri."

"Oh, what's to bash? It's farms and hills. I love Missouri." Everett gives me a twinkling smile and slips onto the bar-stool next to me.

"Then why don't you live there?"

"Because of all those farms and hills. I'm really more of a rock-strewn canyon and swimming pool man, that's all." He picks up a swizzle stick and bites it, letting it hang out of his mouth like a kid playing pirate. "I felt a little claustrophobic in Missouri, like all those waving fields of corn and picturesque vales of trees were just holding me down."

"Having their way with you," I suggest.

He grimaces at the joke. "You cannot trust a crowd of trees."

"I think they call that a forest."

"No, you're thinking of crows. It's a murder, a lot of trees."

"Right." I look at him for a moment, wondering where a guy who sings about anxiety and nervous breakdowns falls in the hierarchy of hippiedom. Probably he isn't even ranked amongst his ancestors. "I definitely see you as a city guy. L.A. makes sense for you. New York might have made even more, though."

"I tried New York. Great town, but, again, the swimming pool to person ratio is just not ideal. I need a *lot* of chlorinated water to survive."

"I actually agree. Did you know I chose my apartment complex because I liked the pool so much?"

"No, but I respect that decision. Is it fancy?"

"It's not fancy, it's just ideally positioned. Close to my front door, gets morning and midday sun, some shade in the afternoon when it's the hottest. I like to take a dip on my lunch breaks sometimes."

"You're really living the lifestyle, Cassie. I approve."

Our martinis arrive, along with a promise that the prawns are on their way. I imagine shrimp with backpacks running breathlessly along a concourse, shouting, *hold the plane, we're almost there!* Phew, do I ever need some solid food. Oh well.

The vodka will have to do. I take a gulp of Grey Goose and smile.

"What do you do for lunch on any given day?" I ask Everett.

He frowns around his martini glass. "Sometimes I nap."

"Oh, nice."

"Sometimes, I go out to the garden and beat the hell out of a punching bag."

I raise my eyebrows. "Violence?"

"Solves everything."

"I wouldn't have expected that."

"Oh, I'm not really doing it to be violent," he says. "More like, to just get the tension out."

"Work stress?"

"Everything stress," Everett admits, and suddenly I see vulnerability in his eyes. "You know, life doesn't get easier just because a few hundred thousand people in the U.S. and Canada know you by name."

"I think it's a few more people than that," I say gently.

"When you include the rest of the world, possibly, but it's not a *lot* more," says the man who has released a certified platinum album and received a Grammy nomination for best alternative song. You know, the category where your parents go, "What does 'alternative' even mean? And who are these bands, anyway?"

"Well, however many people, I know that being semi-sorta famous doesn't make life easier," I tell him. "But it *can* buy you fancy dinners at famous restaurants, so it's always best to look on the bright side."

"This restaurant is more famous than me," he laughs. "And they're only buying us dinner because now my ex-girlfriend actually is famous, or about to be."

I'd somehow managed to forget about her role in all this, but now the drama of their fight comes rushing back, along with all the weirdness I've been tugged into: the harsh insults, the trashed room, the naked photo, the kiss.

The kiss.

I feel my own lips go dry and I can't help licking them, a motion that doesn't go unnoticed by Everett. His gaze flicks to my mouth, then back to my eyes.

Then down again, where it lingers.

I feel my teeth creep out to tease my lower lip, biting at it without even meaning to act sultry or seductive. He just makes me want to feel things, and if I have to be the one to satisfy those longings, that's just the way it has to be. Right now, I want someone's—*his*—lips to take away the tingling in mine; I want someone's—*his*—teeth to nibble at my lips and tease the sensitive skin there. I want someone—*him*—to kiss me so thoroughly that my entire body sings with sensation.

"Your prawns," a waiter announces, leaning between us with two glasses heaped with fat, pink shrimp. "And your table should be ready in about twenty minutes."

The waiter withdraws and leaves Everett and me staring at each other. We're both feeling it. The desire to leave these drinks, desert these prawns, and find a dark corner where we can make out until the cops are called.

He's the first to pull himself back to reality. "We'd better eat something," he suggests, reaching for a shrimp. "Or I'm pretty sure we're going to make fools of ourselves in this fancy restaurant."

"Yeah," I echo, going for a shrimp of my own. "Fools."

I'd better be careful, or I'm going to end up right where I want to be by the end of the night. And that's not how the long game is supposed to be played.

I find my way to the ladies room before the table is ready and give myself a quick once-over: no shrimp or herbs in my teeth, no cocktail sauce on my shirt, no obvious signs of unfettered lust on my face. Well, the last one is harder to ensure, but I'm doing the best I can. More solid food, I think. Time to counteract all the alcohol and maybe make myself a little sleepy and heavy, too—then I'll be far less likely to want to jump him. Right?

I check my phone before I head back to the bar, suddenly wondering what happened with the photographer at the bungalows this afternoon. I don't have to search too far to find the pictures: a few music rags are already running them on their timelines. I look at the backs of our heads as we whisper together in the pool, looking past the palms and evergreens towards the rock-strewn mountains just outside of town. *Lovers or haters,* one caption reads, happily drawing from Everett's catalog of lyrics, *as Everett Torby is caught springing for the ultimate in luxury on a Palm Springs getaway just days after ex-GF Liz Astra signs her first Hollywood deal.*

I read it a few times over, trying to puzzle out why the media thinks one thing has to mean something to the other. The implication here is that Everett is having a fling with me *because* Liz got a movie deal. But why would that be his reaction?

Do they think he's jealous?

Or does it serve some purpose for them if they get Liz jealous—more so than she already was?

I tap my lip with one finger, trying to puzzle out their plans. Everything in Hollywood is plotted out like a cookie-cutter script, I know that much. These publicists and marketing heads jerk strings like over-zealous puppeteers. And they have something up their sleeves with the info they're pushing to the music blogs. What's the agenda, though?

If we were told the record labels were hoping to head off the Liz confrontation by proving Everett is happily dating me, the media is certainly doing their best to run it in the opposite direction, with Everett pulling me as his second-choice after the favorite got away. That can't be a coincidence, unless his record labels—specifically, Sheila—are terribly incompetent.

Which would mean...they want me to fail at capturing Everett's attention long-term. They want Liz...*back?*

That can't be right.

I look at my phone for a moment, trying to think of someone I can text, someone who might have some shred of knowledge about Hollywood machinations. But I don't move in the circles I'd planned to when I moved to L.A., and I just don't have any sources.

I'm on my own here.

* * *

"Table thirteen," the waiter says, pride glinting in his eyes. "Mr. Sinatra's table."

"Oh, my," I purr to Everett, who winks at me in reply. "Mr. *Sinatra's* table. Can I hope for some crooning later?"

"I'd curdle your crème brûlée," Everett snorts. "I've never been much of a crooner, I don't think."

"Really?" I glance up from the menu, interested. His own opinion of himself seems considerably different from mine. "I'd say you're about two albums and a greatest hits tour away from being a full-on lounge singer. Wrong?"

"How could you say something like that to me?" His eyes crinkle at the corners; he's holding back a laugh. "Like I'm going to show up in Vegas wearing a velvet dinner jacket and just start singing out of the American songbook?"

"You'd be up to your eyeballs in panties and bras," I assure him. "But you do you. If you want to be an aging rocker, I won't complain."

"What was that Death Cab for Cutie Song? *'Sixty and Punk,'* something like that? I wish to be the sad main character in that song. Gray hairs and safety pins in my jacket."

"You'll be adorable." The idea of Everett at sixty with a full head of gray hair isn't necessarily chilling; I've always had a thing for a silver fox. I survey him for a moment until he squirms under my scrutiny.

"Stop imagining me old, dammit!"

I have to laugh. "You can't stop me from fantasizing!"

Everett shakes his head. "This is turning into the weirdest dinner date ever."

I feel a twinge of anxiety at that idea; I don't want to be Everett's weirdest, I want to be his best. I pick up the menu and try not to gasp in horror at the prices, reminding myself again that his labels are picking up the tab. Still, this place thinks a lot of their beef.

"The Steak Diane is famous," Everett remarks.

"That sounds like something that comes on fire and with a Jell-O mold of asparagus on the side," I reply, and he chuckles.

"You're very close. What's the matter, not feeling adventurous?"

"When the theme is seventies nostalgia, I err on the side of caution."

"It's our most under-appreciated era," he murmurs.

"On the contrary," I say, putting down my menu, "I don't think we can put enough space between us and the decade of brown decor and disco."

"It's weird, when the two things that define the decade don't even go together."

"Drugs are bad," I say blandly.

This conversation could go on forever, neither of us really saying anything but thoroughly enjoying one another's company, and I wouldn't be mad. When the waiter returns with fresh drinks and takes our dinner order, he asks for the Steak Diane and I go for a filet with the house steak sauce. "I really appreciate a good sauce," I tell Everett, and he shakes his head.

He's just about to reply when a shriek rents the room, cutting through the conversation, and our heads whip around. The source of the sound is charging right for us, all smeared mascara and ripped couture.

This can't be happening, I think, scooting closer to Everett and reaching for his hand without even thinking about it.

His fingers tighten around mine as Liz Astra, in all her drunken glory, arrives at our table.

Chapter Nineteen

"LIZ," EVERETT SAYS quickly, holding up his free hand. "Hon, what's wrong? What are you doing here?"

The *hon* makes my toes curl, but I figure it's just habit. At least, that's what I'm going to tell myself.

Liz doesn't seem to get any comfort from the pet name. She's wearing contacts that turn her eyes a crazy shade of purple, and they seem to gleam at me with a demonic light when she turns her tear-streaked gaze in my direction. I feel Everett's fingers gripping my hand beneath the table, and I squeeze back. For strength, for courage?

Definitely for courage. Liz is terrifying.

"You again," she hisses, digging her red nails into the tablecloth. "What do I have to do to send you on your way, groupie doll? This isn't your place."

Probably, I think, I should not engage with the crazy drunk ex-girlfriend. I look past her, to the horror-struck waiter hovering just out of reach. The manager is racing through the restaurant at top speed, weaving in and out of tables. Help is on the way, if they can actually handle this newly crowned starlet.

"Liz, you need to take yourself home and get some rest," Everett says, his voice going husky in that way I usually love. "Come on, babe. This isn't like you."

"This isn't like *you*," she counters, pointing at him with one crimson talon. "I thought you were better than this!"

Again, I am *this,* and I'm not loving the abuse. But as long as Everett has a death-grip on my hand, I know to stay still and ride it out. He's on my side.

"Ma'am," says the restaurant manager, who is also on my side, "I'm sorry, but you're causing a disturbance. We do not want to call the police, so if you could just—"

"Call them," Liz spits, an otherworldly grin splitting her face. "Call the police, call the press, call *my manager!*" —this last part is shouted as she spins around, waving her arms as if to make sure the entire restaurant is witnessing this. "Tell precious Stevie that Liz is on the loose and there's nothing he can do about it!"

She does a drunken twirl, loses her balance, and tumbles across the table. My martini tips into my lap, but the cold vodka has nothing on the chilly eyes glaring up at me. I draw back from her as Everett releases my hand and stands up, shoving himself out of the booth. "Enough, Liz," he growls, and I think that at least now he's using her name, not an endearment.

Everett takes his ex by the hand and hauls her upright; the manager has pulled out his phone and is talking into it like it's a megaphone, and I wonder idly if he is talking to the police or precious Stevie. Our waiter leans over the table and begins plying me with linen napkins, as if that can begin to dry the vodka soaking through my skirt. I want to tell him not to bother, that he's very kind but everything is already ruined, but the restaurant has gone into such an uproar of excited chatter and warning shouts and the occasional shriek from the arguing, angry Liz, that there's no point in saying anything.

I lean back in Frank Sinatra's booth, steal a swig from my date's martini glass, and let the three-ring circus whirl without me.

Dinner in a bag at his side, Everett walks me to the curb and we wait for the valet to bring his car around. He has a morose expression on his face. I glance up at him and try on a smile.

"Cheer up," I say. "Steak Diane is probably fantastic cold."

He can't help but grin at that, and I feel like I've accomplished something. If I don't get him back fast, I'll lose this entire night to Liz and her scene—and I don't have enough time to just grant her whole chunks of my week with him.

But I know it's going to be a tough episode to put behind us. She was eventually dragged out by Stevie—a bald and alarmed middle-aged man who must have been trailing her around Palm Springs—while a member of the local police force scribbled notes and nodded at the restaurant manager's account of what went down. I'm sure we could have stayed and had our dinners hot, but Everett was tired of being stared at, and nervous that there might be photographers lining up to catch us leaving and tail us home. It was one thing to be seen in public, he said, but another one to be followed back to our house.

So when he suggested we take everything to go, I didn't really have any arguments.

"I can't understand what's going on with her," he says now, balancing his heels on the curb.

I sigh. He's going to want to talk about it. As much as I don't want Liz on his mind tonight, there's no getting past it without a conversation—one I'm really not qualified to contribute to, but I'm the only one here. "Maybe she was already drinking too much when the deal came through, and she's having a hard time dealing with the sudden fame, so she's been getting wasted," I suggest. "And when she's drunk, the first thing she thinks of is… you."

He looks thoughtful. "That's actually as good a hypothesis as anything I can come up with. She's also been a woman who really goes for whatever she wants, even if that can be destructive."

Sounds charming. "Well, I guess that's what makes her perfect for Hollywood," I say.

"Yeah. They love self-destruction in this town. Always have." His voice verges back towards morose. "It's just weird that I don't see her for a year and now suddenly she's stalking me around Palm Springs."

I could tell him a few things about life getting weird in a hurry, but luckily, the valet has arrived, cutting the conversation short. I smile up at Everett as he holds the car door for me, but his face is absent, still lost in thought about Liz. It's a quiet drive home, with me studying his reflection in the passenger window, pretending that I'm watching the streets of Palm Springs slip on by.

Everett goes to bed. It's not what I expected, not what I wanted, but I suppose it's what I deserve. I've done some thinking on the drive home, and the conclusion I came to, walking up to the front door of our deserted street (the supposed paparazzi have not arrived), is that I am asking too much of this one-time-only week with Everett Torby.

Clearly, this guy has other stuff going on.

And I don't just mean with his ex, although that's a whole can of worms. There's some weirdness to him about fame, as if he doesn't want to be seen in public, and it's not just about keeping a private profile or maintaining a distance between his on-stage life and his home life. It's more like there's a genuine fear that he might accidentally become a household name, or become recognizable on the street to more than a few random indie music fans—there are only so many of us allowed to gather at one time, outside of concerts, for nerd reasons.

I noticed the way he grew twitchy at the prospect of being seen as we left the restaurant, and the way he spoke about the potential of being photographed with Liz now that she's famous...he doesn't want it, not at all.

Fame doesn't seem that bad to me. I mean, not a George Clooney or Jennifer Lopez level of fame; that looks problematic on every level. A person has to be allowed to walk down a street without constant attention. But there are plenty of rock stars on the spectrum between Everett's status and Mick Jagger god-tier stars, and the majority of them aren't harassed day in and day out. Usually, it's the opposite and they have to *look* for attention. It seems to me that Everett could juice up his career a little and that wouldn't be the end of his personal life.

I can't understand his fear of big-time fame, and the fact that I don't have the least little clue is a tip-off to me that there's more to this guy than what I can learn in a week of play-dating.

So when I head for the kitchen in hopes of making a drink and sitting up with him, chatting, it's purely platonic. I'd like to get to know him better. I'd like to tell him some dumb, embarrassing things about myself. I'd like for us to be friends. Maybe *that* can last beyond this week.

Maybe, if I'm very lucky, that friendship could turn into the *and more* that I still want from him, so badly.

But he doesn't follow me into the kitchen. Instead, he lingers in the living room, pulling his jacket through his fingers, back and forth.

I lean out of the kitchen, whiskey bottle in hand. "Are you okay?"

Everett looks at the floor and mumbles, "I think I just need to head to bed, if that's okay."

Perplexed, I glance at the clock on the microwave. "It's barely eight o'clock," I say. "The sun is still out."

"I know, I'm just...we didn't really get much sleep last night, did we? Either of us. And today we spent a lot of time in the sun, and I know we have some public stuff to do tomorrow..." He drifts off, looking as if he has listed the complete schedule of the President of the United States and added in a few extra jobs for good measure.

I look at him carefully. He does seem awfully tired. Maybe he's getting a cold. Wouldn't that be charming? I could make him soup and pat his head with a cool washcloth.

"Okay," I say, since I can hardly argue the point with him. "I'll be quiet out here."

With Everett shuffling off to his room—*his* room, I notice with a touch of spite, not the back bedroom with the sunset view where he insisted on putting my things, but the room across the hall—there's not much for me to do but pour that drink and head onto the porch. The sun is setting now, throwing splashy color across the desert sky and shimmering golden as it dips beneath the mountains. There's already a shadow over the pool deck, the neighborhood slipping into a premature dusk that awakens a few early insects. Their raspy chirrups accompany me as I walk across the hot pavement and dip my feet into the pool.

With a sigh, I take out my phone. There's no point pretending I was just going to look up at the stars coming out or gaze soulfully into the darkening water below me. I was just going to look at my phone, like I do all the time, like everyone does all the time. But this time, I have a very good excuse for ignoring the natural beauty of the world. This time, there's scandal afoot and my naked breasts have already been part of it once; they certainly could be again.

I scroll through my social media apps one by one, but my boobs have already faded from the national spotlight—or the Hollywood spotlight, which is a little more narrowly focused on what actors, actresses, and their associated hangers-on are up to. I guess I am a hanger-on now. Or maybe Everett is considered the hanger-on, to Liz, and I am just hanging on to Everett.

For dear life, I think grimly.

Liz is making some splashy headlines again, though. There are several pictures of her from helpful tipsters who were in Melvyn's with us, showing the raging Liz charging across the restaurant towards Table 13, where we sat in Sinatra's loving image.

That reminds me, I think, flicking through the pictures of Liz berating me while I cringe up against Everett. I have dinner waiting for me.

My stomach rumbles encouragingly.

Taking my phone and my whiskey back into the house, I lean against the counter and dig into my filet with house steak sauce. Yes, it's cold, but fortunately, cold steak is fantastic and *this* cold steak is amazing. The sauce is spicy and sweet and I'm dipping some cold fries into it when I hear a door click open.

Everett comes into the kitchen wearing a t-shirt and shorts. He gives me a sheepish smile. "Okay," he says, "so it was a little early to go to bed."

"Also, you're hungry," I guess, and he nods. "Here's your Steak Diane, friend."

Everett opens the container and makes a face. "It really doesn't keep."

"Try my sauce," I suggest, feeling awesome and generous. "It's good on everything. I wonder if they sell bottles."

"We can go back tomorrow and see," he says.

I grimace. "I don't think we're welcome back at Melvyn's, like, ever."

"You heard the manager, didn't you? He wanted us to stay. I'm sure we're welcome back."

"He probably just knew what Steak Diane would look like after it traveled home in a styrofoam container. There's no way he wanted us to stay."

"He did," Everett insists, pulling the steak sauce closer. "I just didn't want to risk more exposure."

"But I thought we were supposed to be getting exposure."

"Like that?" He shakes his head. "I don't see how that's helpful for anyone."

"Well, it makes Liz look crazy, which is good for you and me," I say. "Because if someone on her team is telling her that she needs you back, there's probably not a good outcome for you in that scenario." Suddenly, that seems like the most obvious answer to this whole press debacle. Everett's team isn't the one trying to get back Liz—but Liz's team is definitely trying to get back Everett.

"How do you figure?"

I shrug, hoping it doesn't look like I've given this situation a ton of thought—although of course it's been on my mind ever since we left the restaurant, Liz and his aversion to drama and the whole thing. "Because maybe Liz's management sees you as a good influence on her, and thinks she'd be easier to keep under control if you were taking up some of the slack?"

Everett stops chewing and stares at me.

"Or I could be way off," I mutter, looking away.

He swallows with an effort and clears his throat quietly. "No," he says. "I think you're dead on. She's a handful, for sure. Maybe her team is just realizing that."

"So if they need you to be her babysitter, they might pull out all the stops to get the two of you back together, or at least make it *easier* for you to just take her back. Because you're worried about her." Now it's really starting to make sense to me. "They're going to appeal to your empathetic side. They think if they rile her up and send her after you, constantly, it will be impossible for you to turn your back on her. But it's going to have the opposite effect, because your team won't want you to be seen with an off-the-rails actress. Right?"

"Sheila would hate that," Everett agrees. "Wow, I really think you're on to something. How do you know so much about the devious minds of Hollywood?"

"Because for some strange reason, it's the only place I've ever wanted to work," I confess with a sigh. "I guess I know a little too much about how the place works."

"So, they want scenes in public that make me desperate to end it by taking her back," Everett muses, stealing a few of my fries while I swipe at him, "and my team wants you and I out on some dates enjoying ourselves in public to show that I have no interest in taking her back. This is really gross, you know that?"

"The cold fries, or the world we live in?"

He snorts and laughs. "Honestly both."

"Then stop stealing them," I say, and as he goes for my fries with both hands, I catch his hands in mine and the sparks between us flash so brightly I swear the kitchen could catch fire in an instant.

Chapter Twenty

EVERETT LOOKS AT me, and I see the blue overtaking the gray in his eyes. I take a step closer, then another, until our bodies are almost touching. It feels bold, but right now I feel bold. Ready for anything. Ready to take all the little steps we've taken today and turn them into that giant leap I've been longing for.

His free hand rises and his fingers stroke my cheek, soft as a feather.

The shiver that runs through me is full body, from the top of my head to the soles of my feet, and *everywhere* in-between.

When he speaks, his voice is so gentle, so soft, it's barely a whisper. "You have the softest skin," he murmurs.

It's probably not the softest skin in the world, if we're being honest, but we are not being honest. We are being very, very horny. So I reach up and touch his face, just above his cheekbone, the line where his stubbly beard gives way to bare skin. His eyelids flutter and I nearly swoon at the line of his black eyelashes as they drop. "Your skin isn't bad," I whisper in reply. "I like this spot here—" and I stroke along his hair-line, right next to his eye.

Everett sighs raggedly in reply, and I can't help my lips curving into a sly smile. I knew that spot would get him.

When he leans down to kiss me, I'm still smiling, my other hand coming up to grasp the nape of his neck, my fingers coiling into his hair. "Everett," I gasp against his mouth, just to reassure myself that this is really happening, that this entire day has not been one long fever-dream.

"Cassie," he growls, his lips pushing against mine. His hands slide up to my cheeks and he cups my face for a moment, taking his time with a long, leisurely kiss that stokes the fire within me to a roaring blaze. Forget sparks. We're talking about full-on fireworks here.

Somehow I'm shoved up against the kitchen counter, and then Everett's hands slide down to my waist and he lifts me gently, placing me on the countertop. The marble is cold on my bare thighs, and for a moment I instinctively go to pull that damn short skirt down—but he catches my hand, slides it out of the way, and runs his hand up my thigh instead, pushing the skirt out of the way. I gasp with surprise and pleasure as his fingers reach my panties and teasingly tug at the narrow waistband.

"Oh, you want in?" I whisper, placing kisses on his lips, his cheeks, his neck. "You think I should let you?"

"Yes," he growls. "I think you should let me do whatever I want." He slides his fingers beneath the waistband, and now his entire palm presses against my hip, his thumb sliding downward, tantalizingly close...

"What's in it for me?" I'm not usually much of a tease, hardly ever vocal in bed, but Everett is different. Everett makes me feel safe, and free, and maybe just a little bit out of control. "Tell me why I should let you."

His mouth is on my neck, and he bites down—not hard, but enough to make me gasp and arch my back. It's rougher play than I'd have expected from soulful, tender Everett Torby, but I'm not mad about this side of him at all. His breath is hot against my skin as he replies, "Because I'm going to make you scream with pleasure."

A girl can hardly say no to that, can she?

In reply, I nip him right back and then let my thighs slide apart, giving his hand all the freedom it wants to explore beneath my skirt. With a growl of pleasure in his throat, Everett slips that thumb of his all the way down and presses ever so slightly against my skin. Like a lightning bolt zinging through me, I feel his touch in a hundred places, as if his hands are all over my body instead of just touching that one secret spot. My back arches in reply and I dig my fingernails into his arms, holding on for dear life while he dips his head and adds his mouth to the fun.

Well and truly wet now, I'm all in when Everett murmurs something about the sofa and scoops me up in his arms, carrying me around the corner and into the living room. I dimly register that the curtains aren't closed, but no matter, it's dark outside and the street is still as empty now as it was an hour ago. More empty, even. This neighborhood is fast asleep.

Everett tugs my skirt down, then focuses on his own clothes while I wriggle myself out of my blouse and bra as quickly as possible. My skin is crying out for his, my back tingling against the rather rough cotton of the sofa, and when he's satisfied the condom is on and finally comes down on top of me, I feel like I'm simply going to burn up and blow away, ashes all that's left.

My hips are game and lift, thrust for thrust, while our hands are ripping through each other's hair, kissing and gasping and crying out as the game gets very, very real. When I scream out, he looks at me with those dark blue eyes, and the sight of him, the literal man of my dreams, takes me farther than I've ever gone before.

I come back to life slowly, sensation returning to my limbs and my eyes fluttering open. Everett is slumped against the back of the sofa, still half on top of me; his breathing is regular, but I don't think he's asleep. I would be impressed if he was, though. It's a very odd position. Next time, I think, we'd better head for the bedroom.

Then I hear something.

Something outside.

Something which makes me stir and try to sit up. Everett pushes back from me slowly, and for a moment I admire his chest, the muscles in his arms and shoulders standing out as he rises above me. Something inside me flutters, something which ought to be satisfied for now.

He makes his way to a sitting position and I scramble up to join him, tugging the throw blanket tossed across the back of the sofa across the two of us. "It got kinda cold in here," I say, shivering a little as the dry desert chill settles across my sweaty skin.

"It did," he agrees, leaning against me for a moment. Then he leans forward, frowning, and I realize I hear it again.

A tiny beep and click.

It's coming through the front window.

"Everett," I whisper, "there's someone out there."

He reaches for his shirt. "I'm going outside," he says in a normal tone. "You call the police."

There's a rattle of leaves and a shadow races from the front yard. Even with our reflections on the window, I can see the camera dangling from his hand.

"I think we just got paparazzi'd."

Everett just shakes his head. But I can see the change in his expression. He's not happy.

Chapter Twenty-One

OVER WHISKEY AND a bag of M&M's apparently left by the last tenant of this rental, Everett slowly unwinds. And as he does, he starts talking.

I've studied Everett Torby's words for years now. Interviews. Instagram captions. Lyrics, over and over again. But getting this story, straight from his mouth to my ears and my ears only, feels like the missing piece to understanding this man I have loved from afar for such a long, long time.

"Did you ever disappoint your parents?" he asks. "Like, the kind of disappointment where they get up and leave the room when you come into it, to show some kind of united front against your decision?"

"God." I swallow a burning sip of whiskey. "I mean, I am a constant disappointment to my parents, but not to that extent. Why would they do that?"

"They thought they were too doting when I was a child." Everett grins at his whiskey; it's a bittersweet smile, though, without any real humor in it. "They thought if they'd been tougher on me, they'd have gotten what they wanted. A professional son without all the rock star ambitions."

"But you never wanted to be a rock star," I interrupt, then I put my hand to my mouth, embarrassed. It's a frequent line in indie mags and blogs profiling The Emergency and, more recently, Everett's solo work. But I feel incredibly stupid quoting Everett back to himself—especially when I know he only said it once, more than a decade ago. It might have been his mood that day.

"I didn't," Everett replies, looking up at me through his lashes. Should men have such long eyelashes? Maybe he's uniquely blessed. "I didn't, and I used to tell myself if things got too serious, I'd get out. But now, I don't know what else I would do. Even with the level of fame I've got, who else would I be, if I wasn't Everett Torby?"

I know what he means. You reach a certain point where you become unemployable, when being an entertainer is all you've done and all you've got. Everett has had one job since he was just out of high school. He's a smart guy, but he's only qualified to sing for a rock band. "You have a degree, though," I remind him. "You could get a master's—but wait, why are we deciding what you'd do if you didn't make music? Are you—you're not *quitting*, are you?"

"Of course not. But..." He swirls his whiskey. He's like the picture of a meditative artist. A parody of himself, maybe, but a very attractive one who gets all of it right. "It's just weird to go down a road and then look back and realize how much distance you've put between you and the life you expected. And to realize there's no turning back."

I'm not sure where this is going. I push more M&M's his way. Sugar can only help. "So, your parents. Are they still mad that you pursued music instead of something more, I don't know, easy for them to understand?"

"Something suburban," he says.

It's the song, of course. "Something Suburban" was their first radio hit, and it's one of my favorites, about cookie-cutter houses, pulling into the wrong driveway, kissing the wrong woman, playing catch with the wrong kids. I realize at that moment that it's not a friendly joke of a song about American culture and subdivisions that all look the same; it's the life his parents wanted for him, and the life he ran away from, and the one he has felt breathing down his neck for so long that he didn't realize when it disappeared from the rear-view mirror.

Yeah, it's a big epiphany, but you have to remember I have *studied* this man.

"Parents don't want us to get hurt," I say, feeling like I've had this conversation with myself a thousand times before. "They can't always dream as big as we do, and when we go outside the safe boundaries they've already drawn for us, that's scary for them."

"They scare because they care?" he asks, grinning for real now.

"Yes, Pixar fan number one," I snort. "They scare because they care. They are the real monsters."

"They got over it, I think," Everett says, switching back to his meditative voice. "But I'm pretty sure I never got over it. And something in me says they're right, that I can never be as big as I thought I'd be. That if I did get big, and this is unrelated to them, that would be somehow destructive. It would ruin me."

I push my hand across the table and take his hand. He grips it and meets my eyes with his. The trouble there digs deep into me, and for a moment I imagine being the mother of this teenage boy, sweet and sad and filled with music, and what that vulnerable look of his must have done to her when he kept insisting he was going for that golden ring, to be a rock star and play in front of fans every night.

It must be terrifying to be a parent.

"You wouldn't be ruined by fame," I tell him. "If you're afraid of moving up in this crazy world, well, don't be."

"That's easy for you to say. Look at Liz."

"But she was never—" I stop myself from saying *normal.*

He knows it. "Yeah, fair point."

"You could handle a couple more photographers in your life. It wouldn't wreck you. You're a very grounded person."

"My therapist says otherwise."

"That's a therapist's job."

"True." Everett sighs and runs his free hand through his hair. "Listen, it's late. We should go to bed. For real, this time."

I don't want to go to bed; I want to sit up and listen to Everett all night long. I want to take his fears and put *them* to bed, one by one, until he sleeps like a baby with a smile on his face.

But maybe that's not a one-night job, I remind myself. A man who has made a singing career out of anxiety is probably not the kind of person you can fix in a few hours.

"Okay," I say, and throw back my whiskey. "Just so you know, I'm a light sleeper."

He lifts an eyebrow. "I'll try to be quiet."

"And a late sleeper," I add, standing up.

"Me, too."

"Brunch tomorrow, then?"

"Brunch," he agrees. "I'll make sure Sheila has a place lined up for us."

Ah yes, I think, as Everett and I hug goodnight (no kissing, more's the pity). Sheila, the great brain behind our time together. I wonder if, by the end of the week, I can make him forget there's a puppet master in the background, twitching our strings to make us dance for the cameras.

I'm a light sleeper; I didn't make that part up. Add in that I can't get over the unreality of the past twenty-four hours, and the knowledge that someone very possibly took a picture of me having sex with Everett on the living room sofa, *and* his presence in the room across the hall, and there's an insomniac waiting at the end of this equation. I toss on the soft sheets, thinking feverishly of Everett in between wondering if my reputation, whatever that might have been before, will suddenly vaunt me into starfucker territory by tomorrow morning.

If so, I'll have to own it. Because I'm not taking back anything, not denying any of it. That's not the agreement, anyway. I'm supposed to get caught. We're supposed to be seen. As uncomfortable as that fact is, I wouldn't give this up for anything.

Suddenly, I hear movement in the hallway. A door latch, hinges squeaking ever so slightly. I freeze in terror; did someone actually *break in* to catch us in the act?

My door slowly, slowly opens.

I take a breath and make a decision. "I've got a knife!" I shriek.

"Oh my god," Everett says. "Do you really?"

"Everett?" Nervous laughter bubbles up. "Jesus Christ, I thought you were a photographer."

"It's two o'clock in the morning. They're home emailing their editors." He comes into the room, wearing only boxer shorts. In the dim light filtering through the window, I can make out the lines of his body and my own body stirs to life.

"What are you doing here, Everett?" I ask softly, hopefully.

"I couldn't sleep," he says. "I wondered if you felt the same way."

"Get into this bed," I say, flipping back the sheets. "I absolutely feel the same way."

Chapter Twenty-Two

 restaurants is superb, or at least, she's very good at reading Yelp reviews. Instead of an expensive it-place like Melvyn's, she has a car drop us off at a casual spot with a wide patio overlooking the mountains and a menu full of eggs, brioche French toast, and multiple flavors of bacon.

"Obviously, I'll be having the bacon flight," I announce as we unfold our menus.

"Me, too," Everett agrees. "No way I'm sharing it."

"What about the cinnamon rolls? Would you share one of those?" I saw one of the pastries on a table as we were shown to our seats and despite my love of a good salty breakfast, there's really no turning away from a fantastic-looking cinnamon roll once one has crossed my path.

"For you, I will share a cinnamon roll," Everett proclaims grandly. "Ordinarily no, I would need the whole thing for myself."

"You're too kind, sir," I gibe, but leave off the banter as an interested-looking waitress pours us coffee.

I watch Everett drink his black. "You don't have to resist ordering a moist cappuccino just to impress me," I tell him. "Look, I'm dumping six sugars into this, and a whole pint of milk."

He looks pained. "At least taste it first. This is very good coffee."

I take a sip to please him. It is rich and dark and makes my stomach tie itself up in knots instantly. "Oh, god, this is like drinking very flavorful, um, acid?"

"Fine, milk it up. At least you tried it first."

"Thanks, mom." The milk in its little pitcher is thick and creamy, possibly more fat than most Los Angelenos would consume in a week, but hey, I live in Orange County, baby. No rules. "I'm going to get the chilaquiles. How about you?"

He shakes his head at the menu. "Do you think Sheila would be mad if we ordered one of everything?"

In the end, we narrow his choices down to five: eggs Benedict, corn fritters, yam and sausage hash, a mango waffle, and the heirloom tomato sandwich. The waitress, a patient woman named Margie, is very pleased with our decision. "Everything out at once?"

"Except for the cinnamon roll, Margie," I tell her. "You can bring that out first, if you don't mind."

She grins, shakes her head, and heads for the kitchen.

"We're still sharing the cinnamon roll?" Everett asks. "After all that, I assumed we'd just get one each."

"We don't want to be *extravagant*," I tell him, and he laughs so hard a few people glance our way.

Then they glance back again.

The classic L.A. double-take in action.

"Don't look over to your left," I say, coffee cup close to my face to hide my lips. "But those people recognize you."

Everett leans back in his chair, says something casual about the beautiful mountains, and glances towards the people sitting nearby. They turn their heads again, but it's pretty obvious they are trying to get a view of us without being caught in the act. It's weird; I feel my cheeks redden and lean forward to let my hair fall across my face, hiding the blush.

Everett is busy on his phone now; he flicks his finger a few times across the screen, skimming through social media. When his thumb stills and his eyes rove across it, I know he's found something. I wait, dreading it, until he looks up and says, "They recognize you, too, my dear."

He holds out the phone. I steel myself for the carnage, then take the phone.

It's not just a post, it's a whole article. And it has everything. My boobs. Liz's mascara-streaked face. Everett onstage at the hotel two days ago. The Emergency in an early press photo, Everett and the other guys looking baby-faced in their twenties. A LinkedIn photo of me smiling after I got my internship at that first and only production company in Hollywood that would have me, sure I was on my way in the glittering world of the movies. I look so young and hopeful. I really need to change that photo out.

"Well," I say finally, skimming the text, which is heavily focused on Liz and barely mentions me, except as the woman who stole her man. "I guess we're making those headlines, just like Sheila wanted."

"Earning our brunch," Everett agrees, but he looks pained. "I'm really sorry about your boobs."

"I'm just glad the sex pictures aren't in this article."

Just as the words leave my mouth, Margie arrives with our cinnamon roll and gives me an uncertain smile. I know I'm not the first person in her restaurant to say something like that, so I just tell her thanks and let her get on her way. It's show business, Margie. Sex pictures happen.

"I wonder if they didn't turn out," Everett says, flicking through his phone again. "Oh, wait—I think—yeah, here they are."

"Are they terrible?" I'm weirdly curious to see, but that seems like a really indelicate response to knowing there are pictures of me having sex on the internet, so I just put my hands in my lap and try to look appropriately distraught.

"Actually..." Everett holds his phone out again. "It's surprisingly..."

I look at the black-and-white picture, which is not at all what I expected. The entire picture window is captured, along with the low roofline and some of the rocks at the base of the house. The flash is visible in the window, and beyond it, the outlines of our bodies, entwined on the couch, are centered there as if we were posing. It's grainy and gray-scale and really, really...

"Sexy," I finish aloud for Everett to hear. "They're surprisingly *sexy*. What the hell? Were we visited by some artist last night?"

"An artist named Michel Stephens, according to the photo credit," Everett says. He takes the phone back and looks at it again. His face is oddly absorbed.

Well, not oddly. Someone has made pornographic art out of a paparazzi shot. I want to look at it again, too.

I kind of want to buy a print and frame it.

Shouldn't this Michel Stephens send me a copy, though? How does that work?

"Everett," I say, and then repeat, *"Everett,"* because he's still engrossed in the photo. "Are you okay with this? The way everything is working out?"

It's about the newfound fame, the fear of photographers, but he gives me a long, thoughtful look before he puts down the phone and nods. "I'm fine with all of it," he says. "Are we ready to try this cinnamon bun, or what?"

We're halfway through the bacon flight—the jalapeño is burning my tongue delightfully—when the fan arrives. She's a curly-haired young woman, maybe twenty-two or twenty-three, if that, and she's looking at Everett like he's the second coming.

I instantly stiffen in my chair, my spine pressing against the back.

She barely glances at me, all eyes for Everett. "Hi, um, I'm really sorry to bother you, but I'm *such* a big fan!"

Everett smiles politely and gives her a few minutes of chit-chat while I poke at what remains of my bacon and steam in silence. It's not just that she's shown up and interrupted our brunch—something I would never have done to Everett if I'd seen him out in public! It's that she's so *young.*

How could she have any notion of what Everett sings about? Everett, the rest of The Emergency, and me—we are all in our thirties. We are tired. Our backs are starting to hurt in places they didn't use to hurt. It's getting harder to find cool shoes that don't make our feet ache after half an hour on the pavement. We have responsibilities. What does this little chickadee have going on in her life? She probably works at a social media agency and says things like, "I'm creating stories to illustrate my company's corporate goals and achieve brand relevance."

I'd heard that line recently, and it really annoyed me.

"Thank you so much," she gushes, as Everett signs a napkin she's pulled from her purse. "I just love you."

I chew at my tongue as she finally takes a selfie and then moves on, heading back to her table.

"Oh my god," she says to her friend. "I am *shaking!*"

Everett picks up his fork and goes back in for more of the yam and maple sausage hash. He sees me looking and lifts an eyebrow. "It happens," he says.

"What is she, twelve?"

"Probably at least fifteen." He winks at me. "You sure fame wouldn't be a little annoying?"

"Okay, somewhat annoying," I concede. "She didn't even look at me, did you notice that? It was like I didn't exist. Like yes, please come hug and kiss my date and tell him that you love him, it's fine, I'll wait."

Everett looks down at his plate and concentrates for a moment on his sausage. When he speaks again, his voice is thoughtful. "You know, it's not like they really love me. It's just fandom. It's just—extreme appreciation. Nothing to get jealous about."

I suck in my lower lip, considering this. Maybe for that girl, giggling with her friend as they leave the restaurant, meeting Everett was exciting in a detached, *wow I met a rock star* kind of way.

And for me, meeting Everett was something much, much different.

The moment that would change my life forever, for better or for worse.

I wish I could think of a way to explain that to him, but when he flicks his gaze up and smiles at me, some part of me thinks that he already knows.

I'm changing for a swim when my phone buzzes and Angie's face pops up on the screen. I'm surprised it took her this long to call me. "Hey," I say, hitting the answer button without picking up the phone. "What's up?"

"What's up? Are you kidding me?" Angie's voice is deceptively calm. "Where are you?"

"I'm in Palm Springs, right where I said I'd be."

"Mom has seen the article."

"What article?"

"The one where you're the pretty interloper who stole a Hollywood up-and-comer's handsome boyfriend, ruining her moment of triumph."

"Well, I think we all know *that's* not true, so—"

"No one knows anything!" Angie interrupts, her voice raising at last. "We're all over here reading tabloids and wondering what the hell my baby sister is doing, running off with rock stars and getting her tits all over the Internet. This is like Mom and Dad's worst nightmare of what would happen when you went to L.A. It just took almost ten years for it to happen."

"Yeah, don't remind me of the wasted ten years while this wasn't going on," I snort. I've got the black bikini on now, tied properly and everything, so I prop up the phone on a jewelry box on the dresser. Angie's eyes widen.

"What are you wearing?"

"A very expensive quarter-inch of fabric," I reply. "Like it?"

"No, I don't like it. I don't like any of this! What are you thinking? Is this a mid-life crisis?"

"Quarter-life, at best. How dare you imply my life is half-over already? And should I leave my hair loose or in a bun? What do we think?" I draw some tendrils in front of my ears, curling them around my fingers. The messy mermaid look is so good, but hard to pull off.

"Cassie. What is going on with Liz Astra?"

I shake my head at her. "It's some kind of weird publicity stunt by her management team. I think they want her back with Everett—it would be good for her brand and her drinking. And

I'm in the way, so she's taking pot-shots at me. They haven't been together in a year, though. It's not happening."

"But why are you with Everett? That's the part none of us understand. Why you?"

I stare at my sister for a moment. She still has this skeptical look on her face—at this point, it's probably engrained into her skin—and I have to tell myself that she has no idea how hurtful that question is. *None of us understand.* I imagine Angie, her husband, and my mom and dad all sitting around the picnic table in the backyard, discussing how bizarre it is that Everett Torby is being seen in public with little old Cassie.

Something suburban, I think. All the things I said to Everett last night, being so wise about his parents disapproving of his life choices, when in their own way, my unbelieving parents have been doing the same thing to me for years, and this disbelief is just an extension of that.

The constant refrain of *Come home, get married, have kids, be normal,* just revised for the current situation.

They'd stand on my head and drown me without ever realizing that was what they were doing.

"Why not me, Angie?" I ask coolly, looking back in the mirror. The tendrils are working. I am going with bun and loose curls around my ears, final answer. "Why shouldn't I be with Everett? Am I not good enough to be with someone famous?"

"It's not that," Angie tries to back-pedal, but she has nowhere to go.

"Of course it's that," I say, and I end the call.

"I'm not that famous," Everett says, peeking around the door-frame.

I jump. "Oh! You were eavesdropping!"

"You hung up? I was trying to surprise whoever that was."

"My sister. She wants me to move back to Ohio."

"Jesus. Why does she hate you?"

I laugh. "She doesn't hate me. She just doesn't think like we do." I glance at him, wondering how he'll react to the use of *we*.

Everett takes my hand. "Most people don't," he says. "Come on. The pool looks amazing."

Chapter Twenty-Three

THE POOL TRULY is amazing, even if I have to get Everett to wrestle a sun umbrella into place so that we have a refuge from the midday sun. We settle into a routine of lazily waving the water at each other, looking at our phones, and refilling each other's drinks. *This could be my whole life,* I think, as Everett brings out a glass of coconut water and puts it onto the ledge at my side. *Just me, and Everett, and this pool until the end of my days.*

It would be enough. What else could I possibly want?

"This is a nice day," I remark occasionally, and Everett smiles and says, "Mm-hmm."

I flick between social media, reading up on all the thousand and one ways people hate me now—gosh, women are mean to other women—and when that gets a little too negative for me, I try to read a book. But it's hard to concentrate on someone else's story when my own is suddenly so interesting, and eventually I go to my email, hoping for something more interesting than the usual marketing.

So when I realize I've received an email addressed from Sheila@eightballmanagement.com, my eyebrows go up.

Hello, Cassie—

Thank you for managing things so well during this unusual request of ours. Everett's photos look great and you're doing fantastic keeping the media on their toes. It's really appreciated. One thing—we sent some girls to meet Everett this morning and you kind of zoned out. If you could look more jealous of other fans, maybe that would help with the profile we're trying to build for him. You don't have to pull hair or anything, haha! Just make sure that you don't look happy with the girls when they show up.

"Uh." I stare at the phone in shock.

Everett asked, "Hmm?" without opening his eyes.

"Sheila *sent* that fan this morning?"

"What?" Now his eyes are wide open.

"This email!" I hold out the phone with a shaking hand. "She wants me to act more jealous in public."

"What the..." Everett skims the email and looks at me with very credible surprise. He's not in on this—that's a relief, anyway. "Why on earth would she want to make *you* jealous, too?"

I take the phone back and read it again. "I don't know, but the words, 'the profile we're trying to build for him,' do not read like this was the original plan to use me to get Liz off your back."

"Let me see that again," Everett says, reaching for my phone.

I sip my coconut water while Everett reads the email over and over, wishing my drink had some rum in it. That might be my next stop—the liquor cabinet.

"I don't understand this," Everett says at last. "I'm going to have to email her and ask—"

"No, don't do that. I don't want her to think I came crying to you because I didn't like the message she sent me."

"But this is...weird."

"It's weird, but if she's up to something she doesn't want you to know about, she's not going to email me again with more instructions once she knows I'm letting you read the emails. She'll just keep us in the dark while she keeps messing around with us."

"You think so?" Everett sighs gustily. "I've always trusted Sheila. This is...not great."

"It's really not," I agree. "Maybe it's nothing. A misunderstanding."

"Those words are pretty clear," he says.

"Yeah." I close my email and put the phone on the side of the pool. "They are."

The profile we're trying to build for him.

That's so freaking weird! What could it mean?

"I wouldn't panic about it," Everett says eventually. "I'm sure there's a rational explanation."

"It's a dangerous game, assuming everyone in Hollywood is rational," I tell him.

He grins and shakes his head, acknowledging the simple truth in my words. "I mean, yes. But look. They can't force us to do anything we don't want to do. And we're having fun, right?"

"Yes." There's no denying that part. We're having an amazing time.

Everett slides over to me and puts a hand on my waist. My skin lights up from within. "You don't sound very enthusiastic," he murmurs.

"We're having...*some* fun," I say, shrugging and turning my face away from his. I can feel the power of his thousand-watt smile blazing against my cheek, and it's all I can do not to lean against him, giving in before I've played a little hard-to-get.

"Some fun!" Everett's stubble rubs against my cheek. I have to curl my toes against the bottom of the pool, rubbing them over the smooth concrete like a wide expanse of worry-stone. "I think we're doing better than that." His voice drops to a growling whisper. "I think we're a little more than some fun..."

I close my eyes as his lips find the corner of my mouth.

"A little," I admit, just before he turns me to face him and devours me with a hungry kiss.

The sun is slanting over the mountains by the time Everett and I are up and dressed for dinner.

"Oh," I say, pausing in the hallway the moment I can see through the front window. I take a step backwards. "I think I see where Sheila was going with this."

"What are you—" Everett bumps into me. "Why...oh." He peers around my head and takes in the view. "That's...um... bizarre."

I can't help but sigh in irritation. "Is it, Everett?"

There are girls on the lawn.

Well, women on the xeriscaping, is probably a more accurate way to put it.

The rock garden out front has become a camp-out spot for more than a dozen young women, most of whom are wearing Emergency t-shirts and holding poster board signs. The signs are covered with various messages pleading for Everett to fall in love with them, or fall into their beds, whichever works best for him.

One of them just reads, *Me Next!*

I narrow my eyes at the young woman holding the sign on her lap. Does she think I'm the flavor of the week for Everett?

Is that the message Sheila is trying to send to Everett's fans right now?

"Well, now we can't go out to dinner tonight," I say, "so that should show Sheila her little plan isn't working."

"Unless this has become the plan," Everett sighs. "Maybe she decided it would be more interesting to get us on lockdown because there are so many salivating women, rather than to send us out for photos in public. I mean, there are already pics of us out there...she probably figures that trick is used up."

"So are we agreed then? This was the plan all along? To use the Liz thing to boost your profile up to stalker-worthy status?"

"I think it is. And I'm not happy about it." He takes another look at the broad front window, then shakes his head. "They're going to see us, but the hell with it. We can't stand in the hallway all night."

I follow Everett into the privacy of the kitchen. After an afternoon in bed and a lengthy nap, we both woke up hungry and eager to see where dinner would be tonight, but it's pretty clear DoorDash is going to be the best option.

Everett opens the liquor cabinet and takes out the gin. "Cocktail hour," he announces. "You do drink gin, right?"

"Like a queen," I laugh, and I take tonic water and limes out of the fridge. I notice a ripe avocado and a wedge of brie and pull those out, too. "Hey, we can have snacks! All is not lost."

"Well, at least she isn't trying to starve us into submission," Everett jokes. "Look for crackers and stuff while I make us drinks, okay?"

I put together a tidy little plate of cheese, avocado, and water crackers while Everett slices the limes and makes a pair of very attractive G&Ts. He glances at the pool deck, then shakes his head, discarding it as too public. "Air conditioning for a while, I think," he says, and puts the drinks down on the dining table overlooking the backyard and the mountains. Through the front window, the girls wave their signs, but stop short of actually beating on the glass. That's something, I suppose.

We drink in silence for a few minutes, and poke at the snacks. Everett gets up, roots in a cabinet for some everything seasoning, and puts that on his avocado.

"A man after my own heart," I joke. "Everything seasoning goes on everything."

"Listen," he says, suddenly urgent. "Do you want to keep this up, or do you want to go home? I understand if this is getting uncomfortable."

I stare at him for a moment, uncomprehending. "Uncomfortable?" I whisper. "But we just—"

I stop myself from saying *fucked for an hour and then slept curled up in each other's arms,* but I think my meaning is pretty obvious when I glance towards the hallway to the bedrooms and then back at him.

Everett sighs and leans forward, sliding a hand over mine. I feel the callouses on his fingers from decades of guitar strings. "I didn't mean I'm not enjoying our time together," he says. "I just don't want you to feel like you're on house-arrest with me. This isn't what you signed up for."

He really doesn't get it. My rah-rah brain cells wilt in defeat. I know it's too much to ask that Everett falls in love with me after two days but also—*is* it too much to ask? I mean, it certainly hasn't been an issue for me to fall hopelessly, deliriously in love with him. Why are we playing with two different sets of rules?

"Everett," I say, rubbing a thumb along the palm of his hand. "I didn't sign up for anything but being with you."

He looks at me and for once, I can't read his expression. That fact alone sends a shiver of fear down my spine. He cannot end this. I can't bear it if he ends this.

I had a week. Not two days.

"Okay," he says finally. "I just didn't want you to feel trapped."

I swallow, choking back the words I want to say: *I don't think you understand that I'm not one of those girls out front. I don't think you understand that I'm in love with you. Not Everett Torby, not like that. I'm in love with you, just Everett. And your fame, that fame you hate, is making it impossible for you to see it.*

It seems insane that I can't say that to him. But obviously, I can't.

So I just pick up the hand with his fingers wrapped around mine and bring it to my lips. Slowly, tenderly, I kiss his knuckles. I feel the tension in his skin, the way his grip tightens.

I hope that it means something to him. It means something to me.

Chapter Twenty-Four

WE SLEEP LATE into the morning again.

When I wander into the kitchen to make coffee, I pause for a moment to admire the mess we made of the place. Two days ago it was pristine, but we've managed to scatter takeout containers and glasses over half the kitchen counters. There are empty bottles lined up near the kitchen sink, and the remnants of a dozen limes have been tossed into a bowl. I'm not much of a cleaner myself, but it's pretty clear that today, on Morning Three, the time has come to clean up this kitchen.

I pop a Nespresso pod into the machine and survey the damage while my coffee noisily brews. What a shame Sheila didn't send us a cleaner. But we were supposed to take all our meals out, to be seen.

Until she decided that we should have to run a gauntlet of fans just to get out of the house. We ordered in last night, a huge feast, and pulled the curtains over the front window so we could eat in private. But they stayed out there until late, those girls and their signs.

The memory of them camped out on the rock lawn makes me angry all over again.

Was this really what we signed up for when we agreed to spend a week making the world think we were dating? Grainy black-and-white pics of us having sex in the living room, fans camped in front of the house, that awful sign one of them had. *Me next.* Leaving me wondering if I was supposed to be temporary, this week's girl.

When of course, I am. That's all I'm supposed to be.

Sugar and milk go into the midnight-black espresso, and I take a sip while I start dumping lime wedges into the garbage. I'd like nothing more than to go out for a good latte, but there's the fan encampment to think about—are they still out there? I glance around the kitchen wall, towards the big window overlooking the front yard. The curtain hangs over the expanse of glass, a closed eyelid twitching gently in the air conditioning. I'd have to move the curtain to peek out...unless I can see around it without touching...

I tiptoe over to the window and train my eye on the tiny gap between the curtain and the window.

No one's out there. Just rocks, a few sprigs of cactus, and the silent neighborhood where no one else seems to be living. A small brown roadrunner trots idly down the street, destination unknown.

I let out a sigh of relief. Maybe the fan-girl phase is over. Maybe Sheila got word that it wasn't working and called off her dogs.

Everett comes into the kitchen just as I finish wiping the counters. "This place smells like lemon and my mom's house right before a party," he says, smiling. "I didn't know you were a Martha Stewart."

"Is this the bar for being a home goddess? Wiping up the kitchen?" I turn and face him, grinning—then lean back on the counter I've just cleaned. I figure the movement just hides the weakness in my knees when I see him for the first time on a new day. I mean, I left him in my bed, but he was half-covered by the duvet and facing away from me. Now, wearing a fluffy robe that falls open over his chest, his hair pressed to one side and a morning stubble that's almost a beard after he skipped shaving yesterday, he's too handsome to look away from.

"I guess I haven't been with a lot of women who clean up," he says sheepishly.

"Well, let me make you a coffee and show you what a *real* woman can do," I announce. Theatrically, I remove a Nespresso pod from their jar and drop it into the machine. Then I punch the brew button. The machine hisses to life. "That's right, buddy. I'm Suzy Homemaker now."

"That's so hot," Everett deadpans, grinning. "So, what's on the agenda for today? Do we have anything for breakfast?"

I do a quick search of the fridge. "We do not. And we're out of limes and tonic and...everything else. This wasn't the *most* stocked kitchen."

"I guess that means we go back out there," he says. "I'll just check what Sheila—"

"No," I interrupt, placing my hand on his arm. "Let's do our own thing this morning. Do we really want to go where Sheila expects us?"

He studies me for a minute, then nods. "You're right, obviously. Let me get some caffeine in me first, and then we'll go out on our own."

We end up driving outside the city limits of Palm Springs, heading over to Rancho Mirage, where we stop at an upscale diner attached to a hotel and head inside. No one expected us; better yet, no one seems to know who we are. The clientele is mostly over the age of fifty, and even if they've seen any news about some indie rocker having a messy breakup with a newfound starlet, they probably wouldn't care. In a corner booth overlooking the parking lot and a sliver of the hotel pool, we order pancakes, home fries, toast, scrambled eggs...and put it on Everett's plastic, not the record label card.

I consider offering to pay him back, but that seems weird, so I just resolve to get lunch for us later.

"You think they'll make me a moist cappuccino?" Everett jokes, leaning over and pointing to a towering, old-fashioned espresso machine sitting behind the vacant bar.

"Our waitress's name is Dorothy," I remind him. "The chances that she'll know how to make a moist cappuccino seem slim at best."

"I'll stick to coffee," he says, conceding to my wisdom. "We can try to find some decent coffee later."

"I'm always up for a coffee field trip. Is that what we should do today? Drive around the desert in search of the best coffee?"

"I've had worst days." Everett studies his napkin. "Or we could check out these caves I've heard about. Do you like hiking?"

"I do like hiking, but *caves* sounds a little scary. Wait, you're not a closet cave-explorer, are you?"

Everett looks at me mischievously. "And here I thought you knew everything about me already."

Oof. I lean back in the booth, blushing. He's got me there.

"I'm just kidding," he says, taking my hand and stroking it as an apology (which totally works). "Come on, now. I give interviews, and people read them. I guess it would be pretty embarrassing if I'd told reporters so much about myself over the years and no one actually knew any of it."

"Sure, it's just..." I can't finish the sentence, can't say that I need him to know I'm not *just* an Emergency groupie. Because honestly, I feel like he should already know it. And if I say it, I'm just denying things too loudly, denying accusations which haven't even been said.

"It's just funny what gets reported and what gets left out," I finish lamely. "Like, I had no idea you liked moist cappuccinos."

"Well, obviously, I couldn't share that information. We didn't even have the term until a few days ago."

His smile is so warm, reminding me that now we have shared experiences, inside jokes. That counts for something.

The waitress starts setting plates in front of us with grim-faced determination; breakfast food can be weirdly heavy, now that I think about it. The platters of crisp potatoes and pancakes, eggs and toast, are huge. If you ordered breakfast in L.A. and got this much food, you'd have to invite over several other tables' worth of diners to get enough people to eat it all.

"We're not in the clean plate club," I remind Everett as he grabs a bottle of ketchup and gets ready to overload his home-fries. "Don't forget this isn't our hotel, so we can't sleep this breakfast off."

"Maybe I'll get us a room," he says.

"Check-in time is probably three o'clock."

"Killjoy." The ketchup begins its slow ooze, overwhelming the potatoes like lava inundating a village. "I guess you can't just drive me around the desert while I snooze?"

"I mean, I could. But I don't think you want me to do that."

"Why not?"

I take the ketchup bottle from him. "Because I have no sense of direction."

"What? What does that mean?"

"It means," I say, squeezing out what's left of the ketchup—there isn't much, this man may have an undisclosed problem—"that if you set me in the middle of any town, country, desert, or even the beach, I will not be able to find my way home without the use of GPS, asking several people, and getting lost at least six times. And yes, I mean all of that *in unison*."

"So if I take you to the Pacific Ocean, which I think we can all agree is in the west, and then say, walk north to Venice Beach or whatever, you'd get lost?"

"Yes."

Everett whistles. "That's impressive."

"I think it's a sign of an underlying neurological disorder, but that's just my personal opinion." The ketchup bottle is done for. I put it back and reach for the salt. "So now you know. I could say we're going back to L.A. and you might wake up in Las Vegas."

"Exciting. Like a roll of the dice. I wonder if every road-trip with you could be a new adventure."

I look at him for a moment, my heart so full I feel tears pricking at my eyes. Just the idea of a life where I road-trip around the country, getting lost with Everett...

"Your tour manager would have to take care of us," I say briskly, pushing the thoughts aside. "Or you'd never make your gigs."

"Well, I am taking that year off," he says, forking potatoes into his mouth. "Remember?"

As if I could forget anything he's said to me. But since he hadn't mentioned it again, I'd thought it was just a passing idea, easily ditched. "Are you really? I wasn't sure you were serious."

"Dead serious. Especially now."

He goes on eating serenely, as if I am supposed to know what *especially now* is referring to.

"What do you mean?" I ask at last. "Especially now?"

"Well, just that...my tour is over, and The Emergency won't have studio sessions again for a while, and now that this whole thing with Liz has been blowing up...it just feels like the right time to disappear for a little while. The guys in the band will want a break, too, or they can do some solo work. It's up to them."

I nod and concentrate on my food for a moment, although I'm chewing without tasting. The definition of empty calories. Why did I think I might be part of *especially now?* Why would I expect to be figured into a decision to give up the road and recording for a year? What, so he could spend more time with *me,* the girl he met four days ago, right after she broke up with her boyfriend so that she could spend more time concentrating on how much she fan-girled over him?

Honey, it is high time you stop thinking so highly of yourself, some unkind brain cells say to me.

I wish the rah-rah section would come back.

"Wow," Everett says.

"Hmm?" I look up, only to find he's gazing at my plate with appreciation.

"I've never seen anyone eat a pancake so quickly."

"Oh." My empty plate stares up at me. "Yeah, um, I was hungry."

"Do you want some of mine? I feel like I'm going to fill up on potatoes."

"No, no, that's fine." Look at me, the girl with the healthy appetite. Famous for getting the guys, that particular

Hollywood archetype. "I better eat my eggs, though. Protein to counteract all those carbs."

He nods encouragingly and pushes a bottle of Sriracha my way. "In case you need some spice in your life."

I do need some spice, I think. That's exactly what I need.

Spice, and some perspective.

"So what do you want to do now that you're going to have to find another job?" Everett asks.

I bite my lip, keenly aware I don't have an answer.

We're driving across the desert, the highway stretching straight in front of us and behind us as if we're crossing some massive table. Everett is sure there's an excellent coffee shop somewhere in the distance. For now, we have bottled water and no cell phone service, an alarming reminder that we're alive for the moment, but we could be stranded out here to bake in the sun without much warning.

Would death be preferable to answering this question? I don't know how to answer it, that much is for sure. I didn't want to be a small town theater promoter, and I sure as hell don't know how to turn *failed* small town theater promoter into a better job, especially in southern California. The emphasis out here is not on recovering from your failures. It is on vaunting your successes, again and again and again, until everyone is either so sick of you they hire you to shut you up, or dying to have you on their team.

And it brings up the uncomfortable possibility that I've run the course of opportunities I was given in California. That there's nothing left for me out here and I'm going to have to leave. Find some other small town somewhere else in the country with a theater in desire of being run into the ground by my lack of skills, or go back to school and find a new line of work, one in which I don't destroy cultural institutions through my own inability to draw a crowd.

The last one is the most likely, and the least palatable, because the only way I can afford to go back to school is if I move back to Ohio and stay with my family.

No. There has to be another way out of this.

"Sorry," Everett says, and I realize my silence has been stretching between us for several minutes. "I didn't mean to pry —"

"No, it's fine. I just don't have an answer. I have absolutely no plans."

It's embarrassing to admit, but there's no one else I could be this honest with. Not even Angie will ever be allowed to know that my life has come to a crashing halt.

Especially not Angie, actually.

"I wanted to work in Hollywood," I say eventually. "Isn't that ridiculous? I thought I could work in a movie studio, for a production company. I didn't really care what I would do, I just wanted to be part of the whole lights, camera, action myth. I studied film and television production in school. A terrible, pointless degree. I got an internship. I thought I had it made. And then...nothing. I ended up in Phoenix Canyon and there, that's my professional life. Honestly, it was over before it started. I've just been denying it for all these years."

Everett is quiet for a few miles.

Then he says, "I'm sure it's not all bad."

It's so sweet, so pointless, so without any facts to back it up. I love him for saying it. "Maybe it isn't," I concede. "I just haven't figured out what to take away from it yet. I mean yes, I've done marketing and publicity, two things which are always very in demand. I could probably set myself up as a freelancer, or get a job with a small agency and do some classes and work my way up to a larger group."

"Maybe even for a studio," Everett offers.

"Maybe. I guess it's something to think about."

We pass a sign for a town we've never heard of. It's the first road we've seen in miles. We fly past, still heading east. I only know this because the rear-view mirror has a little compass built into it and the letter is E.

Everett says, slowly, as if he's thinking about each word before it leaves his lips, "For our first five records, we all had back-up plans. Mine was to get an engineering degree. It seemed like the safest thing I could do for myself if music didn't work out. But I used to dread it. I would wake up in the night and imagine myself bent over a computer, or working on some production line. I didn't want to do any of it. I still have a dream, every now and then, where the band didn't make it and I'm sitting in a lecture hall, failing physics."

"Are you naked in the dream?"

"Naked?"

"In my experience, most back-to-school nightmares involve being naked."

"I guess I find the mere suggestion of school terrifying enough," Everett says, "because as far as I know, I'm always clothed in them."

"Lucky you."

"Nudity would be preferable to the way I feel in this dream. Like I'm nineteen and about to fail at my entire life."

"That sucks," I say. "But you guys were always growing. The first record didn't do a lot, but every album afterwards had kind of hit. So you didn't really need the backup...did you?"

"We had *indie* hits," Everett corrects me. "College radio hits. Those do not equal paychecks. When I wrote the lyrics to 'Something Suburban,' it was called 'Suburban Nightmare.' The guys made me change it so I didn't alienate anyone. We were that afraid of losing potential listeners!" He laughs.

"I guess that makes sense. That might be one of the problems we had at the theater, honestly. We always did safe, family-friendly classics. *White Christmas*. That kind of thing. What if we'd gotten edgy? Maybe we'd have gotten some reputation as the weirdos down in the O.C. who don't let local standards hold them down. Maybe people would have started driving down and catching our stuff." It's an idea I've had before, but never said out loud. That by chasing the easy suburban dollar, we were just setting ourselves up to fail. Eventually, people would get bored with us.

And they apparently did.

"It's possible," Everett says. "I've written a few weird plays and never shown them to anyone for pretty much the same reason. Reputation. The idea that people might find out I've got other levels in me besides the one they're used to. I mean, what would fans think they'd get in an Everett Torby play? Suburban angst and failed marriages?"

I'm staring at him. "You wrote plays?"

He smiles, but it's self-deprecating. "Yeah. I have a hard drive full of them. I mean, not full. Five or six. But they're weird, like I said."

"I want to read them. All of them."

Everett glances at me. "Maybe," he says. "Yeah. Of all the people in this world who would want to see them, just because they're mine, I feel like you'd actually appreciate them."

There's that feeling again. Heart full, eyes burning. I open my mouth to tell him that I love him, and then, thank god, he sees the sign for the town we're heading to, exclaims "Almost there!" and cuts me off before I can make a fool of myself in the middle of the desert.

Chapter Twenty-Five

DRIVING BACK TO Palm Springs in the evening feels like capitulation—like we're heading straight back into Sheila's snare. I can tell that Everett has the same feeling; all day he's been cracking jokes in between sharing stories with me, and now he's sitting more quietly, his knuckles tense on the steering wheel. The sun is blazing in the windshield, making things even more uncomfortable. We're hot, sore, miserable. Thank goodness we're smart enough to keep our mouths shut and listen to the radio instead of bitching and moaning all the way home.

When we get back to the house and see the car sitting in the driveway, I stiffen—but he doesn't change his expression.

"Is that her?" I ask, my fingers curling over the seat-belt.

He nods.

"Did you know she'd be here?" I ask. "You don't look surprised."

"I suspected she might show up. We went off grid today. That wasn't part of the plan."

I expect her to open the car door after we park, so I'm totally shocked when the house's front door opens and a tall, slim woman with wavy dark hair is waiting for us. It never occurred to me that Sheila would have the door code. But of course she does; she's the one who rented the house. She's the one who orchestrated this whole thing.

And now we're in trouble for going off-book.

"Everett," she says cooly as we walk up to the door. "I was beginning to wonder when you'd be back."

"Why didn't you just check the AirTag you put on my car?" Everett asks.

My eyebrows go up; so do Sheila's. Her cheeks flush a little as she says, "You know about that?"

"It notifies the driver every time it starts moving," he says. "It's an anti-stalking measure."

"Well, we aren't stalking you," Sheila replies, stepping back to let us through the front door. "Just keeping an eye on you, in case someone *else* has ideas about you."

Her gaze flicks over to me.

I understand my place with Sheila instantly. I'm a fan. I'm an ordinary, everyday fan with a crush on Everett Torby that she is going to use until it's no longer necessary to keep me around, and then she'll try to pay me off again before she sends me on my way. Before I get stalker-ish, for example, and she really feels like she needs that AirTag to keep an eye on Everett's whereabouts.

"You two freshen up and I'll make drinks," Sheila says, whisking herself to the kitchen.

Everett and I start for the bedrooms. When we pause at the opposite doors, I look at him hopefully. I want us to be a united front against Sheila. But he just gives me a little shrug and disappears into the front room. As the door closes behind him, I feel a sharp twist in my center, like I've lost something precious.

"We'll all go out tonight," Sheila declares.

I look at her from over the rim of my vodka and soda. The fizzing glass was waiting for me when I came out of the bedroom. I carefully dressed myself in capris and a light sleeveless blouse, hoping I wouldn't look like the small town hick I know myself to be.

Sheila is dressed in the expensive black of a professional with an expense account. She gives me an encouraging look, lifting her eyebrows, and I know my job is to be enthusiastic so Everett will be, too.

"Where are we going?" I ask cautiously, not willing to step into the role she's envisioned for me. I still want to be a team of two, Everett and me against the world.

"We'll go to the Santa Ana," she says. "It's a new restaurant at the Tropical Hotel. I think you're familiar with it?"

The Tropical Hotel, where the bungalows and pool are. She wants to take me back to the scene of those first pool photos of us?

"It's going to be a mob scene when people find out we're there," Everett says, "if the lawn party last night was any indication."

"That's the deal," Sheila says cheerfully. She regards the ice in her glass for a moment. "Trust me when I say the labels and I only have your best interests at heart here, Everett. We are taking advantage of what's been handed to us. This is free publicity."

"Hardly free when you consider the bills," Everett jokes.

"Trust me, that's a minor investment. As long as our girl is on a bender and pining after you, the media is waking up to the fact that Everett Torby not only exists, but is very talented and very hot. You're going to be fielding offers from Hollywood yourself in a few days, if we keep this up."

I glance at him. "But that's not what you want."

Everett keeps his gaze on his glass.

Oh, I realize. *Fine. I'm out of this.*

Every scrap of pride I've got wants me to excuse myself, head out to my car, and disappear on the road back to Orange County. But unfortunately, my pride is not in control here. My ridiculous, unstoppable devotion to Everett is. And I know I'm going to stick by his side until the bitter end.

Hey, if nothing else, I am loyal.

"So, Santa Ana. Eight o'clock. Everett, until then, I have some business I'd like to go over with you."

Sheila's gaze wanders over me.

I take the hint. "I'm going to take a dip before dinner," I tell them. "Since we have plenty of time."

It's only five. I plan to take some snacks to the pool with me, because I'm dying for an early bird special over here.

"Angie," I say, as she blinks at me in surprise, "I need your advice."

My sister is jiggling a toddler on her hip. "That doesn't sound like you," she tells me.

"I know. But I'm surrounded by vultures. At least, I think I am. And that's usually your speed."

"I thought you were already in the thick of those Hollywood vulture types with your theater," Angie says.

"Oh, yeah right. Try O.C. housewives." I snort. Maybe I painted my career in a flattering light for my family, but that's all over now. The exaggeration *and* the career. "No, this is the real deal. Everett's manager showed up, and she's taking us to dinner tonight. She's pissed we didn't go out the way she planned today and she's here to take us in hand."

"So? So go to dinner and do what she says. That was the deal, right? Eat out with him a lot, get your picture taken. Why'd you go back on that, anyway?"

"Because it got too intense. She sent a crowd of fan-girls to the house to camp on the lawn. They brought signs."

"Like they're picketing you?"

"No." I swallow, remembering the sign that said *Me Next.* "No, like 'Have my baby, Everett', signs."

"Ooooh." Angie's *oh* is eloquent. "And now you've realized you're one of them."

"No!"

I say it loud enough that I'm afraid Everett and Sheila have heard me. But a glance into the house shows that they're still locked in intense discussion, a laptop open between them. Poor Everett. So much for our week away from the world. "I'm not one of them, Angie, that's the point. I'm the real thing. We have a connection. We are actually—we have *potential,* is what I trying to say."

Anything to avoid saying we're meant to be, we're soulmates, because even I can hear the desperation in those terms should I be foolish enough to use them out loud, in the hearing of others. Regardless of what I believe.

Angie puts down the toddler and sends her running for the playroom, squealing like a piglet. "Jesus. Cassie, listen to me. *Please.* You can either get through this week without succumbing completely to your Everett obsession and move on with your life, or you can quit right now and leave if you don't think that's possible. But it's so, so important that you let up on the 'I'm different, I'm special' complex. You're not, okay? I love you and I'm telling you this because I love you, but, you're not different. You're a *fan.* You stumbled into a unique situation, and I love that for you, but don't let it send you around the bend. Please."

My sister's speech is heartfelt, and that makes it so much worse than if she'd just sounded exasperated with me. My sister truly believes that I am just like everyone else.

And if she does, Everett probably does, too. And I *know* Sheila does. And the photographers. And the media, and the label managers, and everyone else in the background of this ridiculous play Everett and I are supposed to be acting out. They all think I'm a fan-girl who was in the right place at the right time for their purposes.

This should have ended when I apologized for kissing him. *Sorry I kissed you,* I said. And he never said it back.

And that's the part they don't know.

It's what I'm holding onto. Everett's not sorry about any of this.

"Angie," I say, taking a breath for courage. "I know what everyone thinks of me, but I'm just asking you to trust me on this one."

"Oh, because you know what you're doing? Because Cass, I don't think—"

"No, I don't know what I'm doing," I interrupt. "I have *no idea* what I'm doing. And I never have. I'm not like you. I don't have a plan. I don't know the right way to do things. My life is a mess, if we're being honest here. But the one thing that makes sense to me is Everett. So I'm going to stick by his side, okay? Until he's done with me or—or—"

The words stick in my throat, still too ridiculous to say aloud.

"Until he falls in love with you?" Angie asks softly.

"Yes," I reply.

"Okay."

There's a moment of silence.

"Why did you call me, Cass?" Angie says at last.

I sigh. It's hard to admit, but— "I just want someone on my team. I wanted to hear you say I could get through this."

"Cass—"

"I don't have many friends," I admit. "My life is all wrong. I live in the middle of nowhere, I work with much older people, I was dating a guy who didn't get me at all because I didn't feel like I was ever going to meet anyone else who was interested in me. And when I wanted to get some support from someone who loved me, well—I thought of you."

"Oh, Cass." Angie swipes at her eyes. "Honey, I love you and I support you. If I tell you to stop chasing this man, it's only because I love you so much I'm afraid to see you get hurt."

"I know," I say. "Thank you."

With Angie off the phone and my glass back at my lips, it's a struggle to recover from that admission. I mean, yes, I have known things weren't going well for me. I already know I live in the wrong town and I am missing the people who should be my friends, and I was wasting my time with Barry. But to acknowledge it all out loud, in the face of this emotional rollercoaster of a week, is a lot.

Part of me really has to wonder if I'm clutching to Everett so hard because he seems like a way out of the doldrum life I've created for myself.

But no. I won't let that doubt overcome me.

I throw back my drink and put on a smile; Everett has gotten up from the table and he's coming outside.

Alone.

Chapter Twenty-Six

HE SITS NEXT to me and dangles his feet in the water. I hold back from the desire to lean against him, even though every inch of my skin is longing to touch his. He glances at me and his smile is apologetic, like he knows what I'm thinking.

"Sheila wants us to be ready in an hour," he says. "She says drinks by the pool at Tropical is the perfect way to be seen."

"Is that what *you* want?" I ask.

He lifts an eyebrow. "It's Sheila's game. We're just playing it."

"It's your life," I remind him. "And I think her definition of winning might be different from yours."

"You mean the Hollywood thing? That I'm going to get snapped up for a movie?"

"Yeah, exactly. A long way from taking a year off and writing plays."

"I don't know that I believe her, though," Everett says. "Nothing's going to come of this. It's all just to separate me from Liz before she does something crazy. The world just has to see that I'm happy without her." He squeezes my hand. "With you."

I sigh. I could swoon about his hand-squeeze, but there are bigger factors to deal with right now. Everett is refusing to see that the lines are being redrawn all the time. So much of his adult life has been managed, made streamlined by assistants and specialists. He might not be Mick Jagger, but he's still a rock star, with a distorted view of the real world.

I take a moment to gentle my voice before I say, "You know that's not all this is anymore, though, right? You're raising your profile alongside Liz's, and at the same time, you're making her crazy by being out in public with me. You're accomplishing two goals, for two different parties."

"What are you saying?" Everett shakes his head. "Don't make this a conspiracy, Cass."

"You *know* what I'm saying," I say, "and it's not a conspiracy. Everett, what if Sheila is working with Liz's team?"

He stares at me. "You're asking if Sheila and the record labels are partnering up with Liz's publicist to make her seem crazier?"

"No," I say. It's all become so obvious to me in the past hour, while I've been sitting out here thinking about my life and telling Angie about the situation. Speaking to someone removed has given everything a new, sharp clarity. "I'm saying they're trying to get the two of you back together in the most toxic, Hollywood-ready couple way they can imagine."

"What?"

"And then they're going to cast you in movie roles that are smaller than Liz's for a while, just to make her happy, and then switch it and give you something bigger than hers, to make her unhappy, all so they can put the spotlight on the two of you constantly. You'll always be in the news. One of you, anyway. The Hollywood couple that can't quite get it right."

Everett shakes his head and looks out towards the mountains. "That's crazy."

"It's not crazy. It's Hollywood."

"What would make you think something like that? Sheila only has my best interests here. And yours, too. She's the one who wanted to pay you five thousand bucks, remember?" Everett's voice sounds harsh, as if I've really pissed him off and he's trying to cover it up. "Why the sudden act that Sheila's the enemy? Just because you wanted to have dinner alone with me tonight, is that it?"

I bite my tongue for a moment, considering him. His face is still trained towards the mountains, but I can see the rigidity in his neck, in his jaw. He's avoiding looking at me, but it's taking everything he's got.

"She told you to watch out for me," I say softly, realizing I was part of the discussion in the house.

"No, she didn't, and you're being ridiculous—"

"She told you to be careful because I might try to use you. Because it's *Hollywood,* and everyone in Hollywood is playing their own game. Didn't she?" My voice rises now and I push away from the side of the pool, facing him, willing him to look back at me. Slowly, his eyes lower to mine. I resist their magnetic gleam, but only by concentrating on my anger.

"Well, Everett, what you forget is that I'm not *from* Hollywood. That town didn't want me. I live in Phoenix Canyon, California, and out there in Hicksville we don't just use people for our own ends. We have actual feelings and we care about people."

I know I sound like a nut now, defending a town I literally live in only because my job is there, a job that's winding up now. I'm hardly the Phoenix Canyon Booster Society president. But I think my point is sound. Everett's been tied up with the media and their machinations for too long; I can see them for what they are because I'm an outsider.

At least never getting my dream job worked out in this respect.

"Sheila is playing the game," I tell him. "And you're one of the pieces. She doesn't want to be a manager for an indie rock band forever, not when she could move up the ladder and start managing major-label bands. And your little labels? They wouldn't mind selling your contracts on to Atlantic or Sony or whoever is interested in boosting you and The Emergency to the next level. Every single one of the people behind this week of ours is poised to make a lot of money off your notoriety, as long as they can keep Liz crazy and you just out of reach. Until you can't take it anymore and you give in to her. And *that's* a headline everyone will love reading."

"Including you?"

I stare at him. "What?"

Everett is glaring down at me; suddenly he slips into the water with a little splash and walks towards me, his speed impeded by the depth. We're both chest-deep, but he's taller than I am and my shoulders are nearly covered by the water; his rise out of it and their defined muscles give him the look of a Greek god.

I can't catch my breath, watching him stride so slowly and purposefully towards me. It's enough to knock the fight right out of me. Advantage: Everett.

"The headline," he says, stopping just short of touching me. My skin sizzles with want. "When I'm back together with Liz. What will you think when you read it? Will you be happy for us?"

I can't tear my gaze from his; it bores into me, the blue and the gray of his eyes like a storm cloud over the mountains. "No," I say. "I won't be happy, because you're wrong for each other."

"And who is right for me?" Everett murmurs, his whisper somehow thunderous in my ears. "Is it you? Do you think I should be with you? Admit it."

"*Yes!*" I burst out, no longer ashamed—at least, for this moment. "You *should* be with me! Dammit, Everett, isn't it obvious? We're good for each other. We have something. We—"

And then I can't speak anymore, because Everett scoops me up in his arms and presses me against him, his kiss so hard and demanding that it's a long time before I can breathe or think again.

Chapter Twenty-Seven

I'M NOT SURE when we mutually decide that tonight, we are troublemakers. It just kind of happens. Like Everett and I decided with our lizard brains (the ones that are completely giving into the sexual chemistry between us, duh) that we are going to show Sheila who the real bosses in this show are. She thinks she's pulling our strings? We're just here for the free food.

Arriving back at the Tropical Hotel gives me a weird burst of nostalgia—for a time period that was just a few days ago. Yeah, I'm being dramatic. But we were almost innocent then, playing in the pool and just getting to know each other, staring at the bed in the bungalow and wondering if either of us would suggest it be the next place we fool around. I feel some regret for that big bed that didn't see any action, and wonder if there's a chance we can acquire a bungalow for the evening. Just in case we can shake Sheila altogether.

She doesn't want to lose us, though. Sheila keeps an eagle eye on us all the way from the host's podium to the table, which is nice, but not the nicest one in the house. She either doesn't have *that* much pull, or someone much more important than Everett is going to be here tonight. Probably several somebodies much more important, if we're being honest here. I wonder if Sheila recognizes that with a few skillful moves, she could be the manager with the biggest client in the city, and if that knowledge gives her the drive she needs tonight, to push past our giggling facades and dig down to our rebellious hearts. She has no patience for silly lovers, not when there's a glittering world out there to conquer.

I slide into the chair next to Everett and scoot it a little closer to him. Our thighs touch. He runs a speculative hand along my leg and I giggle up at him, feeling drunk on his touch.

"I like this joint," Everett announces, looking around.

"Me, too," I say. The vibe is tropical tiki; the lighting is low and the blue of the pool, lit from underneath, flickers over the ceiling and our faces. A blue glass replica of a Polynesian buoy, wrapped in a netting of twine, sits at the center of our table and emits an eerie glow. We're all a little blue tonight, I think, and giggle again.

Everett leans over to me and whispers, "Something funny, Cass?"

Sheila gives us dagger eyes—well, she gives *me* dagger eyes—and unfolds her cocktail menu, which is long and expensive.

Luckily, by now I've gotten used to Palm Springs pricing and I'm able to cheerfully order a Zombie which costs twenty-two dollars and is supposed to come in a mug shaped like a skull.

"I love a good skull drink," says Everett, who has ordered a Navy Grog. "I like to pretend I'm drinking the brains of my enemies."

"The brains? Wouldn't that be chunky?"

"You puree them," he explains, "then pour them back in. Add a tiny umbrella and a mint leaf for garnish."

"So pretty," I coo.

Sheila has ordered a Dark and Stormy and she looks annoyed with us both for our choices. "Did the two of you just order based on the sheer amount of rum in those drinks?"

"Yes," we answer in unison, then look at each other and giggle like children.

I am having *such* a good time, and there's not even rum in me yet!

Fortunately, soon there is rum inside me; the bartender here is very fast. "The Zombie packs a serious punch," I inform Everett, who promptly steals a sip, making an elaborate face at me as he sucks on the purple silly straw my skull has been festooned with.

"Whoooo I feel the zombie!" he declares loudly, pushing his fists into the air. "Brains!"

"Oh god, please don't," Sheila scolds. "That's not why we're here. *You're* not the one having the breakdown, Ev."

He shrugs. "Maybe I am and maybe I amn't."

She rolls her eyes. Sheila is bound and determined to be the fun police tonight. "So, listen. Let's order a few rounds of starters and take it easy on the booze, I plan on staying here for a while. We have about two hours before they insist on turning this table, and in that space of time I expect some pics to be taken, the media to pick up on our presence, and Liz to show up and make a scene." She looks satisfied with herself. "Yes," she says, almost to herself. "It should be a big one."

"A scene's not good for anyone," I argue, poking my drink with the silly straw. "I think we should do the opposite. Eat something and get going before she can find out we're here. Let's take it easy on poor old Liz."

"You're not the publicist, that's easy to see," Sheila says.

Well, that gets my back up a little. "I most certainly am a publicist," I inform her. "I have been a theater promoter for the past six years!"

"I know about Phoenix Canyon theater." Her tone implies she knows everything about it. Including its demise. "But we're on different levels here, sweetie."

Everett points his own straw at her—pink, with a couple loops, like a water slide. "Hey. Don't go condescending to Cassie. She has a lot of talent. You know how hard it is to get in with the right team in L.A. Maybe you can help her!"

He makes this last suggestion with a sloppy smile on his face, which makes me wonder how much of that rum he has downed in just a few minutes. I tip the glass towards me and lift my eyebrows.

"You can drink fast when you want to," I tell him.

"They call me Speedy McGreedy," he says impressively, waggling his eyebrows.

I laugh; this guy's ridiculous and I love him for it.

When I get up to the go to the restroom, Sheila puts down her copper mug and comes with me. I make a face at Everett, not bothering to hide it from her, and trip towards the toilets, which are hidden behind a fishing net covered with shells.

Inside there is an ocean wave track playing, and projection-lit bubbles traveling up the walls. I feel like I'm Ariel in her cave, looking at all her stuff.

"I'm totally doing this with my bathroom at home," I say once we're both standing at the marble sink, washing our hands. "Or maybe Everett's bathroom."

I glance at her to see how she takes the joke; 'not well' would be the correct answer.

"Oh, calm down," I tell her. "It's highly unlikely I'll move in with him right away."

"You know, if you work with me here, there could be a job in it for you," Sheila says suddenly.

"A job?" I'm startled; this is kind of the last thing I'd have expected her to say. When she followed me to the restroom, I anticipated some kind of admonishment for the way Everett and I had been behaving—too close, too happy, when she was clearly trying to get him back with Liz in the most showy way possible. Anything but an offer of employment. "What kind of job?"

I am suspicious, but I am also dangerously unemployed and have zero prospects. I can't afford to not listen.

"There are a million things a person with your experience could do on our agency's team," Sheila informs me, picking up a hand towel and fastidiously wiping her fingers dry. "You know how theaters work, so you could do tour booking. You could work on a publicist team and work your way up to managing your own group of artists. You could move into marketing, if you want. There are plenty of options."

"In exchange for stepping back and letting Everett get swept off his feet by Liz, I suppose."

Sheila shrugs. "*That* is going to happen. You can either cooperate and I'll bring you onboard, or you can make it more difficult than it needs to be, and go back to your little canyon town, where I assume you'll try to freelance until you realize there are a million freelancers already doing the work that you want to get, for less money and more experience. Oh, and all of that work is being replaced by AI, anyway."

She has her finger pretty much on the pulse of things, I gotta hand it to her.

"You're making a really nice offer," I admit, "but it's not as simple as just stepping back. Everett and I are—close."

I think he might be falling in love with me sounds a little too arrogant for this conversation, but it flutters in the back of my mind, a hopeful, foolish butterfly.

Sheila scoffs and shakes her head like she can see the butterfly and it's in everyone's best interests if she squashes it. "Listen to me for a minute. I know you think you and Everett are like, meant to be. And I know you don't believe me or anyone else when we tell you that you're just like a thousand other girls. Maybe ten thousand. But here's a truth you *can't* just shake your head at. Everett doesn't get to have The One. He doesn't have a meant-to-be story. He's a celebrity. That's not how it works for people like him."

I draw back, recoiling from her harsh outlook on Everett's life. How can she turn him into a commodity like that? I burst out, "He's *not* a celebrity, he's a human, and—and anyway, he's not *that* famous—"

"He's going to be," Sheila says. She tosses the towel in a basket. "When I'm through with this project, Everett Torby is going to be America's Sweetheart. He sings, he dances, he writes tearjerker ballads—he's the whole package, plus a few decent movies, and boom." She dusts her hands. "Celebrity. It's in his DNA. It's who he *is*. I have been waiting for this chance for years. And you, as cute and nice as you are, cannot ruin that for him. I won't let you."

I stare at her for a moment. "So you're saying you'd go against everything Everett says he wants—"

"I'm giving Everett who he *is*," Sheila says. "And when you work in this game long enough, you'll learn to see the signs, like I have. This is the opportunity to put him through his paces and show Hollywood what he's got. This is the opportunity he's been born for, even if he doesn't realize it yet. And you, Cassie —you *cannot* stand in his way. But you can help him once he's on his way."

"How? If I were to agree to work with you." Which I'm totally not doing, but it doesn't hurt to get all the info, right?

"How'd you like to work on The Emergency's management team?" Sheila asks, her smile showing me she knows exactly what she's offering—the dream, minus being with Everett. "You could be essential to the band, work with them one on one, even tour with them if that's what you want. I can do that for you."

Her offer leaves me speechless.

Because before last week—before I knew what it was to be Everett Torby's girlfriend, I'd have called *this* the dream of my lifetime. To work with The Emergency, with Everett and the rest of the band—to be friends with them, to be essential to them, to be on tour and stand on the side of the stage as they play, night after night, to have inside jokes with them and see their process first-hand and grab their coffees and sit up for a late-night beer after a show...

That would have been the impossible, perfect dream.

A week ago.

"You can think about it," Sheila tells me, clearly seeing my hesitation. "But in the meantime, no more shenanigans like last night. You've made your point and you've played your part. It's time to let natural selection handle the rest."

Her meaning is clear—the natural partnership for Everett will be Liz, not me. If I let the universe do its thing, they'll come together and the Hollywood angels will sing.

If I get in the way, I thwart the powers that be, earn myself a blacklisted name, and lose everything.

Except, my last poor rah-rah brain cell whispers, *except a shot at being with Everett.*

Oh, good god, brain. You've been so *stupid* for so long! How can I listen to you now?

Across the room, Everett looks up and our eyes meet. There's no faking that sizzle of electricity between us; I feel instantly connected to him. He's the one.

That's the problem.

If Sheila's right and Everett doesn't get to have *the one,* where does that leave me?

Chapter Twenty-Eight

Dinner is cleared and we're discussing dessert before Liz shows up. And when we hear her drunken bellow from across the dining room, I don't imagine the smile that tugs at Sheila's cheeks.

"You called her," I say accusingly.

Sheila shakes her head. "I didn't have to. There are pictures of you two here, and that's all she needed."

Everett looks between us, confused, but he doesn't have time to ask questions. Liz is already crossing the dining room, looking the worse for wear in workout clothes. Her hair is dyed a furious tone of red tonight, clearly matching her mood. "You again!" she shrieks, but she's looking at Everett, not me.

Interesting.

I guess in terms of being yelled at in public, the novelty has worn off, because I don't feel trembly or horrified like I did at Melvyn's. Instead, I just lean back in my chair and wait for the show. (The rum may be contributing to my calm, too.)

"Liz," Everett says cautiously, "I don't know what's going on, but you have to stop this behavior. It's not good, babe. It's bad for your career, no matter what they're telling you."

I glance at him sharply; in my peripheral vision, I see Sheila does the same thing.

Liz barely notices. She's so drunk I have to wonder how she even got here, let alone came storming across the restaurant without falling into a decorative fishnet. Did someone drive her? Just an Uber, or was it something more sinister, like a rep from her new agency?

She leans across the table, her hands planted on either side of Everett's plate, and leers at him. "You miss me yet, babe?"

I guess they're calling each other *babe* tonight.

"Liz, I want you to go home and sleep this off," Everett says.

"I'll go home with *you!*" Liz cackles, showing all her teeth.

"No," he says, keeping his cool. "I want you to go home, sleep this off, and move on."

Liz's Joker-smile retracts, leaving something hurt and helpless in its wake. "I don't want to go home alone," she whimpers.

Beneath the table, I feel my fingernails digging into my thighs. She's either amazingly good at acting—which could be, since she has this new movie deal—or she's desperately sad without Everett. I'm fifty-fifty on which it is right now, and when I glance sidelong at Everett, I can tell he is, too.

I could lose him, I think, and something inside me snaps.

I stand up, pushing my chair back with a rattle.

Liz's neck swivels like a periscope to take in this new threat. "You again." She snorts and shakes her head. "What do I have to do to be rid of you?"

Everett's hand is reaching for mine, plucking at my sleeve, but I ignore him. There's a real desperation to my actions at this moment; if Liz's pleading touches that soft heart of his, however false she might be playing him, she'll win. All I can do now is shoo her away like the dangerous stray dog she is, and hope he hasn't already fallen for her act. "Time to go," I announce, slapping the table next to Liz's hands.

She jumps backward, her eyes going wide. I guess she didn't expect someone to fight back. "Watch it, woman," she warns me, but her hands are up in a defensive posture.

"You're the one who should watch it," I counter, feeling emboldened by her scaredy-cat response. "I think everyone has had it with your tantrums. Take your crybaby self back to Hollywood before your movie deal disappears!"

It's a calculated reminder that she has a new career as a movie star beckoning. If her management really isn't behind this stunt, she'll take my advice and leave. Even drunk, a woman in this business knows that contracts are only worth the paper they're printed on, and a movie isn't a done deal until the crowds are at the multiplex.

For a moment, it looks like she's going to take my advice. Liz edges backwards, her hands falling to her sides.

Then Sheila stands up, shaking back her hair like she's a starlet on the rise, too. "You're not wanted here, Liz, so take your tacky ass back to L.A. and leave Everett alone!"

The words come out like rehearsed lines; there's a reason Sheila's a talent manager and not an actress. She did this solely to set Liz off.

"What is this," I snap, "an episode of *Real Housewives*?"

She shakes her head at me, like I don't get it and I never will.

Liz takes the bait, clenching her fists and giving us all a wild-eyed look. I think a table's about to flip and I take a step back from the one I'm standing behind—I like this blouse and I don't think any of the dishes on the table will improve it. But a house security guard has stepped up behind her and he deftly twists Liz's wrists behind her.

"Time to go, ma'am," he says wearily, like he's wrestled Liz Astra enough in the past few days.

She wriggles and moans, but the fight goes out of her pretty quickly.

Everett watches Liz get frog-marched out of the restaurant before he turns back to me. "I'm worried about her," he says.

I nod. It's the last thing I want to hear, but another part of me knows it's the right way for him to feel. He should have empathy and concern for the woman he used to love. It shows he has a real heart in his chest.

One that's too good for Sheila, Eight Ball Management, and the Hollywood machine that is waiting to eat him alive if they get their way.

"We should go home," I say, taking his hand.

"Good idea," Sheila says. "Our work here is done."

I have to bite the inside of my cheek to keep from yelling that the invitation didn't include her. And judging by Everett's weary expression, he's wishing she'd stop inviting herself along with us, too.

But he doesn't tell her that we'll find our own way home, and in a few minutes we're waiting for the valet to bring Sheila's BMW around. One big happy family.

"Good morning," Everett says.

I push my tangled hair behind my ears and join him at the table overlooking the pool deck. He's been up for a while, judging by the half-empty carafe of coffee on the table. I just woke up, startled out of unconsciousness by the emptiness in the bed beside me. When I'd fallen asleep last night, he'd been next to me.

"I slept so heavy," I say, embarrassed, as Everett pushes an empty mug my way. "Didn't even know you'd gotten up."

He smiles. "No need to get up just because I did. I wanted to let you sleep."

"Thank you." I pour coffee and stare at it; the blackness stares back at me like a pitiless eye. I decide to get up for milk and bring back a few sugar packets from the depths of my purse as well. "I feel like I should be hungover with the amount of rum in those drinks last night," I say.

"You have impressive tolerance." Everett grins. "Maybe you're really a pirate."

"Deep down, I long to swashbuckle," I say, throwing a third sugar into my coffee.

"I've only just found you and now I must lose you to the sea."

I look at him. He's still grinning.

Don't say things like that, I think.

A knock at the door makes us both jump, and then the handle turns.

"I guess that was a courtesy knock," I say caustically.

Sheila shuts the door behind her. "It's ten o'clock in the morning," she announces. "I had a breakfast reservation for you two half an hour ago. What are you doing, playing house?"

"I really miss the days before Sheila lived with us," I tell Everett.

"Our honeymoon, and we didn't even know it," he replies.

I *really* wish he wouldn't say things like that!

"The next reservation is available at ten thirty," Sheila announces. "So, get yourself dressed," she says to me. "Everett, you look fine as you are."

"I'm not even hungry," I say, but my stomach rumbles, cutting me off.

"Betrayal," Everett says. "It comes from within."

I decide this isn't a battle I can win and stalk off to the bedroom, carrying my coffee with me.

"I thought I made it pretty clear I wanted a year off," Everett says.

I take a step back into the bedroom. When I closed the door to get ready for breakfast, I'd suspected they might get into some business discussion she didn't want me part of; but now I'm dressed, clean, and ready to eavesdrop.

Sheila replies with cool dismissal. "We aren't having this discussion right now. I have to get back to L.A.—some of us have to work and go to meetings to make sure your career stays on track. You can have the rest of the week for whatever mayhem you two want to get up to. But be at my office on Monday morning at eleven—that should give you plenty of time to figure out what you're doing with Liz."

"What I'm doing with Liz? I'm not doing anything with her. That was the point of all of this, remember?"

"That was five days ago," Sheila says. "Things move fast, Everett. Try to keep up."

She's right, I think. As much as I hate to agree with her, things in Hollywood do move quickly...and she's trying to keep Everett in the thick of the action. The problem is that she doesn't care whether he wants it or not.

Or maybe she's right, and Everett doesn't know what he wants. Maybe Sheila really sees stardom waiting for Everett, just one leap from the plateau he's been crouching on since The Emergency became indie rock stalwarts.

The front door opens and closes. I step out of the hallway and glance through the front window in time to see Sheila's BMW backing down the driveway.

Everett is standing in the living room, shaking his head.

"Hey," I say.

He looks at me like a lost child. My heart lurches in my chest. I want to wrap my arms around him, give him comfort.

But I hold myself back.

Sheila has confused everything with her plots and her demands. She's in charge of Everett's career, and I'm afraid of how much power she holds over him. Not the emotional power to sway him from what he wants, but the professional power to withhold what he needs. I don't want to be the reason Everett disappoints her; I'm too worried she might strike back by turning down opportunities he and The Emergency might need in the future.

Just so she has economic pressure to force Everett in the direction she wants.

Would she do that? I think she would. Sheila is ruthless.

Or at least, that's the vibe she gives me.

"Did you hear any of that?" Everett asks, looking at the empty driveway.

"Some of it."

"She's insane," he says.

"She's trying to do what's best for you," I hedge, hating myself as soon as I say it. I don't know if that's true or not. But if Everett had a shot at real fame, wouldn't he want it? Despite everything he's said about trying to stay out of the spotlight, who would really turn down the opportunity to be a superstar?

The potential future superstar throws himself down on the sofa and says, "Well, I've been thinking about your theater closing."

"Oh, yeah?" I join him at the far end of the couch. Our feet almost touch. I pull them a little closer. "Why not think about something more cheerful, like orphans or the rising sea level?"

"Because maybe I can help you out," he says.

If he brings up payment for this week again, I'll jump through the front window.

"It's fine," I say. Feigning nonchalance, I flick through my phone, looking for pictures of Everett and Liz from last night. Luckily, this kind of self-torture is very easy. Liz's face is splashed across all the major media outlets, and the industry rags are full of speculation about her ex-boyfriend, the mysterious indie rock singer who has gone to ground in Palm Springs with a nobody—only to reconnect with Liz?

"Unless you already have something else lined up," he says.

"No," I say. "Nothing."

"Do you want to work for the band?"

I nearly drop the phone. "Excuse me?"

"For The Emergency," Everett says patiently. "I was talking to Sheila, and she said she might be able to find a place for you… some kind of junior promoter thing, I don't know. It might be a step in the right direction, if you're still interested in working in entertainment."

I can't believe it. She went to *him*. She knew he was the most likely person to convince me to play by her rules, and she turned it into a favor, something nice *he* could do for me.

He's paying me off and he doesn't even know it.

"I don't know," I say, turning away so he can't see my expression. "That's a generous offer, though. I'd have to think about it. I haven't really decided what I'm going to do next."

"Yeah, it's been a busy week," Everett says. "Running around taking care of me instead of worrying about yourself. But maybe it gave you the space you needed, I don't know. Like you can go back and tackle all that with fresh eyes since you had some time away from your life."

Go back. Tackle all that. My life. My apartment. My cat, who has probably revenge-eaten every leaf from my potted plants. That's why they're all cat-friendly plants, but damn, Tilda can chomp her way through an apartment garden when she's mad at me.

"I just want to be sure you're settled," Everett is saying, his voice somehow far away. "Don't want to have to worry about ya, y'know?"

Because you're not planning on seeing me again.

I nod, unable to trust myself to speak. If I open my mouth, the dam will break, and I'll either cry or tell him I'll love him forever or both, and either way I will make a fool of myself in ways that have hitherto been unexplored by the human race.

We had a week, I tell myself. We had a beautiful week and I will learn to cherish it forever as a fond, fun memory—that time I went wild in Palm Springs with my favorite singer. I'll tell it to my future husband someday, and he'll say, "I can't believe you thought you were in love with Everett Torby, the movie star," and I'll reply, wistfully, "He wasn't a movie star when I met him."

And I'll know that I had something to do with that rise to fame, too, and I'll feel good about it.

I hope.

Chapter Twenty-Nine

WHEN THE FANS show up at breakfast, I'm not even surprised. They parade past in a queue of fawning Coachella princesses, all bare skin and braids and feathers. Everett catches on pretty quickly, too, his sigh erupting every time a new one comes squealing up to our table and offers him a slim hand to shake—ignoring me, of course.

I turn down the offer of a second cup of coffee and push aside my half-eaten omelette. Everett takes it as the cue to leave.

"I'm sorry," he says in the parking lot. "I don't know what's gotten into Sheila."

I hear the telltale beep of a digital camera across the lot. "I know exactly what's gotten into her, and so do you. Congrats on being super famous now, Everett."

He opens the door for me and I slide into the car-seat. "This isn't my fault," he tells me.

I look up at him, savoring the stubble on his jaw. He'll probably shave before we head back to civilization, so that vacation beard is just for me. And the photographers. "I know it's not," I say. "It's just not what I imagined."

He gives me a cynical smile and closes the car door.

Back at the house, we close the curtains and go to bed, but we're both tense and the magic just doesn't happen. Everett throws his head back on the pillow and looks at the ceiling. I coil myself beside him, tucking my heels up, and put a hand on his chest. "What do you want to do?" I ask him.

"Pool, maybe," he says.

"No," I say. "About all of this. About Sheila and the fan-girls lining up outside the house right now. Do you want to keep doing this? Because if you let her run the show, this becomes your life."

"I don't know what I want," Everett says, an edge coming into his voice. One I haven't heard directed at me before; it makes me draw back my hand. "I'm being placed in a really difficult position here."

"You either want to do movies or you don't," I say. "It seems pretty straightforward to me."

"Yeah, well, that's because no one has ever posed this situation to you before," he snaps. "Walk a mile in my shoes and you might think differently."

I roll away from him, thankful for the distance allowed by a king-size bed. With this thing, we could be in two different ZIP codes. And right now, I think that's exactly what I want.

But almost immediately, my anger cools. He's tense and unhappy because of Sheila, not because of me. Still, he has to make this decision. Wouldn't it be better if he makes it with a supportive friend at his side, not in isolation? "Everett, you already know what you want," I say.

"Do I?" He still sounds angry, but I can't help but wonder if he's angry with himself, not me. "Tell me what that is."

"You want to take a year off and produce a play."

He's quiet.

"Don't you?" I ask eventually. "That's what you told me. You've written these plays, and you want some time off the road, and—"

"No one wants to see my plays," Everett says.

"Of course they do! I do—"

"Fans," Everett says bitterly. "Fans want to see my plays. Because I wrote them. Not because they're any good."

I sit upright in the bed and look down at him. He avoids my gaze. "First of all, people will want to see them because you're an amazing writer. Second, what's wrong with people being fans of your work and wanting more of it? Isn't that kind of the point of all of this? People love your lyrics, Everett, you make them feel like they know themselves better, and—"

"Don't give me the fan spiel, I beg of you," Everett interrupts, rolling onto his side to face away from me. "I am so tired of being worshipped. I am so tired of having all the answers for you. I am just as confused and miserable as you are."

The *you* takes me aback. I stare at the back of his head, the curling tendrils of his pale hair.

He's just thrown me back into General Admission with the rest of the fans.

I get out of bed and start pulling on the clothes I tossed on the floor a half hour ago.

Everett rolls over again. "Where are you going? Don't go."

"I have to," I tell him, not looking up. I tug on my capris. Tight. Well, of course they are. I've been eating like a king this week. "I walked away from my life to spend this week with you, and it feels like it has run its course, so I'm going."

"No." Everett gets up, the sheet falling away. I can't help but look now, and he knows it. A mean trick to play on a measly little *fan* like me. "I shouldn't have said that. I'm feeling sorry for myself and that's gross—"

"You can feel however you want," I say airily. "I just don't want to fool myself into thinking this is more than it is, and I'm afraid maybe I'm on the way—" *long gone, actually* "—so I'm making the decision to get dressed and get going."

"You said you'd stay for a week," Everett says. "It's been five days."

"You can have the house to yourself for the weekend," I suggest. "Get to know yourself a little better, without me distracting you."

"Dammit, Cass, this is ridiculous!" he bursts out. "Can we just go back to the way things were? I don't need this kind of crazy right now."

"Too bad. This is the only kind of crazy I can offer," I say, and I duck out of the room before I start crying in front of him.

In the kitchen, I mop up tears with a paper towel while I make myself a cup of coffee. I hear a few drawers slam in the bedroom and then Everett comes out, dressed and ready to keep fighting for me.

I hope.

But instead he just leans against the counter and folds his arms over his chest, watching me fiddle with the Nespresso.

I pour sugar and a disgusting quantity of milk into the coffee as soon as it's done brewing. It's practically a milkshake now. That's what I want, I think. A big, frothy milkshake. Maybe I'll get one on the way home.

"Did things get too real?" Everett asks quietly.

I look at him. His gray eyes watch me, patient and understanding. I think of how they look when he's overcome with lust, the way his pupils dilate as if his body can't get enough of seeing me, the way the blue rims of his irises become bright as the desert sky.

"Everett," I say softly, "things were always real for me. And that's what no one will ever understand."

Girls will say they love him, at every meeting, every day, from now until forever. It will be up to him to figure out who really loves him and who loves his work, the way he makes them feel. If he can't decipher that, if he can't see that what I have for him is real, then there's nothing else I can do about it. I can't even blame him for missing the signs. Who could figure out the real from the fake in a world like his? And it's only going to get worse. Because I know he's going to let Sheila lead him into the thick of Hollywood, and I know he's going to do well.

She said he'd never find the one, that it wasn't his fate, and I can see now why she said it.

Stardom found him first.

And like he already knows, fame ruins everything.

Everett reaches for me, but I take a step back.

"What do you want me to do?" he asks.

Fall in love with me, I think.

"I want you to do what you want," I say instead. "I can't make these decisions for you. No one else can, no matter how much you want them to."

"I'm not asking someone else to make my decisions," he says. "If I'd done that, my parents would be very proud of their son, the civil engineer."

"I think that was true when you were eighteen, but maybe not now." I sip at my sugary coffee, narrowly avoid making a face. I've wrecked it. What a surprise. "You can't even make yourself take a year off, because no one else is making you do it."

His expression sours. "This again? Why don't you just run my career for me, if you're so good at it?"

I laugh mirthlessly. "I would, Everett, and I'd be good at it. But that's not what I want with you. I don't want to run your life. I want you to run your own life."

"Sheila says it's the right move for my career," he says suddenly, changing the topic so fast I blink at him.

"The movies," I say.

"Yes."

"But it's not what you *want*." I feel desperate to get that through his skull. He shies from cameras but wants to raise his profile? Make it make sense, someone, please.

"It would be good for everyone," Everett says. "This isn't just about me. There's the band to think about. Five guys and their families all depend on what I come up with. That's kind of a lot of pressure, did you ever think about that?" Now he's angry. With me? I take a step back, shocked, as he continues in a hard voice. "Everyone thinks it's all about Everett, Everett, Everett. But I am the livelihood of a *lot* of people. Do you know how many people are employed by a touring band, Cass? Do you know how hard it is to make a living as a musician? I took them on this ride with me. Every single one of them could have had an easier, more secure life. I did this. I made The Emergency. And I owe them every scrap of fame and work I can find for them."

He takes a breath, but he looks spent. I suspect he's never said any of this out loud before.

"That's a big burden to carry," I say after a minute.

"It is," he says.

"But you can't hold yourself responsible for their career decisions."

He glares at me.

And that's when I know for sure that this is over. I can't fight with him about this—there's no point, when he's been carrying this kind of guilt for god knows how long. Everett is the frontman, the star, and the focal point of Sheila's attention, so he's not even used to being told he's wrong anymore. Nothing I say can change his mind.

"I have to go," I tell him, putting down the coffee mug.

"Why, though? Why won't you stay and see this through with me? Why does this bother you so much all of a sudden?"

I smile sadly, looking at those luscious lips I won't kiss again. Why not just tell him? It doesn't matter anymore. "Because I love you, Everett," I say, watching as his eyes widen, as those blue irises gleam. "I love you more than you'll ever know, and I'm not going to fight with the man I love."

Chapter Thirty

"Did you have a nice week, then?"

Ronnie is sitting in my favorite armchair with Tilda curled up in her lap. I'm still six feet away, hanging my purse on its hook, but even at this distance I can hear Tilda purring. My cat blinks at me slowly, enjoying every minute of this.

"I had a really nice week," I say carefully. Told a guy I loved him, threw my stuff in a bag, walked out the door, and didn't look back. A hell of a week. I slide off my shoes. "So nice. Thanks for watching Tilda. Guessing you guys had fun."

Ronnie strokes Tilda with one hand and the cat arches her back appreciatively. "We had such a nice time."

"Please don't steal my cat, Ronnie. She's all I've got."

"Fine, I won't," Ronnie agrees, but she looks a little disappointed. "So, I guess you and the rock star..."

"Had fun."

"And now you're..."

"Home again. Ready to live my real life."

She nods. "That's good."

Something in her tone makes me cock my head. "Why is that good?"

"No reason," Ronnie says. "Except..."

"What."

"Of course, you were too busy driving home in weekend traffic to check Twitter or anything."

"Well...yes." The truth is, I deleted Twitter from my phone. And Instagram. And Facebook. I don't want to see anything that reminds me of Everett for a long, long time. The posters on my walls are not helping this resolution, though.

Ronnie nods. "Well, you might want to do some catching up. Or I can do it for you."

I sit down on the sofa. "Ronnie, what don't I know?"

"Everett and Liz were spotted coming out of a pancake house in Palm Springs about an hour ago."

"I left two hours ago," I say, shocked.

Sheila must have been just down the street, waiting for me to leave so she could get to work on these two as quickly as possible.

I feel my forehead crumple as tears start to prick hotly at the back of my eyes.

"Hey," Ronnie says, her voice creaking with unusual levels of sympathy. She's not good at this. It doesn't matter. She brings Tilda over and sits beside me on the couch, my cat purring and kneading my legs as Ronnie tugs me close and lets me cry on her shoulder.

"I love him," I say around sniffles.

"I'm sorry," Ronnie says.

That's about right, I think. The best answer anyone could have.

Sleeping all day does not solve my problems.

I wake up groggy and miserable, with a head full of snot and a heart full of concrete. Sunset is washing over the street outside, and Tilda is poking at the sad remnants of a plant on the living room windowsill. She glances up at me with an inquiring expression as I shamble into the room, as if to say, *Mom, we need a new plant.*

"You're such a bad cat," I tell her, and she mews.

With Tilda fed some actual cat food, I turn my attention to myself. Not hungry? No problem. I order too many burritos from a local Tex-Mex joint, tip the delivery boy as lavishly as if I was still employed, and then stare at the metal containers on my counter. The plastic lids are steamed over and I know there is enough cheese in this single order to feed a small town. I think of the pretty black bikini which I now own courtesy of Everett's record labels, and how I'll never have the heart to wear it again, and then I take out a fork, pop open the first container, and dig in.

Three hours later, I wake up again on the couch, still feeling sick from the three burritos I ate, but oddly interested in inspecting the other three in the fridge. Instead, I pour myself a slosh of whiskey and soda to settle my stomach and turn on the TV. So many options for streaming. So many not-live things to watch which will have absolutely no bearing on my life. I choose a Hollywood gossip show on a local channel which was filmed in the past few hours and will probably break my heart all over again.

"New Hollywood hot-couple?" Right on time, a curly-haired woman digs into the news I crave. "Indies are taking over this town as folk-rock crooner Liz Astra has been the name on everyone's lips, thanks to her upcoming movie with Sideline Productions, but now she's got her man on her arm and there's talk of a new leading man from the ranks of indie rock. Long-time leader of The Emergency, a broody pop powerhouse with legions of devoted fans, Everett Torby! He's been spotted all over Palm Springs this past week, seeming to stay one jump ahead of his estranged wife, but now Liz seems to have Everett back on her arm. Here they are looking cozy at a Palm Springs pool this afternoon."

Cut to a shot of Liz lounging on a float while Everett hangs next to her in the water.

I feel the burritos edging around the top of my stomach, looking for a way out, and swallow some more whiskey. *Nope,* I think. *You're staying in there.*

I want to text Everett and ask him if it's true, but that's not the deal. We were on a contract. Still, I open my phone and look at my texts, just to prove his number is in there. His words to me still exist. I flick through them, wishing we'd been apart more, just so I'd have more to read now.

A notification pops up from my bank app as I'm savoring Everett's short texts again and again. Brow furrowing, I click the banner, and go through the seemingly eight-thousand steps to log into the app. Once I finally get there, those burritos make another bid for escape.

Deposit: $5000.00

"Goddammit," I mutter, throwing the phone onto the sofa. It slides off and hits the floor, and Tilda gives me a slit-eyed glare from the easy chair where she's been sleeping, no doubt mourning the loss of Ronnie's lap. "Yeah, give me the evil eye, Tilda. It's fine. No worse than getting five grand for fake-dating the guy I'm in love with."

Over the next few days, I sink into hibernation mode, wallow there for a while, and then slowly—and to my own surprise—I begin to emerge. Sooner than I would have thought possible, I'm on my laptop answering emails from my coworkers at the theater, getting my department shut down in a practical and polite fashion. There are contracts to cancel and deposits to forfeit and apologetic letters to sponsors and foundation members to pen, and all of that falls under my job responsibilities.

Shutting down a failing community theater evokes a visceral response from the community whose apathy and lack of support ensured its failure, so then there is the public opinion to deal with, as well. Against my will, I am interviewed by several journalists, including a sympathetic woman from the L.A. Times who suggests she comes out to the theater to interview me in person "in the place where it all happens."

Marlena Rodriguez is beautiful enough to play a TV reporter in the movies, wearing a floral dress with frilly cap sleeves and a floating hem that skims just below her knees, along with the kind of heels that would kill me in two seconds flat. She waltzes into the empty theater lobby and looks around at the hand-carved wooden features.

"Wow," she says. "No wonder everyone is so unhappy about losing this place."

"They didn't come when it was open," I say with a shrug. "Now they want to come and it's too late. Typical, right?"

Marlena lifts her eyebrows. "You ready to begin?"

"No," I sigh. "I don't want to come off as bitchy. Can you kind of, I don't know, warn me if that starts happening? I'd like to be civil and diplomatic, but it's been a hard couple of weeks and I don't always know how to do it."

"Of course," Marlena says, sounding sympathetic. "Honestly, this is a local interest piece, so it's best for both of us if you sound like everyone gave it their best shot, a loss for community theater everywhere, et cetera et cetera. You never know, sometimes these pieces can be a shot in the arm for a closing business."

"I don't know that anything could make a difference now. The local paper has already run something, and we've gotten maybe two emails from potential donors. One of those was actually an offer to buy the building and convert it to condos that quote 'respect the building's heritage', so, you know. I think it's over."

Marlena smiles. "Well, this is an L.A. paper, not your local one. There's a sizable difference in the readership. You might get seen by the right people, who knows?"

I feel like I've had enough run-ins with the right people for a lifetime, but I am determined to be diplomatic and do what's best for my theater. So I shrug and say, "Who knows?" before showing Marlena to the box seats I've dusted and prepared for our interview.

We chat for an hour, and it's surprisingly cathartic to get out the emotions surrounding the theater—both for me and for the people who have written to say how sad they are about its closure. And while I don't touch on the shock and misery of unemployment looming, I feel like Marlena understands when there's a personal edge to my words and gently guides the conversation to more neutral waters.

Finally, she turns off the app that's been recording us and caps her pen. "Thanks for being so candid about everything," she says. "Now, can I ask you a personal question?"

I shrug. I feel raw on the inside after our chat, so I can hardly see how it will get more personal. Am I worried about finding work? Absolutely. Do I have a plan B? Yeah, B is for parent's Basement.

"Were you paid five thousand dollars to be seen in public with Everett Torby last month?"

My mouth falls open. "What?" I manage to sputter, just barely avoiding *How did you find that out?*

Marlena's gaze is unwavering. "I have it on good authority that you were hired by his publicist to get spotted all over Palm Springs with him in order to drive Liz Astra back into his arms. And gain him some much-needed publicity in the process."

I shake my head spasmodically. "That's crazy," I babble. "Who would do a thing like that? I don't even know—"

"Cassie," she says, like we're old friends. "Come on. This is off the record. Phone's off, see?" She waggles her iPhone at me. "But I heard some rumors and frankly, that's what really interested me about you. The theater is a good story, but I wanted to meet the woman who got paid to pretend she was dating an indie rock star on the verge of his big-time debut."

"His what?" I whisper.

"Don't you know?"

"I've been so busy with the closure..." I realize I'm not even denying my interest in Everett now, but there's nothing I can do to stop myself. "Did he get a deal? What did I miss?"

"He's on the verge of signing with Pacific Pictures," Marlena tells me, smile glinting in the footlights. "Everyone's talking about it back at the offices. It's going to be a huge deal, perfect for his audience—romantic lead, quirky comedy—"

"Everett's not a comedian," I say.

She tilts her head. "He didn't tell you a lot of jokes during your week together?"

Just the funny joke that we might have been something.

"I mean—what I meant was—"

I falter into silence.

Marlena taps my knee with her hand. "You did this for him. You deserve more than five grand, you know that?"

"They offered me a job," I admit. "Sheila, his publicist..."

"If you're really in the market," Marlena says, "you better call her and take it. I can't guarantee I can keep this theater open for you, but I *can* guarantee she'll pay you a living wage. Which I'm guessing is more than you've been getting here."

"It's complicated," I grouse.

Marlena shakes her head. "Honey, I know this particular spot is the canyons but, this is Hollywood. Go and take what's yours!"

Chapter Thirty-One

THREE WEEKS LATER, the community theater is being bought by a group of Hollywood directors who want it for a pet project, and I'm looking around my new office at Eight Ball Management. The whole thing is a bit of a shock to the system. But there's definitely something soothing about the number of potted ferns and rubber plants leaning against the tinted windows in this joint. I can't help but think Tilda would absolutely love to be an office cat here, munching her way through the greenery.

Sheila teeters over to me in a pair of heels that make her taller than me and says, "Not bad, eh?"

She's been saying that to me all morning. As I walked into the reception area and was greeted by a young intern with a cup of coffee and a bottle of water, as I looked around the open-plan office with its little conference rooms and sprawling sofas, as I inspected the cool white desk that will be mine as I work on up-and-coming artist campaigns. "Not bad, eh?" will be locked into my brain every time I sit at this desk, I just know it.

I have a lot of work to do getting the sleek iMac in front of me personalized with all my own accounts, so I just give her a smile and nod, assuming she'll move on to do her own work.

But Sheila sits down next to me, grabbing a rolling chair from the empty desk next door and wrapping her slim legs around the cushion. "I'm really glad you're here," she says.

Oh, so now we're friends?

"I am too," I agree cautiously, although I'm still confused about how I really feel about being here. This is a dream job, no doubt about it. But, my dreams have a different flavor now. They're a bit more melancholy. Maybe that's a consequence of being a somewhat sad adult, used to having my dreams thwarted on a regular basis...but, did the daydreams that were supposed to get me through the boring doldrums of real life have to be painted gray, too?

It's that The Emergency and Everett are all over this agency. And how am I supposed to get over him when he's part of my office architecture? Especially now, when Sheila has made good on her threats—on her promises, I should say—to make him more than an indie star. To make him a *real* star. Everett's a top priority right now. I've seen his name pop up on multiple all-hands emails in the inbox I've barely had a chance to dig into, and again on conference room doors where meetings without him will take place, deciding his future.

All he'll have to do is sign where they tell him to, show up when they tell him to, say the words they tell him to say.

He didn't want that, but maybe he does now. I don't know. I'm not with him.

And I should be.

And it sucks.

There's even a framed Emergency poster in the break room, and I don't know how to cope with looking at Everett's brooding face every time I need a cup of coffee. I might have to be very cliche and send the intern out to the cafe on the corner instead. Are we supposed to tip the interns?

I try to think of a polite way to ask, but Sheila's already plowing ahead, getting right to the heart of things, because she's a busy woman and she doesn't have time to coddle me. Or at least, that's what she would say to me if she explained herself, ever.

"I know it was hard, the whole Palm Springs situation, but as you can see, it was worth it. You've made a great career move, and Everett is finally going to be working in film where he has belonged for all these years—*and* he owes you a debt of gratitude. Don't think we don't all know that." And Sheila admires a diamond bracelet on her arm with an expression which tells me exactly who she can thank for the bonus that put it there.

Me. I bought her that bracelet. When I pretended to be Everett's girlfriend and brought him all the camera-time she needed.

"Will Everett ever be in this office?" I ask, hating how tentative my voice is.

"From time to time, sure," she says, glancing at her phone. "But mainly he's going to be busy on the lot. They're getting final script approvals now and then he's got a lot of production work to do. Learning on the job, with the deadlines they have to meet! And immediately after they wrap, I want him back on solo tour while the Emergency boys do some session work to prep for a new album. Your first task is going to be to book his solo tour. I've sent a list over with requirements for theaters and cities, so you can work with the booking agents to make it happen, okay?"

I nod at her, my mouth too dry to reply. I was supposed to be working on new acts, getting my feet wet. This is probably supposed to be a treat for me, another way to say thanks.

"It's all happening for you!" Sheila says, shaking my shoulder with one hand. She stands up, towers over me in her heels. "I'm so glad you're here!"

And she marches away, leaving me to gape after her.

I'm working on Everett's new tour. In an office dedicated to Everett, Everett, Everett.

This should have been my dream job, but now it's just a nightmare.

* * *

"Maybe he won't come in that often," Angie suggests. "I mean, he's busy being a movie star. You're booking theaters. There's probably not much overlap."

"Thanks," I tell her. "That helps a lot. I mean that." When I decided to call her on the way home from the office, sitting in bumper-to-bumper traffic, I was hoping for a pick-me-up. Did I forget what talking to sister was like? Sudden-onset amnesia, is that a thing? Angie exists to try and bring me back to earth.

She's doing it right now, her tone frustratingly patient as she says, "Cass—why did you even take this job if it was going to make you miserable? You had to know that you'd be working with his career in some way. It's his publicist's office. He's unavoidable now."

I can't explain that I both need him to be in my life and that I can't stand having him in my life—not this way.

Angie will understand the second half, but not the first.

She sighs at my silence. "You're going to be okay, Cass. You're going to get over him."

I don't think I am. I don't see how I possibly could. I'm in *love* with him. That doesn't just fade. They always show people in the movies, in sitcoms, just breaking up and crying a little and moving on. Why must Hollywood lie? Shouldn't there be consequences for their actions? Congressional hearings, committees, someone has to get to the bottom of this.

"Angie," I say, "do *you* believe me when I say this wasn't just a celebrity crush?"

She hesitates. "Cass...I..."

I shake my head. No one will ever believe me.

And maybe that makes it even worse, to know that I found the love of my life, that he rejected me, and that no one will ever believe it was this bad.

<h1 style="text-align:center">Chapter Thirty-Two</h1>

THE AGENCY HAS relaxed attitudes about office hours, and although I'm expected to work in-house most of the week, I find that I can come in for half-days or adjust my day to start and end earlier than the typical nine to five. Since I'm not ready to move out of my apartment and into the overpriced hustle and bustle of L.A. quite yet, this works out great for me. There's never really a time when the commute doesn't suck, but it can suck a lot less if it's not at peak hours, and audiobooks help with the travel time.

Anyway, if I try to move Tilda away from Ronnie, there will be hell to pay.

When I'm not at home, Ronnie comes over and sits with Tilda, and I come home late to find them sleeping together on the easy chair, Tilda purring as she blinks up at me with lazy green eyes. My cat's long-running infidelity with my neighbor is easier to take now that I'm away from home for ten or twelve hours at a time, and she has an excuse, so I start ordering in enough dinner for Ronnie and she becomes my evening companion. We eat together, we sit on the sofa with Tilda between us, purring, and watch a few episodes of something saccharine and undemanding.

It's a nice set-up for me, and Tilda likes it, although sometimes I think Ronnie misses her alone-time. She lives alone by choice, as she's told me several times over the years when I said something dangerously close to sounding sorry for her.

But I don't want to be alone. If I did, I'd work more from home. I'd sit at my desk and let Charlotte wrap her pretty spider-plant arms around me and listen to Tilda breaking things on my dresser or rooting around in the kitchen cabinets, and I would not have any chance of running into Everett.

And therein lies the problem. If I stay at home, I might miss Everett.

And I *cannot* miss Everett if he comes into the office.

Although it would probably be good for me to miss seeing him, or to go ahead and start applying to other agencies, so that I can rid myself of his presence altogether. The decision should be so simple. Go somewhere and work where my soulmate's image isn't on the break room wall, or where he might not walk in unexpectedly and take my breath away?

Forget it. I choose the pain, every time.

And that, I think often, is how I know it's real. As long as it still hurts, I know it's real.

I'm working past seven in a nearly empty office one night when it finally happens. I hear his voice at reception, the intern perking up immediately.

"Mr. Torby!" she exclaims, and I spin around in my chair, my skin prickling.

A few desks away, another young woman glances over at me, eyebrow raising at my reaction. Our eyes meet and I watch her gauge the situation, remembering what she's heard about me and how I got here.

She gives me a tight little smile and turns back to her computer.

That's right, I think. *I'm the Everett Torby hire. The one who spent a week with him.*

The five thousand dollars sits in my savings account, untouched, the dirtiest money imaginable.

But she doesn't know that.

I hear Sheila's voice from reception and realize she's come back to the office to meet with him. In a moment, he'll be walking past my desk on the way to her office.

My heart begins beating so wildly I see spots.

Leaping up from my desk so fast that I leave my chair spinning, I take off, sprinting for the printer room at the end of the office. It's not the best hiding place, but it's better than the break room, where Everett will be looking down at me from the wall and I run the risk of being smothered by the presence of *two* Everetts, and the printer room is all I can think of right now, a place where there's absolutely no chance he'll visit.

Yes, yes, I didn't want to miss seeing him but I also don't know if I can stand *seeing* him.

The printer room is just a windowless, doorless space where a couple of heavy-duty printers, the kind that can basically spit out entire books or spiral-bound presentations, hum away night and day, ready to produce anything a publicist might need at any hour. The room smells of toner and paper, and someone has left behind a pile of informational packets on The Emergency, which have been printed to send out for press inquiries as Everett's movie career gets rolling. With a feeling of inevitability, I pick it up and flip through the glossy pages, as the band that has dominated my life for the past fifteen years age from wary college kids to jaded adults before my eyes.

"Right here, and I'll get the press kit—" Sheila is suddenly in the room. She jumps. "Oh, god, you scared me, Cass!"

"Shh," I hiss, waving at her. The book in my hand flaps wildly.

"Cassie, easy. Those cost a fortune to print." She takes the book. "Can you grab the rest of the pile and we'll show them to Everett? He's just out here."

Heart sinking, I scoop up the stack of booklets and trip obediently after Sheila.

Everett's eyes widen as I appear in the office. He stands up from the chair by Sheila's desk and runs a hand through his hair. "Cass," he says. "Hi."

I wait to burst into flame, but luckily no human torch results from this meeting. Still, my skin is flashing hot and cold, back and forth, and I figure that can't be healthy.

"Hey," I murmur, dropping my gaze. Looking him in the eye is too much. I pile the booklets on Sheila's tidy desk. "Well, I better head—"

"Stay," Sheila commands. "You can give us an update on the tour."

"Of course." I remain standing, because the only other chair besides Sheila's is just inches from Everett, and I can't sit that close to him. But as he drops into his chair, Sheila clears her throat and gestures for me to sit as well.

Skin tingling, brain buzzing, I sink carefully into the chair, praying my knee won't brush his.

Praying that it will.

Somehow, I avoid touching him. I curl my fingers into a fist in my lap and concentrate on not grinding my teeth. My dental plan hasn't kicked in yet, and I can't break a molar tonight.

I'm the first one out of the room when the meeting is over. Sheila hangs back to do some paperwork; I've seen her after meetings, staying far later than I do. I make it to my desk and have just grabbed my purse when Everett appears in my path, blocking my escape.

"Cass," he says.

He didn't really speak to me during the meeting. He listened, he nodded, he said thanks. But he didn't ask any questions, either professional or personal, and I'm left feeling rejected. Again.

Now I'm annoyed at him for just saying my name. That's all he has?

"What?" I snap, far sharper than I should be with a valuable client. Hell, I shouldn't even talk to an unimportant client that way.

He rumples his hair again, looking sheepish. That simple gesture of his, fingers in his curling hair. It makes my knees weak. I used to believe it meant he was nervous around me, but now I think it's just a tic he has. We're all bundles of anxiety all the time, anyway. Doesn't mean a thing about love.

"I'm sorry," he says at last.

"About what?" I look around. "My great job? It all worked out for both of us."

He shakes his head. "The money," he says.

Oh. "That sucked," I admit. "I'm sure it will come in handy, though. Eventually, I'm going to have to move closer to the office and it's going to cost a ton. It will be nice to have something in savings to fall back on, if I have to." I want him to know it's just sitting there. Unspent.

"They're paying you enough, aren't they? Because I can talk to Sheila—"

"It's fine, Everett." His name glides off my tongue and leaves me weak with longing. Why can't this be enough? Working for him should have been all I ever needed, all any fan-girl could ever dream of. But instead, it's worse than never knowing him at all. "Everything's fine," I insist, as if that will make it true. "I hope you're enjoying movie-star life."

"I'm not a movie star," he scoffs. "Far from it. I just show up and say some lines over and over until they think it's right. It's not acting, it's reciting. I learned to do that in elementary school."

"Me, too," I say. "I had to learn the Gettysburg Address."

"And recite it?"

"Yup."

"From memory?" He's astonished. It's actually pretty gratifying.

"Sure did."

"Can you do it right now?"

"You know what?" I tilt my head, thinking about it. "I think I probably could. Do you want the drunk version or the sober one? Four-square and seventy beers ago—"

"No, wait!" Everett laughs, holding up his hands. "I believe you can, seriously. Maybe sometime you can do it for me. The sober version, even. But I have to get going now."

"Date?" I ask, squaring my jaw.

He shakes his head gently. "Early call-time tomorrow, that's all. I'm not used to the movie-set lifestyle. They get up early, like farmers."

"They would hate that comparison."

He smiles. "I know. But maybe it would be good for them."

"Playwrights sleep late," I say. "Like rock stars."

Everett looks at his feet. "Yeah, well. Cass...I'm glad I saw you tonight. I really wanted to be sure you were okay. After... everything."

I consider him for a moment, thinking about my life. It's hard, there's no doubt about that. But I'm alive and, for all I know, I'm thriving. Maybe once the heartache fades, I'll be able to tell for sure. *Start here,* I think.

"I'm okay," I tell him. "And I really hope you are, too."

He runs his hand through his hair one more time, and his eyes bore into mine. "Honestly, Cass? I'm not sure."

"Mr. Torby," the intern calls, "your car is here!"

"I gotta go," he mutters, turning away. Before I can say anything else, Everett is gone.

My heart rent in two by that last minute confusion, I sink into a chair and press my hands against my face.

This has to get easier someday.

Chapter Thirty-Three

AFTER THAT, I don't hear from Everett for weeks. Summer passes and turns into the indeterminate Los Angeles autumn. The commutes get tougher as the days grow shorter, and I have to admit that it's time to look for a place closer to work. I like the job, despite the stress of working on his projects. As time goes by, I start to admit to myself that I'd hate if I weren't close to him in this way. By scheduling Everett's tour dates, working out his itinerary, making sure he has hotels to stay in and crews to take care of him, I'm able to assure myself that his life will run smoothly and safely. It's nice, really.

I'm Everett's fairy godmother, I tell myself as I book suites and send in riders with requests for bottled water and sweet potato chips and dried fruit so that our handsome leading man doesn't get paunchy on late-night room service and beer. *I'm keeping him healthy and safe.*

Ronnie, to my shock, thinks moving into L.A. proper is great news. "I'm moving to Phoenix to live near my daughter," she says. "Didn't know how to tell you. If you're going to live in the city, that takes a load off my mind."

"But—but—" I almost ask *What about Tilda?*

But of course, Tilda's *my* cat, and if I'm closer to the office, I won't be gone for twelve hours at a time anymore. If I'm very lucky and don't get too choosy about square footage, I might even live close enough to head home on my lunch hour. I can eat a sandwich with Tilda, giving her the little bits of turkey or roast beef she accepts as her due for putting up with humans in her space.

"It's weird how things wrap up," I tell Angie as we chat on my midmorning crawl to work. "The community theater is saved, but it's not the same place anymore. I get a job working with the band, but it's not what I expected. And I put off moving because of Ronnie, but she's been waiting for me to go."

"I would like it if things would wrap up that neatly for me," Angie says, sounding exhausted. In the background there is a wail. "But I think I have about twenty years before anything feels neatly tied up."

She gets off the call to deal with her sobbing toddler and leaves me alone with L.A. traffic. I flick on the audiobook I was listening to, then stop it again after about ten minutes. I didn't hear a word.

We've been stopped next to a billboard for Everett's upcoming debut on the silver screen, a holiday release which, somehow, is only about three months away. He looks so gorgeous as a twenty-five-foot-tall Hollywood idol, I can hardly stand to look at him. And yet I can't tear my eyes away, and I guess neither can anyone on the freeway, because we've been inching towards it for the past fifteen minutes.

Is it my imagination, or does he look sadder than the leading man in a romantic superhero holiday romp should?

Has to be me, I decide. There's no way Hollywood put him on a billboard looking glum.

But I can't stop thinking about it, even as traffic slowly loosens up and we resume our dogged crawl towards Hollywoodland.

Sheila's closeted in her office for an all-hands meeting on the Everett Torby movie campaign, while I'm left at my desk to keep plucking away at the tour promotion. By now he's been on the road for three weeks, but his first break starts today. I don't book his personal travel; the agency has an intern specifically for that kind of work, and I'm trying to think of an excuse to wander past Molly's desk and ask blandly if she knows where Everett is spending his vacation week, when suddenly my phone buzzes with a number that hasn't called me in a long, long time. A number I probably shouldn't even have, but that I'll never ever delete.

Everett. His name is blazed across my phone like a banner. No—like a spark, that reignites a flame in my core. A stupid eternal flame for the man I'll never really get over.

I look around as if this must be a practical joke, then answer cautiously. "Hello? Everett?"

"Cass," he breathes, that familiar rasp setting my skin on fire. Great, now it's all ablaze. And wasn't I doing better? Wasn't I almost okay? Gone now. Damn him.

"Hey," I say, then clear the lump from my throat. "I mean, hi. Is everything okay? You didn't call my office line—"

"This is personal," Everett says. "Can you meet me this afternoon?"

"Of course I can. Where?"

"The hotel," Everett says, trusting I know exactly which one. And of course, I do. "Bungalow seven."

It's just a work thing, I tell myself. *Stay calm.* "I'll be there in two hours."

And there he is, wearing sunglasses and looking thinner than the last time I saw him. Maybe I've kept him a little too healthy.

Everett stands up as I approach the bungalow, tapping his phone to activate the app that unlocks the front gate. I remember it all like we were just here yesterday. Playing in the pool. Eyeing the bed. Untying my bikini. Making Liz jealous.

I look around quickly, but she's not here. Wasn't on tour with him, either. While everyone has assumed he's back with Liz, she's been in Europe promoting her movie and Sheila has been fielding questions about their relationship status with such perfect deflection, no one seems to realize they haven't seen each other since Everett signed his movie deal.

Exactly the way she wanted it.

"I'm alone," Everett says, grinning wryly. "As usual."

I give him a wary nod. "I know the feeling."

We look at each other for a moment—trying to size each other up, I think. But he gives up first.

"Come inside," he suggests. "Do you need to freshen up?"

"If that's code for pee," I say, "then yes."

Everett laughs and ushers me into the bungalow. Inside, it's all the same. That's the magic of hotels, I think. Perfect little worlds that exist outside of time, space, and dirty laundry. The gorgeous bed is still made, but there's a crease at the end where he has sat down at some point. I drag my eyes away from it and back to Everett.

His eyes land on mine like he's been watching me all along.

My hands are shaking.

"I'll order us some drinks," he says. "Daiquiris? To stick with the beach theme?"

"Make mine strawberry." It seems crazy to drink a strawberry daiquiri in a poolside bungalow for work, but that's Hollywood, I tell myself. I step into the white-tiled bathroom and tidy myself up, slicking back flyaway hairs and dabbing my face with a damp towel. When I come back out, feeling less travel worn, Everett is standing near the wicker table and chairs, watching me.

I chuckle nervously. "What's up, Everett? Is the tour going okay? I could have fixed anything you needed from the office —"

"I missed you," he says.

I open my mouth to speak, but there's no air to form words.

"I have missed you every day since you left Palm Springs without me," he goes on, running his hand through his hair so that it stands on end, leaving him looking wild and unsettled. "And I knew when Sheila sent that money there was no fixing it, but I wanted to see you again anyway, so I made up that late meeting with her at the office—"

"How did you know I'd be there late?"

"I know your car," Everett confesses. "I figured out your working hours."

I shake my head. "Lime Lucinda is not the only green Prius in SoCal."

"I know. I stalked you. I'm sorry."

The unlikelihood of Everett stalking *me* after all the words that have been thrown my way strikes me as extremely funny, and I start laughing. Hysterically. So hard I have to sit down on the bed and cover my mouth. The tears that spring to my eyes are part mirth and part despair. He watched my car. He figured out my hours. He came to see me. And I told him I was okay.

"You said you were okay," Everett says.

The laughter dries up as quickly as it began. I look at him, standing there with his hair messed up and his face so drawn, and the real meaning of this visit begins to dawn on me. "I wasn't okay," I admit. "I just wanted you to be."

Everett takes a long, unsteady breath. "I wasn't, either," he says.

The rah-rah brain cells are resurrected like an entire flock of phoenix rising from the ashes. *This is happening! It's all happening! Everett loves you! Everett! Everett! Everett!*

"What are you saying?" I ask, in the most still voice I can manage.

His eyes bore into mine. "I'm saying...that I'm in love with you."

HE SAID IT! my brain cells scream in unison. And suddenly they're all rah-rah. Everyone is on the same side. At last.

At last.

At last.

"Everett," I whisper, wishing there was enough air in this bungalow to fill my lungs, "come here."

He crosses the little room in a single bound and sits beside me on the bed. I put my head on his shoulder and tuck up as close to him as I can, feeling the warmth of his body, the hardness of his frame, as if this is our first time together. This is the time for swelling music and passionate kiss as the camera goes fuzzy. But I just want to hold him, and be held by him.

His arms go around me and he clings tightly to me. "Am I too late?" he whispers.

I think about the way my life has turned around since he came into it. A crash, before everything worked out. "You're right on time," I tell him.

Everett's lips find mine and somehow, in the midst of a make-out session to end them all, I manage to tell him, "I love you, Everett."

Chapter Thirty-Four

THE MOVIE PREMIERE is especially crazy, thanks to the Grammy nomination for the song Everett sings in the movie. (Actually, it's performed by The Emergency for the soundtrack, but in the film itself, Everett sings solo while playing a guitar, then proposes to his movie girlfriend, right before a mega-villain unleashes a swarm of mechanical bees to steal the world's honey and has to be thwarted by Everett's powers in time for the small-town Christmas tree lighting everyone's been looking forward to. Look, I don't understand Hollywood's current era, I just let it happen around me.)

I fiddle with the beaded fringe of my black and silver dress, a vintage number that Sheila's fashion guru found for me somewhere in the depths of her underground gown scene. I'd been dubious about attending a star-studded premiere, but when Sheila assured me I'd be styled and prepped with the same care as a starlet, since I would be representing not just Everett's brand, but the agency, I got onboard.

Liz, on a bender somewhere in France, is nowhere to be seen. Her film hasn't been released yet. No one really knows if it's ever coming out. She proved really difficult to work with.

But I don't follow her career closely, and I don't get any satisfaction from knowing she's having a hard time. I don't have any space in my heart for spite. I have Everett, and that's all I need or want.

I mean, the great job is nice, too.

Tonight my job is to make Everett shine, so when I walk into the bedroom of our hotel suite and see him sitting on the bed with his head in his hands, I feel a flicker of panic which is girlfriend first, publicist second. "Hey, baby, what's going on?" I ask, rushing to sit by his side. "Are you okay?"

He rubs his temples. "I'm so tired," he sighs.

I glance at the dresser, doing a quick visual check for his anti-depression meds. "Have you taken anything for it?"

"No, not yet."

"Let's get you feeling better," I suggest. "A cup of tea, maybe, some biscuits."

"Will that fix me, Mary Poppins?" he asks, smiling up at me.

The smile tells me he'll be okay. "Mostly," I assure him. "Plus your doctor-prescribed pick-me-up."

"I know, I know." Everett sighs again. "I feel like I shouldn't need an anti-depressant on the night of my movie premiere. Like, how spoiled am I?"

It's a familiar refrain. He's been more and more uncertain as the date of the premiere crept up, because this isn't what he saw himself doing with his life, and he's still not sure it's the right thing. I don't know that it is, either, but I've told him again and again to just get through his movie premiere. It's what he's contracted to do. After that, if he doesn't want to do it anymore...

Well, Sheila will go nuts, but we can handle Sheila.

"You can't blame yourself for your brain chemistry," I remind him, rubbing his back comfortingly. "Now, let me call room service and get that tea sent up."

"Wait," he says, tugging at my arm. "Don't go just yet."

I look at the mischievous light in his eyes and bite my lip. "Everett! I'm dressed and in makeup already."

"Can't the makeup girl come back?"

"She'll know *why*," I assure him. "And she'll talk."

"That's okay," Everett growls, pinning me to the bed and making me squeal. "I don't mind if the world knows I'm in love with my girlfriend."

Somehow we make it downstairs and to the theater in time, my makeup reapplied—although I don't think it's quite as perfect as it was the first time, and the girl doing it definitely went directly to the reporters in the lobby with an update on Everett Torby's sexual appetite. It doesn't matter, though, because my boyfriend is happy and stunning in his tux, and I'm on his arm, the only place I want to be whether we're talking Hollywood or the 'burbs.

After the movie—which is weird, loud, and confusing, but Everett says that's just how they make movies now—he makes his way through the round of follow-up reporters while I watch. Sheila stands next to me, as proud as if she made him herself. "He was born for this," she says, ten or twelve times.

I don't disagree, but I also know Everett, and he's not loving this like a man born to do movies should be.

Back in our suite, with a late-night dinner on the way up, I ask him to unzip my dress and as his fingers trail down my spine, I ask him, "Do you want to keep doing this?"

He nips at my neck. "Very much so."

"No," I laugh. "This job. Do you want to make another movie? Because if you want to be one and done, now's the time to get out."

"What happens if I wait?" he hazards. "If I want to make more money?"

"You don't work for the money," I remind him, turning and catching his fingers in mine. "You work for the passion. Don't do this if you hate it, Everett. I mean it."

His mouth twists, somewhere between an ironic smirk and a dejected frown. "That movie was stupid, Cass. You have to know that."

"It wasn't our taste, no," I say, diplomatic as a publicist should be.

That makes him laugh. "What should I do, then? I could work with an indie producer? Do you want me to make a Wes Anderson movie? I could probably get a meeting with him. I could talk to Sheila—"

"You could always have spoken to him solely based on your musical credentials," I remind him. "You were already somebody before. On your own. Hollywood didn't *make* you," I add, remembering Sheila's proprietary gaze. "So they don't get to *keep* you on any terms but yours."

"When did you get so wise about the industry?" Everett asks, raking a hand through his hair.

"When I started working for your publicist." I pause. "But you wanted to take a year off. You wanted to produce a play that you wrote. I knew that *before* all this got started."

"Yeah," he agrees. "I did."

"And do you still?"

Everett looks at me for a long moment. "I do," he says at last.

"Well, then, I guess there's your answer."

"Movies suck, plays and music forever?"

"Let's do it," I tell him, pulling him close. "Let's show them what you've got."

"Let's do the break first," he murmurs. His mouth lights my skin on fire. "A long, long break. Just you and me."

"Palm Springs?" I suggest, but Everett shakes his head.

"Let's go farther than that. I say, Bora Bora. Waste this movie cash the way it deserves to be wasted. Let's go all the way."

And we're about to do just that, when room service knocks.

"Break first," I laugh, and Everett kisses me lightly on the lips before he heads to the hotel room door.

Through it all, I reflect, we've never lost our appetites.

For each other, or for life, or for whatever delicious things Everett has ordered for dinner.

And that's really how I know we're soulmates.

Acknowledgments

THANK YOU FOR reading *Sorry I Kissed You*. Writing this novel was one of the most enjoyable writing experiences I've had yet, in more than a decade of publishing and a lifetime of writing stories, and I think the fun shines through.

I'm a fan-girl; anyone who knows me or follows me on social media for any length of time will know I'm fully devoted to a long-time indie band called The National. I've let their work influence me before and I used them shamelessly in coming up with an Ohio-based band called The Emergency whose best work feels like a nervous breakdown set to music. At least, that's what it does for me. And if that doesn't sound appealing, well, it's not for everyone! Unlike Everett and Cass, though, both the lead singer of The National and myself have been happily engaged in very lengthy marriages and we haven't had any swinging fake-dating weeks in Palm Springs. That part is purely for fun! As for making Everett into a frustrated playwright at heart, I just thought that would be such an appropriately cerebral and literary task for an accidental rock singer. It's like he learned how to communicate with the masses in the wrong way at first.

So, thanks to The National and all the other indie bands I love for making art that inspires me.

Thanks so much to my reviewers and beta readers, who jump on every opportunity to read one of my books and share reviews around the Internet. It's especially gratifying when my equestrian readers jump ship with me and play in new genres. Don't worry, I promise to keep writing horse books.

And thanks of course to my subscribers on Patreon and Ream —your monthly support means the world to me.

Find your name here, lovely friends: Kim Keller, Heather Voltz, C Sperry, Rhonda Lane, Lindsay Moore, Brinn Dimler, Tricia Jordan, Sarah Seavey, Cheryl Bavister, Zoe Bills, Liz Greene, Diana Aitch, Orpu, Rachael Rosenthal, Kathi Lacasse, Mary Vargas, Kaylee Amons, Cyndy Searfoss, Heather Walker, Claus Giloi, Jennifer, Di Hannel, Sarina Laurin, Silvana Ricapito, Katie Lewis, Emma Gooden, Karen Carrubba, Thoma Jolette Parker, Christine Komis, Peggy Dvorsky, Kathlynn Angie-Buss, Nicole, Harry Burgh, Mel Policicchio, Nicola Beisel, Leslie Yazurlo, Sherron Meinert, Jean Miller, Maureen VanDerStad, Libby Henderson, Nancy Neid, JoAnn Flejszar, Gretchen Fieser, Tayla Travella, Empathy, Dörte Voigt, Laura, Elana Rabinow, Cathy Luo, Mel Sperti, Heidi Schmid, April Lutz, Becca B., Sally Testa, Adrienne Brant, Megan McDonald, Natalie Clark, Jennifer Williams, Kellie Halteman, Raina Kujawa, Pamela Allen-LeBlanc, Karen Wolfsheimer, Nicole

Russo, Shelby Graft, Erika Thomas, Jocelyn Bissett, Eris, Ashley Swink, Miranda Mues, Renee Knowles, Annika Kostrabulis, Susan Lambiris, Shauna, Lisa Leonard Heck, Dianna, Megan Devine, Michelle Beck, and Lynne Gevirtz.

Thank you all so very much!

If You Liked This, Try...

As the author of books numbering in the dozens, I have quite a few titles out there for you to try. If you liked *Sorry I Kissed You,* let me recommend one of my other romantic comedy series!

For New York City and women striving to find their personal best (along with love) in a city that never stops grinding, try *The Settle Down Society.* Book One, *The Weekend We Met,* is a pocket-sized starter that introduces you to a delightful found family of friends just getting started in New York City.

For country settings and women chasing their dreams of equestrian stardom, try *Ocala Horse Girls.* Book One, *The Project Horse,* brings you into the world of horses and friendship in the beautiful setting of Ocala, Florida's horse country.

All books are available in ebook and paperback editions from your favorite retailer, or direct from the author at nataliekreinert.shop.

About the Author

A FULL-TIME writer, I work from my farm in North Florida, where I live with my family, two horses, and a combination desktop/barn cat. My work has appeared in many periodicals, including *Horse & Style Magazine, Practical Horseman,* and more, but now I focus on fiction about the things I find most interesting: horses, music, beautiful places, and falling in love. I also cohost an award-winning podcast, Adulting With Horses, with fellow author and equestrian Heather Wallace.

Visit my website at nataliekreinert.com to keep up with the latest news and read occasional blog posts and book reviews. For previews, installments of upcoming fiction, and exclusive stories, visit Ream Stories at reamstories.com/nataliekreinert.

For more, find me on social media:

Facebook: facebook.com/nataliekellerreinert

Reader Group: facebook.com/groups/nataliesreaders

Instagram: instagram.com/nataliekreinert

Email: natalie@nataliekreinert.com